AFTERTASTE

Also by Andrew Post

Knuckleduster
Rusted Heroes

Young Adult
The Fabrick Weavers
Fabrick
Siren by Stone

AFTERTASTE

ANDREW POST

TALOS PRESS · NEW YORK

Talos Press books may be purchased in bulk at special discounts for sales promotion, corporate gifts, fund-raising, or educational purposes. Special editions can also be created to specifications. For details, contact the Special Sales Department, Talos Press, 307 West 36th Street, 11th Floor, New York, NY 10018 or info'skyhorsepublishing.com.

Talos Press® is a registered trademark of Skyhorse Publishing, Inc.®, a Delaware corporation.

Visit our website at www.talospress.com.

10 9 8 7 6 5 4 3 2 1

Library of Congress Cataloging-in-Publication Data

Names: Post, Andrew, 1984- author.
Title: Aftertaste / Andrew Post.
Description: New York : Talos Press, [2017]
Identifiers: LCCN 2017006607| ISBN 9781945863103 (pbk. : alk. paper) | ISBN 9781945863134 (ebook)
Subjects: | GSAFD: Horror fiction.
Classification: LCC PS3616.O8375 A69 2017 | DDC 813/.6--dc23
LC record available at https://lccn.loc.gov/2017006607

Cover illustration by Kevin Peterson
Cover design by Anthony Morais

Printed in the United States of America

For Traci.

FRIDAY.

HIDDEN BY HIGH CLOUDS AND MOVING AT A ROARING CLIP, THE
three agents inside the aircraft man their stations. The first, the
pilot, keeps them on course. The second and arguably most
important keeps an eye on their geographical position, scanning
for cemeteries three miles below. The third, currently without a
task, twiddles his thumbs and stares out the window pondering
how the word "cloud" was invented. *Cloud. Cuh-lowd.* What a
weird word.

The flight suits of all three are covered with sigils and runes
and alchemical symbols. Each wears a set of deer antlers glued
to their helmet. Not by choice, mind you. It's just the uniform,
comes with the job.

Receiving a nod from the first agent watching the gridded
world on his screen, the third agent now eagerly unbuckles himself from his seat, draws a pentagram in the air with his index finger as he stands, and steps into the tail section of the aircraft. He
opens a refrigerated drawer, a plume of steam fogging his visor,
and he bends to peer in. With a long, quad-knuckled finger he
skims through the neat rows of vials within. Each is marked with
a hand-written name and separated into two columns—a rough

colloquial translation from the agents' language: TOP PERFORM-
ERS and TOTAL FUCK-UPS.

The agent pauses, having forgotten since takeoff some
hours ago which employee is next. Slightly embarrassed, he
leans his head into the main compartment. "Uh, brother, who's
up again?"

The one watching the grid sighs. "Zilch. Unfortunately."

"Do we really want him on this, brother? Do you remember
how things went sending him after the Insatiable?"

The map-watching agent shrugs, his jumpsuit making a
crunchy sound. "He's up to bat. We can't skip him again. But do
hurry. I've got a useable grave coming up, brother."

"Yes, brother." The third agent returns to the drawer—his
steps knock crooked when they rumble over some turbulence—
and skims down to the very bottom of the total fuck-up cate-
gory, removes the appropriate vial, and gives it a shake, which
he's always been told helps to wake the employee inside, currently in jelly form.

He clicks the glass tube containing the yellow fluid into a
needle cartridge and carefully carries it over with both hands to
load the Employee Delivery Module into the cannon at the tail
section of the craft. He kneels to peer into the cannon's adjacent
monitor, tweaking the crosshairs to settle them over the grave
scudding by far below, helpfully marked with a big red X by the
map-watching agent.

His brother, up front, barks over the intercom: "Fire when
ready, brother."

"Good luck, employee," the agent whispers when the crosshairs and red X align. He squeezes the cannon's trigger and a
thunderous crack trumpets the employee's departure. The agent
moves quickly to watch from the side window the powdery line
marking the rocket's trip as it screams across the sky in a long,

high arc. Then it vanishes through the clouds, hurtling mete-or-fast toward its destination.

The Employee Delivery Module punches through the cirrus nimbuses and down into a bright sunny morning waiting beneath, toward the grave. It breaks the sound barrier twice. Twenty yards, ten, five, and it pierces the world with a muted thud, the dirt only slowing the needle-tipped rocket a fraction. Roaring through five feet of dirt, rocks, worms, and tree roots in an instant, the module continues to advance. The coffin lid gives minor resistance but the rocket, equipped for this exactly this type of obstruction, sprouts a corkscrew and bores. Wood chips fly up and away and dirt pours onto the well-dressed corpse inside. The determined EDM has, at last, broken through. Its needle pieces the corpse's chest with a *fwap*, finding purchase between two gray ribs. It injects the yellow employee fluid into its new vessel and some seriously heavy metal imagery takes place as the body begins to convulse with new life. Hands ball into bony fists and jaws part to silently scream. The employee is being born again in essence, soul finding meat and weird science making things get gooey again, where, previously, there'd only been dust.

In the aircraft, already several miles from the drop-zone, a green light winks on and all three agents, behind their rune-scrawled visors, smile as one. They will go out tonight, for drinks and to celebrate a successful delivery, their job well done. Meanwhile under the table, far from their bosses' prying eyes, they will make bets on the employee's likelihood of success. Saelig Zilch's odds don't look so hot.

THE CORPSE'S FIRST BREATH IS DISTINCTLY SOIL-FLAVORED. And with the realization that, yet again, he's woken up *under-*

fucking-ground, he begins franticly scrambling for the surface, clawing at the dirt, with hands that are not his.

Punching through the surface, he gulps in fresh air with a guttural reverse-roar. It's so bright up here it makes the back of his eyes scream. His vision is at first nothing but a kaleidoscope of mending cones and rods, but with each blink he has a better view of his surroundings, and he eventually realizes he wasn't so far off to begin with: surrounding him are nothing but granite head stones and weeds. Not the nicest graveyard he's ever been reborn into.

Still in the cheap black suit his borrowed carbon had been buried in, Saelig Zilch grabs at handfuls of grass around him, and tearing them out by the roots as he tries to pull the rest of his body free. It is a slow process; the muscles in his new body are atrophied and it wouldn't be easy for anyone to dig themselves out from under several feet of compacted ground. But soon enough he is out, and crawls away to secure some distance from the grave in an awkward scuttle, afraid of sliding back in—because that's happened before. And what's worse than dragging yourself out of a grave? Doing it from the same one twice.

With each ragged pull of the humid air, his lungs wheeze as they repair themselves—the vessel, what remains of it, tailoring to him. Cells rebuild. The nanobugs assimilate or recombinate or whatever the scientific term is—overwriting the DNA of the poor sap who died and looking more and more with each passing moment like Saelig Zilch.

The skin, what the body has left, almost immediately begins to lose its chalkiness for a healthier hue. His eyes balloon back up to refill the sockets, blank white one blink, blue-blue the next. His hair becomes an inky black with twin shocks of silver on the temples, as it had been when he'd last been alive. All of this, mind you, hurts a great deal.

Zilch lies on his back, drops his chin to his chest, and notices the rocket-powered syringe still harpooned in his chest rocking back and forth with each labored breath. He has to use both hands to draw the needle from his new body—it's at least eight inches long and he swears he feels it pop free from his spine, giving him a flash of pain when it dislodges.

He studies the side of the gizmo. A screen flashes *delivery complete* twice and goes dark. There is a switch on the side—it's currently set to DELIVER, the other ABORT. He'll need to hang on the needle for later—this is far from his first rodeo—so he pockets the module and peers down inside his shirt to watch as the puncture wound fills in, making a sound like someone blowing a bubble as it closes.

Things inside him click, crunch, squeak, and gurgle. His teeth reset like a player piano with sticky keys. It gets quiet once things settle, complete, and all he can hear, then, is the machine-gun chorale of the cicadas in the trees and grass around him, the sound thunderously loud to his new eardrums.

He sits up and raises a one-finger salute to the sky. "Made it, assholes."

The inner ear of the formerly-interred gives Zilch a seasick kick once he's standing. One step, then another, tottering like a gin-dipped toddler.

Down the path of the cemetery he goes, wavering, his black suede loafers crunching on top of the walkway gravel. He admires the glint on some of the newer headstones as he passes, the marble of many is still fresh and the carved lettering sharp. A few of the names chime something in him, faraway. And those dates, birth and death. He tries to ignore the nagging feeling of déjà vu. Memories are just stains, and no matter how many times he does it, being reborn is like waking suddenly from a bizarre dream, and it can take some time to shake his head of the fragments bouncing around inside.

He pops the collar of the burial suit's jacket, a mannerism that feels full of fake bravado even to him, as if he's trying to convince himself, *This doesn't bother me, not at all, just another day at the office.* But thoughts continue to be triggered, his brain making damp clicks as vague memories surface, none of which he likes very much. He suddenly remembers how badly he'd botched the last job. How long ago that was is impossible say, because to Zilch the splice between the end of one job and the start of the next is indiscernible—he was screaming and bleeding to death not ten minutes ago, to his mind, then boom, he'd awoken in a different body, buried alive and *still* screaming, as if he'd snapped out of a dream and woken up in a new one. A nightmare loop.

Being eaten alive, that was a fail. And not a particularly positive memory to have lodged in his head. So he closes his eyes, sucks in his breath, trying to scramble his thoughts, to bury that one deep in his subconscious. He does, but immediately another one surfaces, horrifying in a completely different way: her face, her laugh, the color of her eyes and her hair and her cupid bow lips. It may still be a dream, or a memory of a dream, or even a dream made up of rearranged memories. But he suddenly remembers, for certain, that her name was Susanne. Her name was Susanne. Those assholes made sure to leave him that much.

"Her name was Susanne," he says, the last recitation accidentally out loud.

But enough standing around in a graveyard muttering to yourself. *You're here to work, so get to it,* he thinks grimly. Zilch has wasted plenty of jobs sitting around getting all philosophical already; it's a dead-end. He scans his surroundings, squinting past the sun. Task *numero uno:* it's good to figure out where the hell they dropped you.

Clues one and two appear to him over at the graveyard's perimeter, where there are wildflowers beyond the fence, crowded on the grassy shoulder dividing the boneyard property from an unpaved country road. The raw dirt of said road is orange, just like that of the grave he'd crawled out of, iron-rich. Clue One.

Clue Two are the flowers. Zilch tests himself on what he remembers about plants. (They have no problem stealing his memories from his former life but leave the rest the parts of his brain filled with useless trivia. But who doesn't like a dash of insult on their steaming hot injury, right?)

He remembers. That's the gory, spiked head of . . . Bee Balm.

The buttery pastry on a stem: that's Yellow Jessamine.

That triggers a strong memory of . . . salads. In particular, one he's made for a wedding he'd worked as a caterer some years back, with Susanne. It was a salad with wildflowers and radicchio and grated carrots. It had been a big deal among gastronomical trend-followers. The bride had called herself a *foodie* (a term he and Susanne always hated) but had wanted something to represent her groom—a southern boy—and his roots. Virginia. That where the wedding had been, Virginia. Bee Balm and Yellow Jasmine grow in Virginia. It had been about as hot that day as it is today. Except then, Zilch had been sweating out the previous night's bottom-shelf vodka. Now, he just stinks like turned earth—he picks a wad of it out of his ear.

So between Clue One and Clue Two he deduces: *I'm somewhere down South.*

But with the high number of conifers among the growth across the road, it's can't be *too* far south. The orange dirt he just scraped out of his ear helps narrows it down more.

Apparently his nanobugs have gotten his gray matter working well enough to produce a headache—the kind you might get when a dentist misses your mouth and opts for a frontal lobotomy instead of a sucker following a root canal. You know, for the LOLs.

He clutches his head, eyes watering, and turns with the pain as it shifts about his skull—from his left brow to over his right ear. A compass needle demanding to be followed.

Under the hot sun, Saelig Zilch follows the pain compass out the gate and onto the dirt road. *Fuck my stupid un-life.*

THE OSCILLATING FAN STANDS GUARD AT THE CORNER OF THE bed, droning, scanning right to left over Galavance's frame. It was too hot last night for covers, or even a sheet. She's in a Papa Roach T-shirt that's been laundered so many times it looks shotgunned. Poking her finger like a mole through one of the many holes, she considers how much the shirt, which isn't even hers but Jolby's, feels like new pasta. Pasta. Pots and pans. Steam. Kitchen. Time clock. Late. "*Shit.*"

She doesn't feel the hangover—didn't even realize it'd been waiting, coiled inside her head—until she sits up. *Blammo.* Then she remembers the light dinner and a whole bottle of white zin Three Buck Chuck. She stares into the white plastic face of the fan, slowly shaking its head at her. *Tsk, tsk.* Galavance sits on the corner of the bed, begging the clawed thing in her skull to go away.

It's sitting here, staring at her boyfriend's hillocks of dirty clothes (sharing foothills with the mound of clean clothes, dangerously blending territories) that she spots something terribly honest. A pair of his tidy whiteys, crotch-out, with an earth-tone smudge the size of a thumb print driven deep into the fabric. It feels like the skidmark is looking at her.

Jolby keeps asking her to bring leftovers home from work, and she does it because she hates cooking, but Americanized French cuisine—with about ten times the necessary grease—does a serious number on her beau's guts. Maybe Galavance needs to consider which is worse, cooking or doing his butt-burnout laundry.

This was nothing new to her. Soiled underwear, a flecks of orange on the bathroom wall where he'd missed lurching into the bathroom for a loud, three a.m. barf-a-thon, the fact he seems allergic to washing his dirty dishes. But when you've dated someone for going on damn near a decade—*shrug*—that's just how they are, love it or lump it.

"Where else are you gonna go?" he says without saying. "We've been together forever." Imprisonment marshaled with a banal, lazy fist. Partly his, partly hers. She could leave at any time. *Could* being the operative word there.

She's still thinking about fists as she pours cereal into a coffee cup because it's the only clean dish left in the place, wondering how sometimes—okay, often—she'd like to make another kind of fist and render Jolby's head to skull-mulch. She considers how much it pleases her to think about this when she thinks of her hands, her fingers, picking up his shit-stained clothing sans jewelry, engagement or otherwise. Not even a cheap-ass pewter promise ring from Walmart.

*I wouldn't even care if it did turn my fingers green, I want some*thing, she thinks.

That was what she would say, you know, if she cared that much. *I'm a modern woman. I shouldn't need that validation, that existence-confirmation, but at the same time, aren't I fucking owed? I wash his underwear. And I don't (often) complain.*

Having eaten, Galavance steps into her work pants, slipping Jolby's T-shirt off. She snaps a bra, and dons her work-issue polo with FRENCHY's stitched onto the chest. She speedily tries working her white-blond hair into some semblance of a style before giving up opting for a simpler ponytail, then applies her makeup, hastily but with expertise.

Her purse is light forty bucks. Half her cigarettes are gone, too. Along with her lighter. Jolby, for a stoner, is an early riser. He's been gone since before dawn.

With her embarrassingly out-of-date pay-as-you-go flip phone, Galavance punches in the number for work on its cracked screen while stepping out into the morning's soul-burning heat. She tells her boss she's going to be a few minutes late. Her boss, three years her junior, gives a moment of dead air. He's probably shrugging and expecting her to divine that through the phone.

"Whatever," he says at last. "But you remember Patty's coming by today, right?"

Galavance's eyes shoot wide. "*What*?" Whether it's the news, the sudden heat pounding across her, or a combination of both, her stomach turns.

"Ch'yeah, man. Patty's coming for the new test location menu items and shit. Said she was gonna make sure we're, you know, on the ball. And shit."

"You're gonna be there, right?" she asks. Her boss is a fuck-up, the only one bigger than her at this particular location. He'll soak up some of Patty's rage for Galavance, if he's there today. But he just laughs.

"Screw that. I called in. Have fun."

She doesn't say goodbye, just closes the phone and grinds her teeth. Goddamn it.

Stomping across the mildew-stained Astroturf carpeting the patio, she dances between the neighbor's dog's shit piles and beer cans land-mining the front yard, and hops in her bubble-gum pink Cavalier. The dial thermometer hanging on the side of their double-wide says it's eighty-three outside, but in the car it feels at least three times that. Galavance starts the car up and immediately mashes the switches to drop all four windows—one screams and shudders in its reluctant descent. She tests the wheel with exploratory pats. Cool enough. She backs out of the gravel driveway and drives down and out of the court, never bothering to acknowledge any of the octogenarians in their front yards, watering pathetic flowerbeds, even though they wave at her, denture teeth big as playing cards, too white, too widely presented.

Happy old people. Fuck 'em.

The Go-Go's Greatest Hits has been stuck in her car's CD player for months. Some days she doesn't mind. But today the next track is "Skidmarks on My Heart." She cannot help but shake her head—it's too potent a coincidence.

With no time to stop for a coffee, she needs nicotine, ASAP. She feels around blindly for the goddamn lighter. Cup-holders, passenger seat, nope. She knows Kit Mitchell Road like the back of her hand. She's confident she can look away for one little second.

Flame blessedly set to cig (the lighter had fallen under *her* seat), she glances up just long enough to register that there's a pale man in a brown suit coming up fast, too fast to do anything but realize she's going to plow into him and there's no way to avoid it.

Tires scream. She screams. He screams. We all scream for vehicular manslaughter.

Thumpa-thump.

The Go-Go's continue, trapped in the 80s on a spinning plastic disk, undisturbed by the collision. "*Head over heels, no time to think . . .*"

Hands automatically readjusting to ten and two, Galavance stares through the spiderwebbed windshield at the road ahead, now scattered with broken grille plastic. The headlight bracket rolls along like a coin on its edge. All she can say right now is "Oh," over and over again. "Oh. Oh. Not good, not good."

Then, as if her day couldn't get any weirder, in the rear-view mirror, as if only suffering a minor ouchy, the man she's hit (and not just clipped but *bulldozed* over) rises to his feet. The shoulder of his dark jacket flutters loosely, shredded. Tie askew, flopped over one shoulder. One side of his face is chewed and ribbed with bleeding road rash. Something skitters across his face—or is that the sunlight playing tricks on her?—and makes a beeline for the edge of the wound and either vanishes or . . . goes *inside* him?

"You kids have *got* to slow down out here," he says, coming up next to the car, hardly limping.

"I'm—I'm sorry. I didn't see you."

"Well, thank God you didn't do it intentionally."

How is this possible? she thinks. *I saw him spiral through the air like some kind of deathwish ballerina on malfunctioning spring-heels and now here he is . . . talking, walking, goddamn* alive?

The man leans down to the window and looks at Galavance, still holding the wheel as if she's about to edge over the big hill of a rollercoaster. "Are *you* okay?" he asks with raised eyebrows and chin down, the picture of uncertainty.

"I'm so sorry, mister. Hey, I mean, do you need a hospital?"

"Not necessary." He coughs and frowns into his palm. Wiping whatever he brought up on a pant leg, he says, "Where are we?"

"Kit Mitchell Road."

"But, North Carolina, right?"

"Yeah," she says. As gently as if the man's a shaken bottle of nitroglycerin, she asks, "Say, you sure you don't wanna see a doctor?"

"I'm always this pale if that's what you're getting at. Even before—" he cuts himself off. He steps back from the car, hands on his hips, squinting into the morning sun. Up close now, she sees his suit isn't brown, but black, just covered in layers of dirt. He was dirty before she hit him. Why is some filthy suit out here in the sticks?

She places a hand over the shape her cell phone makes in the pockets of her form-fitting khakis. She could call the cops, sort this thing out legitimately, correctly, but doesn't want to. She's seen *Orange Is the New Black*. She wouldn't last long in prison.

"I shouldn't be talking to you," he says. Another car passes and he moves *way* off the road this time. "I've got somewhere to be."

Oh, God. He's like some gangster or something. Did he bury someone out here and his buddies left him? Or, fuck, is he all dirty because he was the one buried? Galavance's hands squeak on the steering wheel, tightening.

He's looking over her Pepto Bismol pink vehicle closely. "Your wheels still good to go? Sounds okay."

She undoes her seatbelt and sighs. "All right, go ahead."

His brow clouds. "Pardon?"

"I don't want any trouble. I'll even give you a few hours head-start before I report it stolen. I'll have to report it, you under-stand?" Killing the engine and stepping out, Galavance presents her ring of keys with its rabbit's foot keychain in matching pink.

"I meant you drive, me ride." He points at her and mimes twisting a steering wheel.

"You want a ride?" She's still holding the keys out at him.

He looks around as if he heard something Galavance has not. His eyes track about, past her, his mouth a hard line. "Yeah," he says after a moment. "I think so." He trains eyes on her the shade of crayon kids always pick to scribble skies. "It feels nearby. Couple miles."

"Okay, well, I'm late for work, so let's get going, all right? If you're ready that is." Slowly tucking a swirl of blond behind an ear, she adds, "Don't wanna rush the guy who just got hit by a car or anything . . ."

He smiles. Toothy, genuine. He steps forward, hand out. There are pale scars on almost every finger. A few flat, shiny sections on his palm, old burns. She works in a restaurant, she's seen plenty of hands like his. A cook's hands.

"Saelig Zilch," he says.

"Saelig?" she says, nearly recoiling at how cold he is.

"Go ahead, I've heard them all."

"I wasn't . . ."

They shake. She waits until he's walking around the front of the car to the passenger side, then furiously wipes her palm on her pants when she's sure he won't see. Crunching through broken plastic strewn across the road, Zilch gets in. "You?"

"Sorry?"

"What's your name?" he says.

"Galavance."

"Huh. I can see why you didn't give me shit for mine, now."

She manages to smile, somehow. The tires slip momentarily, then chew in and dig and they disembark.

SHE SMELLS GREAT. LIKE BUBBLEGUM, FLOWERY PERFUME, AND the good menthols.

Preparing himself for the worst, Zilch summons the courage and folds down the visor on his side to flip open the mirror. He gives himself a reluctant sidelong glance, sees it's not so bad, and eases into looking at himself full-on. The road rash is already gone, healed, but fuck. What a bad start. Out of the boneyard ten minutes and he gets street-pizzaed.

"I'm sorry, but I have to ask," Galavance says, eyes on the road, "but you're not gonna sue me, are you?"

"Trust me," Zilch says with a half-smirk he knows—but cannot help—makes him both more and less trustworthy at the same time, "I'm not going to sue you." He flexes his hand open and closed and finally rests it on his knee. It aches, like his carpal tunnel used to.

You only have so many nanobugs per job, he remembers being told, once, *to patch things up and keep your borrowed carbon in working order.* Getting clobbered by a car probably just exhausted well over half of them. The genuine hurt would come early. Normally, he's three shots of Jack numb, when fresh to a husk. The bugs do a good job; focus on the important things like keeping the blood marching through his veins instead of patching up nerve endings. It's comfortable territory for Zilch, after all. He spent most of his adult years numb by one type of chemical helper or another, so this isn't something new. Still, having exhausted half his little buggies means he'd just cut his time left to do this job by half. Fun.

"You might change your mind later," she says, and it's clear that she's still quite worried about getting in trouble for whacking him. "But if you do, can you wait until at least after the first of September? That's when I get paid next."

"What do you do?" he says.

"What?"

Zilch notices that she startles every time he speaks, that whoever this girl is, she's got a truckload on her mind.

"What do you do?" he says, slower.

"I'm the wait-staff shift manager at Frenchy's," she says, as if giving a bad diagnosis.

"That some kind a titty bar?" He's picturing plus-sized women in maid outfits, shining up metal poles with their inner thighs and that long *shriek* of generous flesh sliding down tarnished brass. It's a weird thought for a walking corpse to have but hell, rotting flesh or not, he's still a dude.

And as if she can see that image in a thought bubble floating over his head, she says: "Ex*cuse* me?"

"Sorry," Zilch says. *She's giving you a ride, asshole. Be nice.* "I guess the polo shirt *does* kind of go against titty bar. Or is it a yuppie joint where they only play Phil Collins?"

"Who's Phil Collins?"

Zilch draws in a deep breath. "He was big when I was your age. We used to ride around on my friend's Brontosaurus listening to him. But what's Frenchy's—if not a strip club?"

"Frenchy's is a *sit-down* restaurant," she says.

"Oh, a *sit-down* restaurant? Pardon me all to hell."

"Kinda hard to be a snob when you're out in the middle of the road at 9 a.m. looking like you just crawled out of an unholy grave or something. No offense. What were you doing out here, anyway?"

He chooses not to answer. "I just find that hilarious, when people use that distinction: a sit-down restaurant. Like *sitting down* for a meal is some kind of big la-ti-da affair."

"So you *are* a snob."

"With food, yes. So what do you serve at Frenchy's?"

"The shit kind," she says. "Food sucks, vibe sucks, the decor is like *holy shit*, but getting a regular paycheck *doesn't* suck and it takes care of my bills. Most of the time."

Galavance has been slowly increasing her speed over the course of the conversation, which Zilch has only recently noticed, and now she's barreling at eighty-five down this curvy dirt road like it's nothing. When she goes around the next corner, Saelig imagines the tires' grip giving out and the car going side-over-side-over-side-over-side in a roll that doesn't end until the car folds around a tree like a wad of dough walloped by a nunchaku. It's not a comforting feeling, given his already-depleted inventory of nanobugs.

"What kind is the shit kind, exactly?" he asks, almost panting, once they're on another straightaway.

"Americanized French cuisine," she says. Fast, dismissive. "But what about you? The way you were asking me where we were back there, seemed like you're a long way from home?"

"You could say that."

"Okay," she says, and he knows it's a bad answer that only makes more questions, but thankfully she drops that line of questioning. "Then what do you do for a living, Mr. Zilch? Or are you one of those people that gets hit by cars on purpose to do the whole ambulance-chaser thing?"

"Christ, what is it with you? Did you get attacked by a pack of rabid lawyers as a kid?"

"Sorry."

Zilch grunts and tries to slouch, but the harness looping under both arms and up his crotch like a baby seat prevents it. He's glad it's there, though; she's power-sliding them around every curve. "I don't know what you'd call what I do," he says, blurting, like he's being tortured with homicidal driving for answers. He winces. *Shut* up.

"So you're like, self-employed?" she says.

"Forget I said anything," he says, bracing for the next hairpin. "I don't want to spoil the ending for you." That last part slips out, accidentally.

"Spoil what ending?" Too late. She's interested.

"Nothing."

"No, tell me. You're getting a free ride here."

"After you *ran me over*, I'd like to point out."

"I did run you over, that's right. And then I watched you get up like nothing had happened, and I watched your face turn from the texture of a seared steak to completely normal, and despite all that, I let you into my car and haven't really made an issue out of it. So, you could just tell me."

Zilch sighs. It's not an illogical argument, and Galavance has already proven herself to be an unusual encounter. His guts somersault when she tugs on the E brake to glide them around another turn. "Okay. You ever think about what happens at the end of your life?" he squeaks, realizing as he says it that he's coming off as creepily murderous.

"All righty, I think I'm going to pull over now." Again with the E brake.

"Wait, I don't mean . . . No, ha-ha, I'm not going to *kill you* or anything . . ." He slaps palms to the dashboard, their speed dropping away so fast he's being lifted out of his seat. "Listen, you asked."

"I know, and now I'm really regretting it. I think if you want to sue me now, that'd be fine," she says. "I think I might have a case."

Zilch sits up and tries to turn to face her but again, the harness has him in a half nelson; he unclicks the buckle and detangles himself. "Look. I was *trying* to tell you, I'd started to, but you drive this thing like it's fucking stolen. If you keep it under mach nine for one goddamn second . . . I'm not *supposed* to tell you, but I will." Fuck it, why not. She's weird. And, aloud by accident: "Can't turn out any worse than the last time I spilled the beans."

"Uh, pardon? What was that?"

"Nothing."

"All right, so go on," she says. "I'm listening."

"Pleased to meet you, Listening. I'm dead."

"Uh, what?" She glances over at him, lip curled. She snorts. "You're gonna have to try a little harder than that, I think. And you can stop with the Dad jokes anytime you like."

"I wasn't finished. It's . . . I'm not supposed to talk about this, tell anybody what I am or what I do. But I'm dead, I get sent back, and I hunt *lusus naturae*. Freaks of nature. Not sure why they insist on the Spanish—"

"I think that's Latin, actually."

"—but that's what I do. And *have* been doing for a while now, with no end in sight. Apparently the world never runs dry of weirdos."

"You don't say."

"Hey, you asked. You asked, so I told you. And there it is, the stone facts of the thing."

"So you kill monsters."

"Yes."

"And these monsters, if I were to see one . . . would they look like monsters, or just random people you run up on and stab to death?"

"What? No. They look like monsters, as monsters tend to do." He pauses, frowns a second. "Most of them. Like 98 percent of the time."

"But not all the time."

"No, not *all* the time, but—"

"So you kill things that look an awful lot like people."

"Sometimes." He groans. "Maybe we should start over. And before I introduce myself, let me preface this conversation by saying: I swear I'm not a psychopath."

"Do you have some kind of doctor's note I could see, to corroborate this?"

"What's your deal?"

"What's *my* deal?" She snorts again. "I've got a nutcase in my car."

"Give me a second. I can explain it better."

"Oh?"

"Give me a second."

"Okay, okay. Go right ahead."

They tool along, still halfway on the road, at an above-the-speed-limit-but-still-quite-reasonable-by-comparison speed of forty-five. She notices he's no longer strapped in, and gives him a devious smirk that a face that adorable shouldn't be capable of making.

"You know, if you tried something, I could hit the brakes right now. My boyfriend, he installed these super-good brakes, and you'd go for a fucking *ride*, mister."

"Go ahead," Zilch says, without worry. "I'm quite sure it won't have the effect you intended." Then there was a slight jolt and he felt *lusus naturae*'s call—that soft thrumming, that foggy arrow in his mind pushing him in the direction of *maybe that-away*. Fuck, did he just think that out loud? Being dead, you forget there used to be "just for me" words and things other people can hear, too.

He says: "Look. You're not in any kind of trouble here. And I'm not threatening you, I swear, I'm kitten harmless. Grandma harmless—"

"Grandmas can be crazy too." She nods to herself. "All righty. I think Galavance has had enough. I have a crazy man in my car, a bad morning has gone nuclear, and I should probably just pull over—actually, I probably should have done that a few miles back."

"It *sounds* crazy, I agree, but I've had the time to . . . you know, get used to how crazy this is, and how crazy it sounds. I'm not good at explaining shit, okay? I appreciate the ride, no harm will come to you, and . . . let's just get there, all right? Double underline: I'm not a psycho."

"But don't psychos, you know, like to lie about *not* being psycho?"

"Exactly. So if I'm addressing it, up front, then that should be a good sign, right?"

"Unless you're trying to do that reverse psychology thing. Say you're not a psycho, when you are—okay, fuck it, you haven't stabbed me yet. I'm not gonna go out of my way, just say stop when you want me to stop. Okay?"

He can't help but grin. "Okay."

∞

It's the sticks, but there's still a backup at the ramp to get onto US-1. Galavance pictures the Frenchy's regional manager, Patty, tapping her foot anxiously, checking her watch, adjusting her too-tight blazer she's always dressed in, prepackaged like the meatloaf Frenchy's serves, wondering where her wait-staff manager could be, waiting to shit-can Galavance *literally* as soon as she walks in the door.

But we're not there yet. That future can be avoided, maybe. Galavance hates the idea of fate. Fuck fate. *I might be making this up as I go along, and sure, it looks like a mess from the outside, I totally agree, it does, but I* can *make this better. I will.*

While they wait for the light, one hand on the wheel and the other keeping her head up, Galavance says, "Talk to me."

"Hm?"

"You're getting a free ride here, the least you could do is make a little conversation—even if it's about whatever crazy shit you claim to be up to. Especially since I'm having to suffer this commute to just go into work, get fired, and turn right back 'round and go back through it again. Not exactly worth the gas if you ask me, but someone's gotta keep the boyfriend in Budweiser."

"You have a boyfriend," Zilch says.

"If you could call him that."

"I don't think I follow."

"He's a *boy*, that's for certain. But as for that word 'friend,' well, friends don't typically shit on each other." Galavance smiles, weakly. She feels guilty bad-mouthing Jolby with a stranger, even if he deserves it.

The light changes. They move along with the crush of traffic, then break off to take the two-lane running alongside the highway.

"What does he do?" Zilch asks.

"Farts around, says he's building a house."

"For you and him? How Abe."

"No, for someone to buy. But it took them almost a year to get the frame up and now—Jolby says—they're putting up the drywall." She pauses. "But I'm pretty sure they're just sitting around all day getting shit-faced."

Zilch is looking out the passenger side window and doesn't reply.

"What do you *really* do?" she says, snapping him back. "And no bullshit this time. Your face, before . . . I mean, I hit you, hard. Now it's like it never happened."

"I told you."

She chuckles, shakes a smoke from the pack, and offers him one. He accepts. Taking the hide-and-go-seek lighter that facilitated their meeting, their fingers brush briefly. His touch is still cold, clammy. He says, "I tell you I'm a reanimated corpse sent back from the dead to hunt monsters, and you're fine with it . . . and you giggle?"

"I just don't buy it, simple as that," Galavance says. "And things I don't buy I laugh at. Laugh, not giggle. I don't giggle. But, a guy *tells* me he has a seventeen-inch trouser goblin, what am I supposed to do? Keel over from how impressed I am? No. Prove it. So you had some road-rash, before, and now you don't. Maybe the light made it look worse than it actually was. Maybe you take your vitamins, I don't know. Drink lots of milk or some shit. But a zombie monster hunter? That's just a flat-ass lie, mister. You insult me. This blond comes from a bottle, you know."

"You asked, remember," he says. "I told you because *you asked.*"

"Don't get loud with me. Ain't nobody allowed to holler in this car but me."

"Sorry."

"Now, if you wanna tell me something true, I'll let you bend my ear for that."

"I got nothing else to tell you. I've been doing this shit for so long I can hardly remember when I *wasn't*," he says. Galavance feels him look over at her again, and suddenly feels bad, gets the feeling that Zilch actually does believe his whole story.

"Anyways, a monster hunter? You'll have to try harder than that. I saw three things on the internet last week alone that were freakier than that. Jolby showed me this one website: there's kids who post videos where they numb their stomachs and disembowel themselves. Call it *scarfing*, because the goal is to pull the small intestine out far enough to wear it like a scarf. Fun, huh? Then there was another thing where they found a piece of a spaceship out in Russia with a bunch of newspapers in it with all of their dates ten years from now. And on top of all that, there's apparently Lizard Men stomping around swamplands jacking cars for parts *in this very state*. There's no surprising anyone anymore."

"Wait. Lizard Men?" Zilch perks, sitting straight in his seat.

"I rattle all that shit off and *that's* the thing you find weird?"

"Lizard *Men*? Plural?" he pressed. "Like, more than one? Are they sure about that?"

"I don't fucking know, mister. Go get online with the other crazies."

"So you *do* think I'm nuts."

"We established that. Look, fella, I went to school with this chick, Maybelline, who swore up and down she was a vampire. I know this other guy who swears when he gets really high he can walk on the ceiling, except it only works when nobody's looking at him. So, not to be a bitch or anything, dude, but you're gonna have to get over yourself—or try a little harder. You hunt monsters. You say you're a dead fella. Okay. Sure, honey. Have fun with that."

"Turn here," he says.

"What?"

"Turn." He's holding the side of his head as if trying to squeeze his brain out his ear like the last of the toothpaste. "Right here, turn."

"There's nowhere *to* turn, do you see a road anywhere?" It's just wetlands on either side; they're on a manmade strip just wide enough for a road to get slapped down.

Zilch's fingertips are pressing dents into his temple. "Stop the car. Now."

He nearly climbs into the driver's seat with her, peering out her window, past her. He's close enough she can smell him; he reeks like dirt. Galavance turns to look where he's staring. To their left, mere feet from the road's shoulder, is brown stagnant water. Spindly trees, willows, cat-tails. Nothing more. Silence. The warm morning air makes it look like the water is steaming. It looks state fair fun house fake, it's spookiness overdone. But she pulls over, careful to not dunk them into the water. Zilch scrabbles out before they're even completely stopped.

She watches him in the side mirror as he approaches the swamp's edge, staring out across the water, but not at any particular thing—like throwing his gaze past what's present. As the door ajar chime dings and dings, Galavance considers reaching over, closing the door, and taking off. Her heart starts to race at the idea. She could be rid of this weirdo, right now. But he knows her name, knows her car. Its front end is all goobered up from hitting him. She's seen those forensics cop shows; she's seen people get the electric chair from one little fleck of skin picked up with tweezers. She ducks her head out the window, watches him standing there in his filthy suit staring off across the murky water that's probably full of snakes, leeches, and God knows what else. It smells bad, too, when the wind tears hot across its surface, like decay. He looks out over the bog for a while, maybe a minute, eyes pinched like he, too, had Three Buck Chucked himself into white zin oblivion last night.

"What is it?" she asks.

Zilch turns, only half paying attention to her, polished loafers crunching in the roadside gravel. "Thank you for the ride," he manages, still squinting, "Much obliged."

He carefully moves alongside the bog's muddy bank, steps squishing, head tilted as if he's trying to avoid his ear drums being punctured by a siren only he can hear.

The cicadas chirrup, the tiny frogs sing their overlapping *glunk-glunk* songs. Galavance's patience bests her. "Seriously? That's it?" she shouts at his back.

"Yep." He continues on, squish, squish. "Thanks."

"You know the Lizard Man thing is just some internet thing, right?" Galavance yells. "Like Slenderman or that other thing, the doll with people teeth."

"They're just internet things *now*," he says without turning around, squelching away.

"Fuck does that mean?" she says. Her focus adjusts past him, and she realizes where they are. Directly across the swamp—Old Man Weatherly's Pond as the locals call it—is Whispering Pines Lane. Jolby, quite likely, is only a mile and a half away, directly across that stinky water, or partly under it, trying to complete the house. She can see some roofs, shingle grit and new siding catching the sun, glistening.

The passenger door is still hanging open, the door ajar alarm singing. *Fine*, she decides. *I didn't have time for this anyways.* Galavance reaches across the seat, pulls it closed, drops the car into gear, and takes off, throwing rocks for a dozen feet behind her. Back to reality. The suckiness closes in around her again. After that weirdness, it's finally time to go get fired.

ᴄᴘ

ZILCH HOPES IT WORKS OUT FOR HER. THAT SHE GETS WISE AND breaks up with her lifeblood-sucking boyfriend before it takes her under completely. Despite the headache threatening to crack his melon open, he pauses, and recalls Susanne—and what he did to her. Galavance's story had hit close to home.

Not liking the taste of that particular memory, he turns to face out into the wetlands again and hopes there's only one Lizard Man, if that's what he's here to find. And if it is, that it's easy to kill.

Led by the flickering needle of his pain compass, Zilch trudges down the road that borders the swamp, glad when the terrain evens out a mile down the road. He comes to a new development neighborhood, and stops to read the bas relief sign plastered on to a stack of bricks: *The Whispering Pines of Picturesque Bay.*

There's a dirt path with lots of truck tread running back and forth through the mud, no pavement yet. He walks in, avoiding puddles, listening to the sounds of electric saws and the whoosh-and-thwack of pneumatic tools. Some of the houses are almost complete, with siding and everything, while others still have their raw pink insulation exposed. Some porches still need railings, only a few houses have mailboxes staked out front. Some near the end of the cul-de-sac are just wooden frames on cement pads, lumber, nails, miles of spooled electrical wire, and so forth arranged in the front lawns. Oh, talk about those lawns. Rolled out like carpet, the gaps between sections still obvious and dark like fresh skin grafts. Unlike most new development neighborhoods, Zilch notices, these are not cookie-cutter McMansions. Each is different. If he were to ever be granted life for more than a handful of days at a time, this would be the kind of spot he might consider. It's nice. Kind of place you could leave the doors unlocked.

These pop-up neighborhoods aren't a terribly new sight to Zilch; that sort of thing was just starting to happen when he'd died for real, for the very first time. But he's never heard of draining a swamp to construct a neighborhood. *That* is a new one.

At the cul-de-sac, the asphalt circle at the end of the drive is half-submerged in murky brown water. There are some trucks set up with long yellow ribbed hoses running out into the bog, gurgling as they pull the rancid water out a gallon a second. It looks like it will take months to finish, and when it rains again it'll probably need to be done all over again. A collection tank sits nearby, he notices, a big swallow of the swamp in its semi-transparent tank belly. Next to it, a strange sight that makes Zilch frown. A backhoe, yellow and new, is up on cinderblocks like the mechanical victim of parking on the bad side of the tracks. All four massive wheels are gone. Is that deliberate or—did someone steal them?

Something buzzes in front of his eye, a mosquito coming in for a fly-by inspection, nearly getting tangled in his eyelashes. Slapping them dead is pointless. He lets them smell him, get the idea, and take off. Nothing worth sucking off of this one, they determine.

Zilch approaches the point where the neighborhood and the swamp start competing for territory. The pain is intense here. Whatever it is, he's on the right track.

He stares, listens. He has spots in his eyes, his ears ring as if he's just left a concert, a watery thrum going and going. He takes a step forward and the pain arrow swings around to the back of his head. He turns to face it and it swings to settle in the corner of his left eye. Facing the swamp, and can see, through the cattails and willows, the road where Galavance let him out. The pain compass is spinning him around in a circle. Something in the center point, between over there and here, is calling. He waits, head throbbing, listening.

"Sit still," he murmurs. There is no accurate read. Just a general somewhere, close by or maybe not. Monster in a swampy haystack. Shifting the pain to the back of his head, he turns back around and examines the row of incomplete houses, all staring out from their lots with vacant, glassless eyes. There's a realty sign posted in front of one building, its yard half-submerged in swamp water. Probably a tough sell, Zilch muses, until they can assure you that you won't wake up one morning to a muskrat swimming in through your bedroom window.

1330 Whispering Pines Lane. The tide, having reached halfway up the house at some point in the recent past, has left behind a filthy brown line. He crosses the lawn and when his footfalls begin to get squishy, he stops. Something catching his eye in the driveway, the rainbow glimmer of a prism, shifting through the color spectrum when he moves. Moving in closer, there is a fragment of a car reflector tucked between the panels of cement. He remembers Galavance saying the Lizard Men were stealing car parts.

The garage stands as the most completed part of the house. On tip-toes, Zilch peeks in through one of its windows. Inside, he's startled to see a big black shape crouched inside. It's huge and gives him a start but after letting his eyes adjust, he realizes it's just a car parked inside. Unable to make out any of its details or see if anyone's sitting within, he heads back around front, stepping up the uneven front walk of the house. Without a door to knock on, he looks around and gives the plastic hanging over where a door will be someday a couple of howdy-do neighborly slaps. Maybe Lizard Man has a timeshare at 1330 Whispering Pines Lane.

No one answers. And the pain compass starts to lose its keenness. He turns to try and catch it, but it's fading too quickly. It winks out and Zilch, though released from the vice around his head, is now also without a trail to follow.

"Fuck."

The gurgling of an outboard engine makes him turn to face the swamp again. He sees a small rowboat puttering along, leaving a broken line of smoke in its wake as it nears. The compass doesn't flick toward the old, bent man driving the boat—but something about how the coot is staring at him as he runs his aluminum watercraft aground tells Zilch he should give this fella some attention. Zilch steps down off the porch and cautiously approaches, his steps sinking into the waterlogged yard.

The old man limply tosses an anchor and its hook sinks into the mud. "Morning, young fellow," he says, friendly enough but somewhat rigid, clapping his hands of dirt in a way that looks like community theater.

"Morning," Zilch says, eyes narrowing, studying the old man.

"Mighty fine day here on the planet Earth today. Is it not, fellow human being?" the old man says. "Temperature levels are favorable and oxygen is low of allergy-causing particulates."

Zilch snorts a laugh. "You can stop anytime you like. It's embarrassing."

The old man in his waders, flannel shirt, and colorful lures pinned to his rumpled bucket cap says: "It was the least conspicuous individual in the immediate vicinity."

"Which one are you?"

"Excuse me?"

"Have we met before?"

"Yes, four jobs ago."

"You never gave me your name," Zilch says.

"Eliphas," the agent says, and pauses to look down at his denim trousers stained with the blood of bait. "Dungaree. Eliphas Dungaree."

"Rolls right off the tongue," Zilch says.

"I'd like to remind you, Saelig, that divulging employee information with the mass uninitiated is strictly—"

"Prohibited, yeah, I remember," Zilch says and pinches the bridge of his nose. "I had to tell her something."

"Not to split hairs, but you actually didn't."

"Fine. It'd just be nice for once, to go on one of these fucking things and . . . not have it just be only about the job."

"That's what you're here to do. That's why you were—"

"I know. But, despite the details of how all of this—" Zilch gestures at everything standing in his shoes "—works, I'm still, by definition, human."

"You feel your emotion-part has become neglected."

Zilch blinks. "Yeah, if those are the words you want to use to describe what I'm feeling, sure. My emotion-part feels neglected, yeah."

"Perhaps this will help," Eliphas says. "You are almost adequate at what you do." He smiles. "Better?"

Zilch sighs. "Yeah. Much. So, what brings you down to terra firma then?"

"What is your compass telling you?"

"It was around here a minute ago," Zilch says. "Out that way." He gestures until Eliphas makes the old man turn to look the way he's pointing, over across the steaming bog.

"Do you know how to swim?" the old man says.

Zilch issues a sarcastic laugh, slaps his knee. "Hoo-boy, what a card."

The old man standing in the boat faces Zilch again. When one of them hijacks some poor nobody, it's hard to tell sometimes but there's a faint violet glimmer in the eyes that can be caught at the right angle and in the right kind of light. Zilch only peeks one small glimpse of Eliphas, inside, when the old man inclines his head, smirking, to say: "I'm not supposed to be here. I slipped off while my brothers were refueling the aircraft. I wanted to tell you I'm pulling for you."

"Meaning you're trying to rig the bet, right? Fine by me. Then help me kill it."

"I cannot risk interfering other than to point you in the right direction," Eliphas says. "Even so much as speaking to you after the assignment is in motion is against the mandate, other than to threaten."

"So you're only here to tell me shit I already know. Great. Good work," Zilch says. "How much?"

"How much what?"

"How much do you have on me?"

"Twelve xabfarbs," Eliphas says.

"Is that a lot?" Zilch says.

Eliphas nods. "A great sum, yes."

"I could've used the help with the last job. I fucking wandered around aimlessly for a week, compass spinning the whole time before the thing, like it got bored or felt bad for me, sprang out of goddamn nowhere and swallowed me whole. *Whole*, Eliphas. While I was still fucking alive. Didn't even give me the courtesy of chewing first to put me out of my misery."

"I lost four xabfarbs on that," Eliphas says, "if it's any consolation."

"Gee, four whole xabfarbs, you say? Sad face." Zilch faux pouts. "I'll remember that next time I'm having some limb-removal done by a skunk ape," Zilch says. "If you can't actually do anything to help, can you at least tell me what I'm after?"

"A creature that can hide in plain sight."

Zilch scans his immediate surroundings; there are no irregular shadows on the ground that might indicate something invisible is casting them. Nor is there anything semi-transparent hanging from the trees, bending the light around itself like heat waves rising off a highway. No faint silhouette watching from the roof of 1330 Whispering Pines Lane behind him either. He puts out his hand to his left and looks at the old man. "Hot or cold?"

"No," Eliphas says, "the trouble lies in the duality of the creature and its host. The host is unaware that they are harboring any affliction whatsoever. And only one—host or parasite—can pilot at a time."

"So we're dealing with something that may not look like a monster, right away." Zilch recalls the conversation with what's-her-name in the car. "Those can be tricky."

"Yes."

"Fantastic."

"With our current data," Eliphas says, "my brothers and I have decided to declare this a class eight *lusus naturae*." The old man smiles, as if Eliphas's happy for Zilch. "The first you've been assigned to, I might add."

"Class eight? What the hell have I been going after before now?"

"Class twos, mostly. The occasional class one."

"What was 'The Insatiable'?"

"That was a class four, but you were assigned to it by accident. Clerical error. We do not blame you for aborting that mission."

"It melted me."

"We know. It did not get put on your permanent record. Our fault."

"With its vomit. It melted me, to the *bone*, with its *vomit*."

"We issued an apology. It's also been appropriately reclassified, to a nineteen."

Zilch shakes his head. "So I'm being handed a class eight and there's no undo button this time?"

"Your failed attempt against the Insatiable was our fault, as I previously stated. It wasn't your turn. This time it *is*—we double-checked—and despite the *lusus naturae* being above your experience level . . ."

". . . welcome to the big leagues?"

"It's your turn. Be warned: if you fail, more of her will be—"

"I *know*, fuckhead. Christ. Are you *trying* to make me feel bad?"

"I'm sorry, Saelig."

"Sure you are." Zilch groans. "Fine, whatever. How do I make it dead?"

Eliphas doesn't make the old man reply right away. He looks Zilch over, up and down. "You've severely damaged your vessel," he says finally, a little aghast. "Your nanobug count is where it should be after four days post-delivery and you've already expired over half of them! What happened?"

Zilch chews on the corner of his fingernail. "I got hit by a car."

Eliphas blinks. "On purpose?"

"Why does everyone keep asking me that? No, not on purpose."

"You'll have less time. And you'll only be allowed to hold onto her so long as you start to succeed at your assignments."

Zilch hands knot into fists, and he squishes a few steps across the soggy yard, closer to the boat. "What gives you dickheads the right to mess around in my head, anyway? I've got dead spots. New ones. Ones I didn't make myself."

"As an employee, the penalty system was explained to you in full," Eliphas says.

"That's *another* thing," Zilch says. "I'm not your employee. I didn't apply for this shit."

"Employee, I suggest you continue with your mission. You have the same information we do now."

"Nope, not good enough. I demand answers, you memory-stealing shit-wizard."

The old man flinches, and looks at his hands, then at Zilch. "Who are you?"

"Nice try." Zilch steps up into the boat with the old man. "You know, I've always been curious, what do you guys really look like? I say we crack you open and see. Personally, I hope you're like that fucking paperclip that was always telling me how to write a resume." Zilch rolls up his sleeves. "Wanna guess what my most recent job title was? Head of the department of kicking your ass."

The old man, hands out, tumbles over trying to get away from him. Zilch, towering, sees that up close, the purplish flicker has indeed left the man's water old eyes, and he's beginning to shake. "Stop, please. Take what you want, don't hurt me."

Zilch groans out his frustration and steps back off the boat, shaking his head as the old man tries to offer him his expensive-looking fishing reel. Zilch leans side to side, the old man's eyes tracking him as he tries catching for that violet glimmer— but he doesn't find it.

"Sorry," Zilch says. "I only called you over because I thought you had a flat tire. My mistake." Zilch tugs the anchor out of the mud and drops it back into the boat for the old man. "Have a good one."

The old man wastes no time wrenching on the pullcord to get his motor started again. He gets the boat turned around and tears off back across the bog in a hurry, trailing a white wake of turned swamp water behind him. Glancing back at Zilch, there was nothing in his eyes but a whole lot of fear and confusion.

Zilch watches him go. "One day, pricks. One day."

Tires squealing, Galavance turns, hard, into a parking lot. The front of Frenchy's kills her soul a little every time she sees it. All that neon and Parisian whorehouse motif by way of pre-weathered fabricated weather-resistant polystyrene. It looks like the "crashed" Disneyland seafaring vessels.

In the clinging humidity and noise of the kitchen, Galavance punches in twenty-three minutes late. Daring a peek into the heart of the grill-line section of the kitchen, she sees Patty has already arrived and apparently has been here for a while. She's going through everything; opening drawers, scouring the reach-in coolers, checking freshness date stickers, prying open the lid of the Tupperware containers and stuffing her stupid fat face inside to sniff-sniff-sniff. She's a Hobbit of a lady, short and ruddy and freckled, but an *angry* Hobbit, perpetually scowling, pissed at all she beholds. And right now, that's Galavance.

Patty sets aside the plastic container of pre-chopped romaine with an unnecessary slam and says, peachy as can be, "Ms. Petersen. So good for you to join us this blessed morning."

"Sorry. I had kind of an eventful commute."

"Must've been," Patty says and scoffs, shaking her head. "Because by the time I have, it looks to be a couple minutes shy of no longer being morning at all."

"I'm really sorry," Galavance says. Every eye is on her. The Mexican line cooks eye their Jordans. The wait-staff, her own people, not a single one of them over the age of twenty-one, all made up like work is some kind of beauty contest, stare as Galavance's cheeks redden. They're all just happy it's her and not them on the chopping block.

"I got in an accident," Galavance says, praying her voice won't break. "I had to figure out everything with the other guy and . . . yeah."

Silence. Somebody please fucking say something, please.

When Patty finally speaks, it sounds prepared. It probably is, a shape-up-or-ship-out competency booster.

"When Francois 'Frenchy' Burdeoix started this restaurant in Limoges, France in 1978, he was a pioneer in his field, Ms. Petersen. He had a dream to come to the American South and turn the traditional cuisine of his adopted home on its ear, to inject culture where there was none. To take the cheeseburger and elevate it into a *fromage sur la viande*. And do you think that the *fromage sur la viande* or any of our other 101 decadent options became world-famous because Frenchy was late to work every day, unable to separate his personal life from his professional one?"

"No, ma'am." She always thought it was weird that Francois, a man from France, went by Frenchy. It'd be like her having the nickname Americany.

Patty gifts Galavance with a few more moments of agonizing silence under the pitying stares of her peers, then, apparently satisfied, angles her square-shaped body to address the entire staff, her seafoam dress suit so starched the fabric makes snapping sounds as she moves, fanning out her arms. "Do we understand?"

"Yes, ma'am," everyone mutters together.

Patty points a talon-like fingernail across at Galavance. "Do *not* let it happen again, Ms. Petersen."

Galavance keeps steady eye contact with Patty as she speaks and it nearly hurts.

"If we find ourselves here again in a similar situation as this one," Patty adds, "Frenchy's and you may have to sit down and reconfigure their relationship. Understand me, girl?"

"Yes."

"So, now that all of *that's* out of the way," the woman says, and after clapping her hands to illustrate the change of gears, she turns back her doom-gaze on everyone else. "What else do I have to do look into before I go? All of you got your performance evaluations—which I hope you'll take home and think long and hard about, since not a *one* of them is worth putting on a refrigerator door—what else?"

The grill cook, Miguel, quietly offers a suggestion: "Walk-in?"

"Good, *Me-gell*! Very good. Yes, let's do that. Come on, everyone. Let's go and see how many outdated freshness labels we'll find in there. But not *you*, Ms. Petersen." An outstretched palm bars Galavance from moving forward with the others. "I think you have some salt and pepper shakers to refill out in the dining area." She checks her watch. "We only have half an hour before we open, after all."

"Yes, ma'am."

As Galavance walks out into the dining room with the canisters of kosher salt and ground black pepper, both roughly the size of paint cans, she thanks God that she's not a psychic, that she can't make things move with her mind. Because if she could, Patty would be ripped limb from limb and all of those loose parts would be going back in, just not in the places they came from. Thanksgiving turkey comes to mind. She smiles at this thought, Patty stuffed with her own parts. That hateful mouth packed silent, forever.

Yikes. I get dark *when I'm hung over.*

She's at table four, refilling the pepper and getting it everywhere, when her cell beeps. She takes it out, using the table to block easy view of what she's doing from the kitchen, just in case Patty comes storming out of the walk-in cooler.

A text message from Jolby.

can u go 2 the bale-bonds place? i got busted w/ a dimebag.

She compiles a text on her phone's cracked screen: "I'm sorry. I can't. I gotta stay my whole shift. You're just going to have to stay the weekend in jail. Maybe next time you'll think twice before going to score with Chev."

Her thumb hovers over the send button.

She thinks about this being it. The final straw. That she'll return to their double-wide (which is under his name, he'll be quick to tell anyone who will listen), pack up her stuff, and take one last look at his skid-marked underwear. But this time it won't be a "Jesus, my boyfriend's a man-child fool who can't wipe his own ass," but a "Now where the fuck am I going to live? I guess he wasn't *so* bad. Here, let me go get my toothbrush. I'll get that out in a jiff."

Galavance can't even break up with Jolby in her own fantasies. She feels awful admitting that to herself, that the alternative, that she'd have to shack up with—heaven forbid—her parents, is worse. For all his awfulness, he does make her laugh, though. He's sweet, generous on occasion, kind. *Fuck, I just did it again.* She holds down the delete key and erases her first reply. "Fine," she writes. "I'll cut out early."

Thx babe. I 3> U sooo much.

She texts: "Yeah."

Patty comes up to the table and nearly catches her with her phone out. Galavance palms it, quick as a magician, and smiles as Patty nears.

"All through?" Patty asks.

"Yep, last one," Galavance replies, slapping down the aluminum spout on the salt canister, done.

"Lovely. We're doing a tasting back here from some of our new menu items. Want to head on back and try some of it with us?" Not a question. Come, slave. The next round of floggings is to be begin promptly!

Galavance follows Patty into the kitchen. On the prep table a few halved green peppers are sitting in a stainless steel hotel pan, stuffed with what appears to be chipped, burnt tires and stomped grapes and something viscous and brown. The smell is unreal. Like how your hair smells after the beach, plus the sharp tang of diarrhea and oniony stress sweat.

Everyone is eating, but it's obvious no one's enjoying it. The kitchen guys politely nibble, and the wait-staff are all on thirty-calories-a-day diets anyways, so they take tiny bites like they're stranded on a mountaintop and it's their best friend's ear they're sampling. Patty, chewing away, is nodding encouragingly for Galavance to take the remaining one.

"Garlic crouton stuffing with sausage and goat cheese inside a green bell pepper. The Culinary Inspiration Team at corporate headquarters named it *poivrons farcis*." Patty attempts to mash the French name through her Dirty South accent and she ends up sounding like Foghorn Leghorn trying to be fancy. Galavance took French in high school (mostly so she could graduate a year early), but knows that every "creation" from Frenchy's Inspiration Team is really just something you'd find it in *The Joy of Cooking* translated verbatim into French. *Poivrons farcis* is literally "stuffed peppers."

One bite and Galavance understands why every other employee around her is trying to not make the "This tastes like the bathroom floor of a meth den and I do not like having it in my mouth" face. The sausage is squeaky between her teeth. It doesn't taste like cow or lamb or pig. It tastes vaguely fishy. Couple that with the richness of the goat cheese, and the mental image she sees is roadkill. Crushed, burst guts sizzling on hot asphalt. She fights to swallow it down, bile coming halfway up to meet it. She swallows again, and takes two of the Dixie cups of water Patty had thoughtfully arranged next to her tray of horrors.

Patty, suddenly remembering something evidently, lunges for her wheeled suitcase. She carefully sets her own stuffed pepper on a napkin and goes through her file folder until coming to a stack of papers that she disperses around the room. It's a review sheet for the stewed ass they've just eaten.

"Everyone, fill these out when you're finished and hand them in to me. Just remember that the Culinary Inspiration Team are fellow Frenchy's family members and that they have feelings too, so don't be too harsh." *This coming from* you? Galavance thinks.

The review sheet doesn't require a name. Galavance can speak her mind anonymously. She jumps at the chance, using the counter of the grill cook's prep area as a desk.

What did you think of the sausage?
It helped me to answer a question I've been struggling with most of my life. Now, I can claim, with zero hesitation, that there truly is no God.

With two words, describe the texture (or "mouth feel") of the new menu item.
"Like butts" comes to mind.

How would you rate the new menu item on a scale from one to ten, ten being stellar?
I've forgotten what numbers look like after you made me put that in my mouth.

While Patty is busy adjusting one of the hairnets of the cooks and lingering a bejeweled hand on his swollen bicep, Galavance takes the opportunity to surreptitiously deposit her questionnaire by the briefcase and quickly make herself scarce, ducking back out into the dining area. She doesn't know exactly why she felt compelled to do it, give it to total strangers guff like that, but all she knows is that after this particularly challenging—okay, downright shitty—morning, she deserves to have a bit of fun.

The restaurant opens. In this corner of Raleigh there are a few office plazas whose workers make Frenchy's their lunch break destination. Galavance mans her podium back by the kitchen door, going through the grid for next week. Getting each of her waiters and waitresses' requests for time off and still having full coverage for every shift is like playing a terrible version of *Tetris* where there is no pattern to the pieces. She gets it looking right just as Patty wheels her suitcase into the dining room and spots her. "Busy, Miss Petersen?"

Galavance keeps her worry—*she's deciphered my hand-writing, she knows it was me*—packed down. "Sure, what's up?"

"There's a cooler in the walk-in. Bring it out to my car for me?" Patty says.

"I'm kind of busy," Galavance says. Schedule done, she now can pretend to be working the rest of the day which requires a great deal of creativity.

"Cooler. In the walk-in. Now." Patty shoves the door open and walks out into the parking lot, towing her briefcase on wheels behind her. Galavance cuts through the kitchen, where a few of the dishwashers are standing around, and wonders why Patty didn't ask them to haul this heavy-ass thing out to her car.

Out in the heat, lugging the kind of Coleman ice chest she's only seen loaded with beers around campfires, Galavance makes her way slowly out to Patty, who is waiting by her rental car. Patty loads her suitcase into the trunk and holds the lid up and nods for Galavance to hoist this thousand-pound thing in by herself. "God, what's in here?" Galavance mutters, accidently out loud.

"The sausage has to come back to the hotel with me," Patty says. "It still has the Inspiration Team's top secret label on it. Can't have my little ants taking samples home and reverse-engineering all of the Team's hard work."

Fat chance of that ever crossing anyone's mind, but okay. "Is it really that special?"

"Didn't you notice a faint fishy taste to it?"

Galavance nods. "I did. Is it supposed to be like that?"

"That's our focus for tomorrow," Patty says and continues staring at Galavance as if expecting her to bow, walk backwards a few paces, *then* turn around to part her wizened company.

"Well, if that's everything," Galavance says, "Drive safe."

"I'll be back tomorrow. And the day after. I'm in Raleigh through the weekend," Patty says, as if she enjoys laying this sentence down on Galavance. "But, listen, Miss Petersen . . . if I could steal one minute of your time before you go back to sending sweet nothings to your gentleman callers on your phone— yes, I saw that . . ."

Galavance fights the urge to cross her arms.

"Forgive me my assumption that you're somewhat thick, but I feel inclined to repeat myself. You need to buckle down if you want to continue working here. I'm glad you have a life outside of work. But to support that life, you need to make money."

"I understand the idea of employment." Daring.

Patty takes the sass, grins a little, and surprisingly decides to ignore Galavance's snark. "But do you understand that *keeping* yourself employed means showing up on time? Being present, being reliable and accountable and *at your job* when you are scheduled?"

"Yes. I do."

"Tomorrow, you and I are going to spend some time together. I can tell by the look on your face you are not thrilled about it. I'm okay with that." Patty pauses, squinting at Galavance like she's the most confusing thing that's ever passed in front of her eyes. "Do you even have any interest in moving up? You're the wait-staff manager. How you got that promotion is beyond me, but is this where you want to spend the rest of your life, at this rank?"

"I don't know."

Patty shakes her head. "See, it's things like that—what you just said, 'I don't know'—that we're gonna work on. You're not alone in this; I think it's a generational thing. None of you know how to make a decision because us old people have always made them all for you. Shame, really. Tomorrow, be on time. Do we understand each other?"

"Yeah."

"Good." Patty gets in her car, slams the door, starts it up, and leaves.

Galavance waits until Patty turns the corner out of the lot and onto the highway before raising two middle fingers above her head. She turns to go back inside, seeing the windows along the front of Frenchy's all have a customer or two framed in the tinted glass. They all saw her do that. Does Galavance care? Not especially. Because if today wasn't bad enough, it's all but certain that tomorrow will be worse.

Galavance spends an hour on Facebook stalking people she went to high school who ended up more successful than her, staring at pictures of them with their kids. She's careful not to accidentally "Like" anything because she's not friends with any of them. When she's green enough with jealousy, she moves over to her own page to update it. But swear words are all she can think of to type in the status composition. Or she could confess to running over a man on her way to work. She decides to not post anything after all and logs out.

Galavance decides Patty's been gone long enough and she's unlikely to return the rest of the day. She uses this to punch out and end her three-hour shift, and reluctantly leaves the air conditioning of Frenchy's for her car, melting in the back lot. At least she didn't get fired. Now to deal with Jolby.

She runs her hand along the man-shaped dent in the hood. Her finger bumps against something hard—it's a button halfway pressed through the sheet metal, like a coin that'd proven too big for its slot. She tries wiggling it loose, but it doesn't come free, it's really in there. Feeling the gaze of her coworkers still inside, still on the clock, watching her leave early after showing up late, Galavance gets in, starts up her car, cranks the AC, and returns to the highway.

An hour later, crossing back through Raleigh, Go-Go's on the radio because she has no choice, Galavance takes the exit for the town of Franklinton, North Carolina.

If one were so moved they could do ass-naked cartwheels up and down its main street and likely never get noticed. There are no open stores anymore—they'd all closed before Galavance was in high school. She passes the old vinyl siding factory—closed, the gas station—closed, and the feed and seed store—closed. Then there's the "black school," the single-level plain red brick building set way off the road, and a block down, the now-integrated school, what was once for whites only, with its stately pillars and three stories and immaculate lawn and fences and army of pristine school buses.

She feels the ghosts of that place as she goes past. She hated high school at the time, but now looks at those three years fondly because, really, it was the only time in her life that things had been simple. She should've enjoyed it. If she knew she had days like *this* to look forward to, she would've. But she cannot look at the building completely fondly—because it's where she'd met Jolby.

He'd moved to Franklin County freshman year. He was beautiful. All the girls fawned over him; they seldom got transplants—he was fresh, hot blood, and they all wanted a taste. The other boys hated him, which only made him more desirable; he was dangerous, a new element among the shallow gene pool. Immaculate Jolby Dawes, back when he was fifteen and gorgeous and funny and knew all the best music and had giant mind-busting opinions about the universe and science and art and drove this really cool car and Galavance, in the passenger seat, would watch the girls he'd rejected in favor of her glare as she went by, seething with jealousy. She'd give them the smallest, sharpest smile—*I win*.

Now, she'd probably accept a trade with any of them, on any terms. Jolby for a pint of expired coleslaw? Deal, he's all yours.

Since her car's mashed front end might raise questions with Sam the sheriff, once she gets to that end of Franklinton—and its only really the one road—she parks around back. The police station was once a general store, and you can still tell; among other things, it has a malt counter. Behind it is where Sam stands, removing his hat because he's in the presence of a lady. Old school. His moustache hides his mouth, nearly to his chin, and it adorably exaggerates his smile. Jolby, on the other side, unlike Sam, is chained to a chair and not smiling. He's slumped in his seat, gut prominent behind his well-worn and food-stained Metallica T-shirt, floppy hair in his face, pierced lip trembling.

Most people wouldn't notice, but she knows him well enough to tell he's been crying. Just puffy around his eyes, the tip of his nose a faint shade of pink. He doesn't look at her, even as Sam, loudly, greets her. Sam was friends with Galavance's mom. They, too, went to Franklinton Public. Galavance wonders how Sam can sit at a large-windowed station every day, directly across from that place, and not end up burning it down. Perhaps because he didn't wind up with some human fail-heap.

"What's the damage, Sam?" she says amiably.

After giving the price to spring Jolby, Sam adjusts his bolo tie and uncuffs Jolby as Galavance writes out a check. Jolby, head down beside her, rubs his cuff-dented wrist.

Galavance signs the check, rips it free, and hands it over.

"Court date's set for the nineteenth," Sam drawls. "Should get him into some kind of program. I like seeing you, Gal, but not for these reasons." Sam cranks the ancient cash register—like the counter, it was too heavy to move when the place became a police station—and slides the check within. Bye, eighty-five bucks. Probably more like a *hundred* and eighty-five, after overdraft fees.

"I know," Galavance says to Sam, but really to Jolby, "but I think he might be a bit too old for obedience school."

Sam laughs and Galavance makes herself smile despite the pinch she feels in her heart. Older men hate Jolby, she assumes because boys like Jolby, to Sam's daughters and other older men's daughters like her, are like sink-holes. Sometimes Galavance wishes her mom, instead of hooking up with Asshole Amos after dad took off, would've gotten with Sam. Galavance could've used some of that Jolby-hatin' encouragement. Someone to send him scurrying off their front door's stairs with a well-timed porch light. Or spray him with the hose whenever he threw pebbles at Galavance's window in the night. But Asshole Amos likes Jolby. Because they're exactly alike. And, well, at least the worst has been avoided. Galavance takes the pills when the dial-a-baby-banishment tells her.

Jolby shuffles ahead of her and out the door, Galavance bids Sam farewell, and the couple goes out into the street. The sun is just at the beginning of its descent. The air is still thick and hot, and a bat who woke up early flits soundlessly overhead against an orange sky.

Jolby hesitates when he sees her car, and Galavance nearly runs into the back of him.

"What the fuck did you do?" he says.

"I hit a deer on the way in to work," she answers at once, ready with the lie. She moves in front of him before he can notice the button wedged into the hood's metal. Even Jolby's smart enough to know deer don't wear things with buttons.

But when she looks at him, really wanting him to make a stink about her car mere *seconds* after she paid to get him out of spending a weekend in jail, he's no longer studying the front of the car, but the passenger seat, his hand hesitating on the door handle.

"What's his name?" he says.

"What?" Galavance says, going around the car and waiting for a pickup to pass. "What are you talkin' about?"

"The seat, Galavance. It's been moved back. So who's been riding in the car with you? What's his fuckin' *name*?"

He can't see his girlfriend is dying from double shifts and calling her mom every other month for money just to keep them afloat, but a fucking seat being slid back an inch? That he sees.

"I gave a friend a ride," Galavance says. "Jesus. Lower your voice, we're in public, you know." There's no one around, just the dead summer wind sliding about Franklinton, but still. It's embarrassing nonetheless.

"I don't fuckin' care. Who was it?" *T*s make Jolby's lip ring click against his teeth.

"Just a friend. Get in, Jolby."

"No. I wanna know who it was."

"Just this person I work with."

"You fucking slut." His voice carries up the block and back. *Slut. Slut.*

Over the top of the Cavalier, she shakes her keys at her boyfriend. "You listen to me, Jolby, and you listen good. I didn't have to pay that just now. It would've been cheaper to just let you sit in jail for the weekend, so you should be nice to me," she says. "Things have gotta change. Because this crap you and I go through all the time, with *this*," she indicates the police station with a backhand slap, "and with you not making any money . . . You're almost thirty goddamn years old, Jolby. It's time to hang up the one-hitter and get some of your life squared away."

Jolby stares at her for a moment, then as if he didn't even hear any of it, begins trying the handle on his side. *Clunka-clunk-clunk*. She hasn't unlocked the car yet and she isn't about to. Not yet.

"Take me to my whip. I wanna go home."

"We're *talkin'* about this, Jolby."

"Right here? Right now?" he barks, brushing hair out of his eye again. "Come on, I'm *tired*. I just spent almost the whole fuckin' day in that place, Gal. All Sam talks about is the root beer he makes in his basement. Unlock the door." He tries it again and again, jerking at the handle until she unlocks it. He immediately scrambles in, slams the door closed.

She sighs, savoring the second she has alone outside the car. Then she gets in as well and they share a claustrophobic silence. Her heart is racing. She really wants to smack him.

"Could you start it up? It's hot in here."

"Babe, we *really* got to get some things figured out here. Can we talk?"

"I'm sweating. Turn on the AC."

You're always sweating. "Jolby. We've really gotta—what happened to your arm?" she stops herself. She hadn't even noticed that his wrist is bandaged. She guessed it was the way he's compulsively always got his hands in his pockets, but now that they're in the car and sitting casually, she sees it—gauze all around his left wrist. Galavance reaches to touch at it mindlessly and Jolby pulls away like a kid with an ice cream cone from a sibling.

"I'm fine."

"Did you give Sam trouble?"

"No, it happened before. At the place."

"At the house?"

"No, before I got busted me and Chev were doing this quick patch-up for this guy, this dude Chev knows. Some of his shingles blew off 'cause of that storm last week, and I was up on the roof and slipped. A nail caught my wrist."

Galavance winces sympathetically. "How does it look?" The bandages are on thick.

"It's fine," he says. "Let's just go."

"Wait. You got arrested doing shingles?"

Jolby sighs, sad and embarrassed. "We were up on the roof. I slipped, did this to myself, and then when I got down—Chev was freaking out, screaming for someone to call 911—and the dude whose place it was came outside with his buddy. The dude went and got a towel and some tape and I made the joke that I was just a skosh stoned and that normally it doesn't affect my work. I guess I said it because I was nervous. There was, like, a lot of blood. And then the dude's buddy is all like, 'Can you repeat that?' and I'm, like, okay and I say it again: 'Being stoned doesn't normally affect my work.' And Chev's giving me this weird look, like, his eyes are all big and shit? And then the dude—not the dude whose house it was but his buddy, this big guy with sideburns—asks if I could empty my pockets and I . . . I . . . he wasn't wearing his uniform, but he was a . . ." Chin down, he sniffles.

"Oh, honey. You got to admit, though, you walked right into that one." The sourness changes and becomes—son of a *fuck*—pity.

"Yeah, I know," he says, corners of his mouth tugging down.

"Aw, come here," Galavance says and it's pure mom-all-the-way. She absolutely cannot stand the sight of anyone crying. Even if there's a kid at Walmart bawling its eyes out in the parking lot that she's never met before, she will run and get him a soda at least, a temporary tattoo from the coin-machines, anything to get a smile. With Jolby, it's a bit different. If he's upset, typically a bottle of some cheap beer or a quick BJ—they're always quick, admittedly—will do, but since they're in public and broke, she just hugs him. She promises she had no one in the car worth fretting about, which is true. The dude claimed to be a reanimated corpse, *eww*, right? She rounds it out with saying everything is going to be okay. Jolby is out-and-out crying now and Galavance consoles him the best she can. A pat and a swirly-rub on the back of his neck followed up with a peck on the cheek.

"Let's get your car and go home," she says. "I'll fix dinner."

"Okay."

"What do you think you want?" she asks, starting the car.

"I dunno."

"We got a frozen pizza still, I think."

"Naw, me and Chev took that over to the house other day."

"*Okay*," Galavance says, pulling out of the spot, and checks her mirror even though there's absolutely no traffic—nor is there ever—to worry about in Franklinton. "What else do you think, then?"

He twists around to look in the back seat. "Did you bring leftovers from work?"

"I had to leave to come get you. I wasn't really thinking about sneaking anything home."

"Can we go out, then? Tacos or something?"

"I just dropped bucks on your freedom, sweetheart. I don't think we should be going out. Besides, you know how Mexican wreaks havoc on your stomach."

"One night of the trots is *totally* worth some primo tacos, though."

"Says the guy who doesn't do the laundry."

"What do you mean?"

"Nothing, sweetness. Nothing at all."

The ride is mostly silent. Jolby takes a cigarette from her pack without asking and lights it, inhaling in little gasps like a stoner taking his pot drag. Old habits. It's annoying. Galavance turns the Go-Go's up louder.

She drops him at the end of Whispering Pines so he can get his car. The minute he's out of sight, at the next stop sign, she is punching the steering wheel and screaming until her throat's raw. She has to pull over to fully void her meltdown from her system. Afraid he might make it to the trailer before she does and restart the whole accusation game about cheating, she uses the mirror to fix her hair where she was tugging at it and uses the hem of her work polo to dab her tears. *The Go-Go's Greatest Hits* is playing "Vacation." Galavance murmurs along with it, finding it relatable, especially the part about having to get away. But the second she makes eye contact with herself, she shoves the mirror in a different direction. "Fuck you."

She beats him home, probably because the guy can't pass a gas station without getting a Slim Jim. After changing—balling up her polo shirt and pitching it into the dark depths of the closet—she comes back outside and has a seat on the front porch in jorts and a tank top, running her bare feet back and forth through the scratchy Astroturf until the soles of her feet are numb. All the while, she examines the damaged hood of her car from where she's sitting. All of the ruined work Jolby's put into it, and the money that, originally, should've been used elsewhere.

The sun dips over the horizon, gone, and the crickets start up. He's still not home. A neighbor goes by in his ancient pickup and waves. Galavance waves back. The guy's window is down and he has "Bad Medicine" going full-blast. She savors the song for as long as she can hear it, before the pickup goes down the trailer park's far bend. Still humming inside, Galavance turns the air conditioner up to the coldest it can go and goes for the third drawer down in the kitchen. Where the corkscrew is. Now, for some *good* medicine.

In lieu of a wine glass she uses a red Solo cup—which is fine, they hold more anyhow.

Cup number one brings about some ideas about what her future might be like. Halfway through cup two, she's thinking that things might one be better day if she actually gets up off her ass and makes some changes. On the final sip of the second cup she is okay with how things are, but she still has some minor complaints.

Stepping back out onto the patio, taking the slurp off the top of the filled cup number three before it spills, she almost misses the seat of the lawn chair and her mind clicks onto the fella she hit with her car this morning. And some tiny part inside her— the one that used to believe lightning bugs were pixies and a big strong man who lived on a mountain threw the Fourth of July fireworks by hand—wants to believe his story, too. She wants to think that life outside of work, grocery shopping, and living in a falling-apart trailer being unhappy all the time might not always be just a fantasy.

Her cup is empty again already. Galavance doesn't remember getting up or going down the patio steps but she's standing in front of her car feeling the crinkled sheet metal and the button still pressed in hard and permanent there. She wants to think there is something to Zilch's story. A part of her wishes she hadn't driven off when he got out of the car. It suddenly feels like she might have left the change she'd been thinking about making standing on the side of the fucking road in the middle of the sticks.

"Good going, idiot," Galavance says to herself, and sits on the patio again, waiting for the other idiot to get home.

∾
⸙

ZILCH, FROM THE FRONT PORCH OF 1330 WHISPERING PINES Lane, watches the last of the workers leave for the day. Tools locked up, equipment stowed, they pile into pickup trucks and rusty beaters and cloud the unfinished road with brown dust, leaving in a swarm of country music and untuned engines.

He's completely alone in the neighborhood now, and Zilch sits and lets his head ache—a dull throb telling him the thing he's after is around here, somewhere. He waits, wishing for God to either give him a little more push in the right direction or throw a pack of Marlboros down into his lap. And a lighter, if He isn't too busy.

Zilch looks over his shoulder at the front of the house. He'd let himself in a couple hours ago—is it considered a B & E if there's no front door?—and searched the building, finding only an old cooler with melted ice, a TV, some kind of video game thing, and some folding lawn chairs. The hood of the car in the garage was cold to the touch and there was no sign of anyone—upstairs or down—to whom it might belong. The pain continued though, and unwilling to venture too far from it, so Zilch, without a lead to pursue, sat on the front porch, eyes closed, letting the ache churn in his mind. He kept trying to picture Susanne, trying to make new memories out of the old, see her face, see her smile, hear her laugh.

"I'm sorry," he tells her, in his mind, once he sees every freckle of his imaginary version of her has been dotted on, perfectly, as they had been all those years before. "I'm really sorry, babe."

And just like then, she doesn't forgive him. She turns away, and leaves, their apartment door slamming shut behind her hard enough to make a framed picture—of them—jump off its nail.

"I'm sorry."

The image echoes painfully in his head. She turns away, and leaves. The door slams, the picture hits the floor.

"I'm sorry."

She leaves. Slam. Picture hits the floor, smash.

A nearby rustling draws Zilch's focus back to the present. He shoots to his feet, wiping at the corner of his eye where a tear had been welling up.

The streetlights are sporadic, only six lining the unpaved road and at odd intervals, but one throws blazing orange light onto the neighboring house, which is almost completed. It's there, out front, that a figure rises out of the shadows. It looks like it's made from the same rolled-out grass it was hiding among, carpeted in bushy greenery. It faces Zilch, but seems unsure if it has been spotted and takes one step backward, bent at the waist, then another, trying to retreat further into the darkness, sneaky but failing. The thing has a bolt-action rifle in its hands.

"I can see you, you know," Zilch calls, hands cupped around his mouth. "Why don't you come over here? We'll talk." Lizard Man is packing heat? Not good.

The figure shifts its hands on the gun, gripping tighter. It doesn't raise and take aim but it does shake its shrub-like head. Zilch notices as it steps through a sliver of moonlight cutting through the trees that the creature's hands aren't covered in green tendrils but are instead flesh tone, its fingers small fat digits.

It takes another slow step back, hesitates, then turns and bolts. Zilch stumbles a few steps forward to give chase but the thing dodges into a small grove of trees operating as a property line between two of the unoccupied residences, and blends in so easily it's like goddamn magic trick. One moment it's there, then it's not.

"Shit," Zilch says, peering into the dark. His heart pounds. He does *not* want to get shot—duh—but he also wants to make the pain in his head go away.

A half-beat later, he hears an engine up the street turn over and a set of headlights spark to life. Zilch watches helplessly as the thing—and now that it's in better light it's obvious that it's just a guy in a homemade ghillie suit—drives off in a black sedan. He stares after it, noticing the car's license plate has been obscured with strips of duct tape.

The car speeds away. Probably just some guy stealing boxes of nails and whatever else he could find lying around in the construction sites. The rifle and bush costume are a bit excessive, though.

Zilch stands in the road, coming to terms with his disappointment and frustration.

Then, a disquieting yowl; wet, gurgling, and prolonged. The sound sharpens up into a shriek, crescendos at a shrill climax, and then lowers into rumbling hiss, almost like laughter, *guk-guk-guk*. The silence following is profound; the crickets all shut up, as well as the frogs.

His headache ratcheting up to the point it makes his ears ring and his mouth dry out, Zilch turns and looks for the nearest thing he can halfway protect himself with. Luck would have it, there's a shovel lying at his feet. Holding it in two hands, he faces the swamp, towards the source of the sound—his pain compass is his third eye now, dead ahead. But he can't see anything. He hears splashing, one sloppy plash in succession after another, on fast approach. Too many hanging willows and tree trunks and cattails to make sense of anything; trying to pick anything out in this confusing mess of things, in the dark, is impossible—but the steps are getting closer, faster as they start reaching the shallows. Zilch grips the handle of the shovel, locks his loafers in the soggy rolled-out grass, and readies himself. If it's just another ghillie man, is he prepared to whack the idiot upside the head anyways?

But then the street lights catch its eyes, flaring two bulbous yellow eyes in the dark. The creature comes splashing up out of the bog water amongst the swamp-draining machines, moving on all fours, and there's no mistaking it for a human. Zilch takes in long limbs, prominent upper body, round skull, and a swaying gait, a nearly comical swing of long limbs like a giraffe in flippers. It pauses, licking the air, and then sits back on its hind legs and lifts its front paws from the mud, standing. The transition from a squatting waddle-walk to a bipedal stride is herky-jerk, as if it's fighting its instincts to make this shift.

Maybe it had heard the car leaving and had come closer to investigate, but the thing didn't seem have a precise lock on Zilch at the moment. He uses this to his advantage and remains stock-still, holding the shovel tight, and watches, trying to keep his breathing quiet. The creature slowly steps forward, scanning the yards of the unfinished houses cautiously. It's not twenty yards away. Zilch can hear its slow breaths in time with its swelling bubble-like throat, laced with veins.

The creature approaches one of the trucks with the pumping equipment in its bed. It goes right to the driver's side door without sniffing around much, prying its fingernails into the door frame. The old clunker opens right up, the lock popping like a firecracker. The thing shambles up inside the vehicle's cab head-first, and from where Zilch is standing, it sounds as if it's has found something to eat. It's ass end is moving back and forth in the open truck door and the sound of *something* being shredded is audible: cracking plastic and ripping metal.

Zilch takes a step forward. His head rings. *I may not get another chance at this.* He takes a step forward—*snap.* "Shit."

After glaring down at the broken twig that gave him away, he watches as the creature's head springs up, framed in the windshield of the truck, bovine yellow eyes locking onto him. It awkwardly swivels around to stand on the edge of the door opening, keeping its unblinking gaze fastened onto Zilch, sniffing the air, arrowhead-shaped nose-slits flaring. It has wires hanging from its mouth, yellow and red. It takes only a second's hesitation to stare at him, to size him up. Then it's bounding—back on all fours—toward him with effortless, silent speed. It cuts across the cul-de-sac in an instant.

Zilch readies the shovel and gives it his best grand slam swing, but the creature glides under the shovel and barrels into him, shoulder to stomach, pitching Zilch onto his back. He brings the shovel handle back down and braces it in front of his face as the monster gnashes stubby, flat teeth uncomfortably close to his face. A shove pushes the creature aside. It flips itself, inhumanely fast and flexible, to its feet, legs and arms bending backwards making rubbery sounds.

It drops into a squat, hissing at him in the mud. Its powerful legs are long enough that its knees stand taller than its head on either side. In an oddly sporting display, the creature gives Zilch time to get up and find the shovel he dropped, wipe the mud from its handle, and get a good grip again. Patient.

The creature's deep-set eyes move up Zilch's body, hesitate temporarily on his belly, and then up to his face. A damp hand rises, pointing with webbed-together index and middle fingers.

"You're missing a button," it croaks.

Zilch looks down. Sure enough. *When do you suppose that*—

A plastic-wrapped load of shingles strikes him dead in the face. Zilch takes the hit as best as one man could, fumbles a few awkward lopes backwards, and regains his posture by driving the blade of the shovel into the soggy earth before he topples over. He glares at the broken pack of shingles, then at the monster, feeling the blood begin to run down his face and drip from his chin. The creature is standing again, approaching him with a typical bogeyman "I'm gonna eat you now, okay?" look in its eyes, a look Zilch is quite familiar with.

He will *not* be shat out again. Zilch readies the shovel. His face hurts and he can actually hear the bugs inside him going to work to repair the damage—angry bees in a burning hive.

"Just let me take it," the creature says, its voice so deep and so phlegmy it's nearly impossible to understand. Its tongue looks swollen in its mouth, flopping this way and that as it speaks. "I just want the radio."

"They sent me to kill you. No radio for you, fella."

The creature moves, finking left and right, and then springs forward with a speckled green shoulder angled towards him. Zilch is fast to move out of the way, but leaves the blade of the shovel in the creature's path and lets its head collide with it, clonging like a bell.

The creature isn't remotely fazed. It grabs a handful of Zilch's baggy dress shirt as it flies past and hoists him up off his feet—tosses him away—all in one fluid movement. Zilch spirals through the air, up over the railing of the front porch and in through the front window of the house. Without glass to break, just a sheet of translucent plastic, he slaps through with little resistance, and hits the rough plywood under-floor. Zilch slides, the chip-board biting his reaching hands as tries to brake himself, digging under his fingernails, until a high stack of sheetrock brakes him. Something in his lower back softly crunches. Through the new pain, he fumbles around, looking for the shovel, but then remembers he lost it somewhere in the airborne trip into the house. He can hear the creature now, just outside, mounting the front porch's steps with damp slaps of webbed feet.

Zilch looks for another weapon. He kicks and slides his feet, swiping blindly across the chipping plywood floor for anything, anything, anything.

There is a rush of air and the creature comes soaring in through the front door and ends its colossal leap alighting mere feet from Zilch. Caught off guard by such a show of sudden velocity for a creature so big, Zilch shrieks and jumps back, and that's when a series of tolls ring out—echoing and hollow and metallic. He's knocked over a leaning collection of metal pipes when he backed away, one of which he quickly takes up in his hands and without hesitation, swings with all of his strength at the creature. It doesn't weave or even duck; it takes the hit to the neck, and the next to the top of the head, and the last—a driving jab to the chest—without so much as a flinch or a big-eyed blink.

"I just wanted the radio," it explains and backhands Zilch, sending him stumbling back into the unfinished wall, his spine slamming up against an exposed stud. He lands funny and now his left arm is hanging at an unnatural angle, fingertips touching his elbow. Zilch's eyes go wide—you never get used to seeing yourself pretzeled. He hears the buzzing swell under his skin, the nanobugs working overtime.

A hot, wet hand takes him by the throat, pinning him to the studs of the wall, pink insulation ticking the back of Zilch's neck. At this intimate proximity, the creature radiates the smell of swampy, slow decay and something akin to a drained aquarium that hadn't been cleaned in a long time.

It brings its face close to his. "Lick me," it says.

Zilch had his eyes closed, certain that this was the end. They pop open. "What? No."

The creature's other hand slaps up around Zilch's jaw, pinching his mouth open with its sticky thumb and forefinger, presenting its slime-shiny forearm to Zilch's crushed mouth.

"Lick me."

"*Luk yahsulf*," Zilch manages.

It doesn't make another request, instead presses its flesh against Zilch's mouth and rubs forward and back, up and down. Zilch struggles, kicks, punches, and after what feels like an unnecessarily length of time of being forced to mouth the creature's arm like a harmonica, is shoved to the floor, discarded, like it'd been Zilch's idea to engage in this weird activity and the creature's sensibilities have suddenly been offended.

Zilch, on hands and knees, arm still bent backwards but mostly operational, spits and gags. "What the hell was that about?" Spit. Hack. Spit. "You taste worse than you smell."

The creature stands by, seemingly waiting. Its arms hang at its sides and Zilch is about to drive a punch into its face, putting his weight behind the blow. Then the entire house moves.

His feet go out to catch himself and his arms are spread wide, like a surfer ready for a bone-breaking wave. Zilch looks outside the window. The house is awfully close to the swamp, after all. Maybe it's finally split from its moorings and is drifting on the water. But nothing is moving outside. Just . . . him.

The creature is grinning, as much as it's possible for it to do so.

Pushing against the skull-cracking ache, otherworldly wind chimes sound in Zilch's head, reminding him of that time he went to South America and his somewhat shady tour guide came back onto their river boat with something cupped in his hands. A brilliantly colored frog. They took turns giving it a lick. Ten hours later, Zilch and Susanne were still having giggle-riddled conversations with a blue-skinned, six-armed George Harrison about the benefits—both financial and moral—of selling your blood to Mogwai orphans.

Zilch glared at the creature. "Oh, fuck. You *didn't*. Tell me you're not—"

The bufotoxins, as they did on that vacation years ago, work fast. An electric green wave hits him and the half-finished home around Zilch twists. Rooms expand and contract and double on one another and become hallways, like something M.C. Escher would've drawn after spinning circles in the yard for an hour. A giddiness hops into Zilch, despite there being a creature in the incomplete room that could very easily kill him. He feels an incongruous chuckle climb his throat and burble out.

"Heh . . . ahem. Heh. Hee-hee." He glares at the creature, and giggles through saying: "You crafty son of a bitch. Heh. Hee-hee. You fucked me up then *fucked me up*, ha-ha."

Zilch manages to back away, still keenly aware of the danger he's in—but he's unable to fight the toxins and the laughs they're chemically inspiring. The true height of the trip is still in the mail; that much is without question. Signed, sealed, and soon to be delivered.

He stops laughing as the floor turns into a gluey wood grain paste and Zilch, even knowing that this isn't real, feels himself sink into it. Just like in South America, this trip, too, takes a turn. His hands slap down hard to catch himself, his arm makes a grinding sound as the broken bones bang together. The floor feels like a paste he's sinking into, waist-deep, then chest-deep. His face falls off. The wind tosses back the plastic sheet and outside the world is exploding with a billion candy-colored Chernobyl fireflies. It's great and bad and stupid and scary, all at the same time.

Managing to determine which way is up for a moment, Zilch sees the frog man is just a set of dark footprints on the floor. On elbows and knees (his hands and feet have departed for the time being) Zilch crawls to the doorway and watches the creature trotting back across the lawn. It stops at the pump truck at the edge of the swamp to reach inside, snatch out the stereo it'd been working on when Zilch had interrupted. Then, wires dangling, it takes a few splashing strides out into the dark water, dives, and is gone, leaving only a faint ripple as any evidence it was ever there.

Zilch drops to his chest and forces himself onto his back. He cradles his broken arm and stares at the sheetrock ceiling, the hanging wires, and the PVC tubes. He can smell the sylvan and chemical reek of the fiberboard, the nostril-burning smell of the paint, the musty fresh cement. The sounds: the crickets are all playing full-tilt again, each in duet with a frog in one big bog song. The hallucinations keep trying to edge in, shifting these normal things to colorful, bendy alternatives. Zilch stops fighting it. He recalls, at five, eating some of the weird-tasting candy he found in his parents' nightstand, his first unceremonious exposure to drugs. He had been left home alone that afternoon, with his eight-hit trip. What did I do then? he asks himself. Oh, right. Nothing. What *can* you do? Once it's in sponged into the folds of the brain, there ain't no scratching it back out.

He goes still now, on what'll someday be the middle of some nice family's living room. He allows himself, if this makes sense, *into* himself. He becomes a body-fist and hears "The Wind Cries Mary" even though nowhere in this empty neighborhood, as far as he can tell, is it actually currently playing. A garage door hums and rattles nearby, retracting. An engine cranks up, revs, and blue-white cuts across him, searing eyes he cannot close.

Susanne appears in the flare of light as it passes over him. Every freckle in place. She bends, smiles, and touches his cheek with the back of her fingers, gentle. Though her hand smells like his hand—blood and swamp water and mud—he closes his eyes to savor the touch.

"I'm sorry," he tells her, touching his own cheek as the nowhere music plays on.

BLUE-WHITE HEADLIGHTS PENETRATE THE DOUBLE-WIDE's curtains, throwing twisty shadows across her. Galavance goes to the window, seeing Jolby's Accord pull up into the driveway behind her Cavalier. She watches him struggle out of his car and pause, again, to survey the damage of her vehicle. He's a particularly perspiration-prone guy, but he looks especially damp, his skin shiny-wet. She watches him notice the button, and try to dislodge it. He can't get it to break free either, the kingdom not meant for either of them. Galavance creaks the screen door aside and steps out onto the porch's Astroturf, still in bare feet, trying to keep how drunk she is concealed from him. She concentrates and plans her greeting so when she says hey from the top step she doesn't slur.

"When the house sells, I'll be able to fix all that," he says, coming up the steps. He's changed clothes, she notices. Linkin Park instead of a Metallica T now. He says nothing about the button hammered into the hood.

"Do you guys have any sort of timeframe on that?" she asks.

"On what?"

She stares down at him, refusing to step aside to allow him in the trailer. Once inside, with a video game going or his headphones on, he might as well be down a well. "On selling the house, Jolby."

"Don't use my name like that." He plays with his phone, thumbing through his empty text message inbox idly. "Don't talk to me like I'm some little kid. That house is my job, not homework."

She doesn't want to, but . . . "It's not a job. A job pays. And how the hell *else* am I supposed to talk to you? Tell me. You *act* like a little kid, you do stupid little kid things just like you did in high school. I mean, getting busted with dime bags? Seriously? Did you even get paid by that guy whose roof you were fixing? And how'd you have money *for* a dime bag in the first place?"

Jolby says nothing. His thumb has stopped moving, so she can tell he's just staring at his phone's screen just so he doesn't have to look her in the eye. Galavance glares at him until apparently he can feel it and he puts his phone away.

In the fluorescent light coming out through the kitchen window, the look he gives her is easy to see. Like an animal with its leg in a trap. She's good at cornering him in arguments, he's easy to outmaneuver. Especially when he's on a pot hangover, as he is now.

Do *not* start crying again, she silently warns him, chewing the inside of her cheek. Do not do that. You *know* what that does to me.

He doesn't. Instead, more talk about responsibility takes place. How this will pay off, eventually. She fires back about how she's the only one living in the present. "And what if that fucking house *never* sells? What then?"

They've been together long enough to get each other's goats without difficulty. They bicker and fight and when it gets loud, they temporarily put it on pause to go inside, then continue right where they left off behind closed doors, even if the walls are too thin to make much of a difference to the neighbors.

"*What* are you *doing* to your *car*?" he blasts. He slaps aside the curtains over the kitchen sink and points out the window at the damage, as if she needed help finding it. "Did you hit a fuck-ing rhino with that thing?"

"I told you it was just a deer," she says. *I saw him see the but-ton. But it's like he forgot. Well, I'm sure as shit not going to bring it up.* She wants to shove the argument off this track, before he chooses to go there. Now is the time to turn the tables. If there is one benefit to Jolby dragging his ass in the making-money department, it's that she can win any argument. She can pull that over on him any time she likes and he can *never* win from that point on. She knows it's low and unfair, but in a case like this when she's already had a super-shitty day, this will cut things short.

"Well, maybe I wouldn't be falling asleep at the fucking wheel if I didn't have to go in at the ass-crack of dawn just to get a fucking paycheck," she roars at him, her voice getting reedy. "And then I probably wouldn't end up hitting any fucking deer!"

"Don't drag all that into it, Gal," he yells back. "Don't. Do not."

"Why not? It's what we're dealing with here."

"You can't drive for shit," he says. "That's the real point."

She lets that one sail past. Too easy. "So if I fall asleep at the wheel to get a job to provide for my lazy-ass man, then that has nothing to do with it? Really?"

"That's not what I said."

"Well, I wouldn't expect you to. You, Jolby, own up to some-thing? *Pssht.* When pigs fly."

"Come on, I thought we just got through with all this bull-shit. We're going in circles."

"What are you going to *do*, Jolby?" she snaps. "What are you going to *do*? I mean, I bust my ass day and night and I go off the road *one fucking time* and you get to cuss me out like this? Do you think this is how I wanna be? I hate saying this shit to you. I really do. Please, let me stop being a bitch. Because you know if I say these things to you, it's *you* making me say them."

Ding-ding. KO.

His posture has changed, his shoulders slumping and his head bending forward. He's letting his hair fall in his face and Galavance knows that this is how Jolby is putting up his shield, when he lets that greasy mop hang in front of his eyes like a blackjack dealer's visor. Next he'll try to hug her. He's already cried, so he's burned that one already. Now it'll be his Hail Mary, his Jolby the Cuddle Bear routine. Just watch.

He stretches out his arms. "Come on, babe. We're both tired, it's late, let's just dial it back a notch."

See?

She keeps her arms crossed. "When, Jolby? When it's going to change? Huh? When?" Her throat hurts and she can't scream any more. It comes out hoarse and low.

He hugs her around her crossed arms. She doesn't soften. He smells like pot. Pot and that cologne-in-a-can he uses—he really doused himself good with it this time. She turns her head aside and he rests his chin on her shoulder. He kisses her neck, soft.

"Stop. I'm mad."

His hands move over her hips, around her waist to her front. He feels his greasy thumb attempting to work at the button of her shorts blindly. Guilt hits her for having spent time with Zilch, and she doesn't know why. *I was helping him. The guy needed a ride. And maybe he's a bit squirrelly, maybe he works for some afterlife* Quantum Leap *set-things-right committee, maybe he's just nuts. But I didn't do anything with him, not even any flirting took place. I never gave him a number, nor took his. Why the guilt?*

She brushes his hands away from her zipper, but he just goes right back to it. He's looking down, having stopped kissing her neck to stare at her crotch and concentrate.

"Is this thing stuck?" he asks.

"Here," she yanks the zipper and he slips her jorts to her knees, her panties, and without even so much as a hello, buries his tongue. The sudden warmth of his mouth is alarming and she has to brace herself by latching a hand onto the kitchen doorjamb—but it's not a pleasurable alarm that's striking her. She's mad and she doesn't want to allow herself to react, to let anything occur down there that would be indicative she's enjoying this. She focuses on all of the awfulness of the world to try avoid becoming wet.

There, that's working—go with it, think about dead stuff. But try as she might, Jolby's tongue is nimble and is hitting all the right places.

Dead stuff, dead stuff, dead stuff—come on. Don't succumb.

She touches his hair, remembers it's damp. "You're soaked."

"I showered at the house. Question is, why aren't you?" he says, muffled, chuckling at his own easy wit.

She's trying to think of more dead stuff, but at the same time something really fun is happening downstairs. And there it is, something's tripped and like a gate cracking off its hinges, splintering, and then fully giving way—she thinks of Zilch and below, a muffled, appreciative humming.

"You like that, huh?"

A *Step by Step* rerun she hasn't seen before is on. Galavance watches, from bed, hating herself. Their bedroom TV is small, and only one speaker works. She kills it and refocuses on the book in her lap. A thousand-page riff on love and tragedy in Soviet Russia that she wants to get through before the movie hits DVD, but every character's last name confusingly ends with -*ski*. She snaps to the next page. So far the entire thing could be summed up with: it's cold in Russia. And everyone is sad.

Jolby is in the bathroom—the walls are thin and she hears him peel off the condom like he's poorly making balloon animals in there—and he steps into the bedroom with his hair actually combed. He's overweight, but has stamina. She wonders how much, secretly, this contributes to her keeping him around. She's changed into her T-shirt nightgown and the same set of glasses she's worn since high school. She gives him a raspberry over the top of her Dostoevsky.

"Oh come on, Gal. You always used to like it when I slicked my hair back like this."

"Yeah, but then it became a thing and every time you did it you may as well have been announcing: I'm horny."

He flops down on the bed and takes the book from her hands and tosses it across the room. She's still holding the bookmark in her hand and looks at the where the ten-pound tome landed halfway to Mount Dirty Drawers. She was somewhere in those thousand pages, but where *exactly* she isn't quite sure. "Hey, asshole."

He kisses her neck. "What?"

His lips and tongue are taking a tour of her neck's nape, moving down into the notch between her collarbone and shoulder. They know how to get each other's goats, but they know each other's special spots too.

"Again? Already?" she says, unable to help but squeak her words, ticklish.

"Yeah, why not?" Between flicks of his tongue, "You're not into it?"

"I'm still mad at you."

"And *I'm* mad at *you*. This is called makeup sex."

"We already did that, didn't we?" she says.

"You got to have fun first, so now it's my turn."

"Is this because you're not going to spend the weekend in jail? You suddenly feel like you need to have sex because you're not"—she shoves him back a little—"going to have to be someone's bottom?"

His face hardens. He still gets weird when anything about anyone being gay is suggested around him, more so when suggesting some of it involving him. He isn't, Galavance knows, but also knows that if Jolby ever actually met a gay person he didn't realize it.

"Fine." Galavance rolls over to reach into the top drawer of the nightstand. "Here."

"Two? I thought you were taking, you know, pills."

"I am." She peels off her T-shirt nightgown. "But you can't be too careful."

Another grunty six minutes and it's over. Five after that, she's asleep and having some very bizarre dreams. Patty's there and she's wearing her Coleman cooler like homeless people wore barrels in those old-timey cartoons and screaming about the end times.

Relieved when it's over, Galavance opens her eyes and can see, through her blurry vision without contacts in or glasses on, that the far paneled wall of the bedroom is illuminated. Jolby's shadow shuffles about. Out in the kitchen, he's clunking and slamming around. She listens to him cough, three times, each hack harder than the one before. She listens to him cough more and more, and she wonders if it's some kind of stoner timer going off inside him: *ring-a-ding, let's get stoned!*

She waits and when she hears the jingle of him pick up his keys, she knows he's going to go and hang out with Chev.

Despite being as quiet as he can manage, Jolby is still stifling coughs and even when he's out in the yard, she can still hear him through the wall of the double-wide. She listens to his car start. He lets it idle for a moment, probably trying to decide on what music to listen to. She feels the bass in her pillow of the track he's selected, some thrash-punk hip-hop garbage he incessantly deafens himself with. This isn't too out of the norm for them— usually he's out of the house at sun-up under the guise that he has to meet Chev somewhere early to pick up building materials when they're on sale, as the stores open. But this is very early. Like still-dark early.

She leans over to click on the oscillating fan, for the noise. She remains in bed, staring up at the water stains on the ceiling. She listens to the crickets outside. Loneliness creeps in quickly but it's such a familiar feeling to her, she would feel even more lonely without it.

SATURDAY.

THE ALARM BUZZES, BUT GALAVANCE IS ALREADY AWAKE AND has been for hours. There were no answers found on the ceiling of the double-wide, but it didn't stop her from looking. She gets up, showers, and dresses for work. Outside, she sees her Cavalier and realizes she'd forgot about the damage from the day before. The hood is slick with dew. Something bites her as she runs her hand across it. There's a small cut on her palm, bleeding, and the button is gone—now just a ragged coin slot punched into the pink metal. *Maybe it fell out overnight, or some bird plucked it out—they're attracted to shiny things, right?* But then she wonders if Jolby removed it this morning before he left. She was glad he didn't bring it up last night, though he probably, really, should've asked. He can forget he saw things, omit truths from himself, like the best of them. Maybe, Galavance realizes, she can too.

When she arrives at Frenchy's, she realizes she's the first one there, other than Patty, whose rental four-door is covered in dried mud that's splashed up to the windows on the sides. Was her boss doing some off-roading last night? Not many dirt roads between here and the Hilton up the road.

Patty meets her at the back door before Galavance can reach for the handle.

"Well, good *mornin'*, Miss Petersen. I see you're not only on time today, but early."

I want to kill you, my boyfriend, then myself. "Sure am," Galavance says, chipper. She isn't sure why she gets this way around Patty, this superfake smiley way. Same way she acts around cops, even when innocent.

Patty leads them into the kitchen. Everything's off except for a few lights. The walk-in cooler as well as the reach-ins hum, and every bit of floor and counter space is spotless. Their night porter is thorough.

On the counter, Patty has some review sheets spread out. "These were faxed over to me late last night, from our other locations," Patty says. "Everyone hates the peppers."

Galavance watches Patty, down in the mouth, studying the words 'awful' and 'disgusting' and 'rubbery' as they appear over the multiple sheets again and again. Why Patty is taking this to heart, Galavance doesn't know. She leaves her work at work, but Patty looks like she was up half the night, much like Galavance, but for different reasons: haunted by stuffed peppers instead of her loveless, dead-end life.

"We really need to do something about this," Patty says. The kitchen lights shine on Patty's glasses, hiding her eyes behind the gleam, but the desperate frown on her wide, doughy face speak volumes.

"Well," Galavance says, backing away, "good luck with it, I'm gonna go get the vacuuming started."

Patty looks positively heartbroken. "Actually, I was thinking . . ."

"Oh, we as in: *you and me* do something about it, like actually you and me?" Galavance says.

Patty nods. "I was gonna have Cheryl"—the head weekend cook, with her toque and clogs fresh from Le Cordon Bleu—"take a look and see, but since you're here . . ."

"What about the Culinary Inspiration Team?" Galavance asks. "Isn't it their job to, you know, make things taste good?"

"They're all in California, appearing as judges for some reality show." She shakes her head, and her hair doesn't move. "It's really a shame; I thought the peppers were quite good." She looks to Galavance, eyes huge behind rimless lenses, expectant, desperate. It was the first time Galavance had ever seen Patty look vulnerable. "What did you think? Someone from this location did a review sheet yesterday, said some pretty childish things."

"I thought they were yummy." Lying always made Galavance's neck feel hot. *Please don't make eat any more of that.*

"Guess it wasn't you then," Patty says, with a tone. She *so* knows. Galavance is suddenly very aware that it's just the two of them, alone. "Anyway, would you want to help?"

"Uh, okay. I mean, I can burn Froot Loops . . ." She knows it's not really up to her: either she pretends to actually give a shit or she's fired. "What do you want me to do?"

"Wash your hands first," Patty says, firm, "then we'll channel our inner Martha. By God, we'll make this recipe item *perfect!* Doesn't that sound like fun?"

Galavance's forcing her smile so hard that her cheeks hurt. "Yeah, totally. It's going to be, like, awesome and a half."

ZILCH KICKS HIS LEGS AND THRASHES AND FINALLY ROLLS onto all fours, back arched, every hair on his body bristling. He had just had the strangest dreams of his life. He looks down at his arm—it's lumpy but has healed significantly overnight and is usable again. His back aches and he can feel the dull buzzing of his nanobugs as they labor away at his mangled spinal cord. The sun cuts in through the open doorway, and he can hear the muffled sound of a radio going somewhere. No, not the radio, but a demonic cacophony of construction noise: the *psht-tak* of pneumatic nail-guns provide the percussion, while wailing belt sanders and circular saws duet on top of them.

Brushing the mud from his cheek, he remembers Susanne. He feels drugged, almost hung over, and the flicker of seeing her, now very much gone, makes him draw the employee delivery module from his pocket. With a snap of the wrist the eight-inch needle telescopes out. He flicks the switch on the side, to ABORT, turns it around in both hands and prepares to stake it through his own heart.

But he hesitates, knowing that to leave now, before the job is done, will mean another dead spot in his mind. The memories of his life with her—the moments he still has left—are already fragmented and incomplete, more like a reverse follow-the-dots drawing—he had a clear picture once, but now it's just a vague outline. Entire weeks where they may or may not've been on vacation, or shared a shift at the catering company together, or taken a road trip somewhere over a long summer weekend. He doesn't know exactly what he's lost, just that there are important pieces missing; he can feel the raw edges of the beginning and end of certain memories, but with nothing in between, nothing to flesh them out and make them real.

To abort now would mean another chunk gone.

He collapses the needle and puts the module back in his pocket, for now.

With the morning light blooming, he can see the inside of the house a lot better now. Dried muddy footprints on the floor, the pipe he tried to defend himself with now bent into a seven. The door connecting the house to the garage hangs open. The car that had been there the night before is gone. The goddamn thing can *drive?*

Ducking under the plastic sheet draped across the front door, Zilch steps out onto the front porch. The water is higher today, lapping up against the steps. He goes to the front of the house, crouching to study the tire marks in the driveway.

The pneumatic slap of the nail gun stops. The saw's scream snuffs. A mob of alarmingly yellow hard hats, pit-stained T-shirts, and holey jeans, are staring at him from the half-finished one-story across the street. One—to call him a big fella would be an understatement—steps out of a pickup truck, the same one the creature had stolen the radio from the night before.

"You lost?" he calls.

Zilch can't think to say anything. He stands up from the skidmarks in the driveway. "I'm a realtor or something. I mean, I definitely *am* a realtor."

"Bullshit." The big guy and his group of lackeys set their tools aside and march across the street in muddy work boots. The big guy, clearly the leader, has a giant gleaming rodeo buckle that catches the sun, flashing Zilch's eyes.

"Whoa, guys," Zilch says. "Wait a minute. What's this all about?" He throws his hands out in surrender at the approaching mob, but none heeds his plea. They circle him.

"Someone broke into my fuckin' truck last night," the big beefy guy says. "And since *you're* the only piece of shit around here I *don't* recognize, that means you jump to the top of the suspect list."

"Hey now, I was just here, sleeping off a bender. Dark side of realty. Saw no one was around, saw no locks on the doors, figured you guys wouldn't mind."

"That right?" Beefy says, half-grinning. He points at the ground next to Zilch's waterlogged loafers. Zilch looks. There lies a thin copper wires that looks a hell of a lot like it may've been keeping Beefy's truck radio operational.

"Wanna explain *that*, hoss?"

"As a matter of fact, no, I *don't* care to explain that, thank you very much," Zilch says.

Six sets of work-gloved hands grab him.

The construction guys haul him like ants carrying a slice of bread, and by Beefy's instruction they drop him on the hood of the now-radioless truck. A couple guys hold him in place while Beefy and another two go to the back and dig through the truck bed toolbox squeezed in next to the pump. Zilch hears the words "bungee cords" uttered.

Might as well go for broke. "Look, fellas. Do any of you know anything about the Lizard Man?"

One goateed guy chortles. "That's *South* Carolina, bo."

"Ever hear of migration? I suppose not since evolution, clearly, skipped right past you guys. Okay, I'll let you fellas in on a little secret, hear me out. That's why I'm here. I'm after the Lizard Man. He's the one who did that to your buddy's truck."

"Yaw, 'kay, hoss. Tell it to yer buddy."

"What?"

"That dumb sum'bitch who tried to make us believe that's what fugged up *mah* car last week. Lizard Man. Gimme a break."

"Hold on, *what* did you say? Who saw it? Who's my buddy?"

The ropey-armed guy with the farmer's tan continued. "Your buddy that says he had a video and he'd seent the Lizard Man, but when 'e went to show it to the po-leece—and me—wouldn't ya know it, the video was *gone*. Someone musta hacked 'im and e-razed it off his phone, so he says."

"You keep saying *my buddy*," Zilch says. "Who's my buddy?"

Goatee harrumphs. "Chev Bertrand. Figgered you were buddies, what with you sleepin' it off in dat shit-shack he and his fat-ass friend beat us out on the gig for." Goatee bobs his head toward the house marked 1330. "Then all they do is play them damn video games and smoke weed all day up in there, making the property value of every other house on the street go down 'fore any of 'em after even finished!"

Zilch recalls what Galavance told him about her boyfriend. He cranes his head around to look over at 1330 Whispering Pines Lane. Jolby was building a house, isn't that what she said?

From the back of the truck, Beefy barks, "Why the fuck you talkin' to him so damn much? Ain't no point in it, Suity-Pants here's 'bout to be scared so shitless he won't even remember his own damn name." Beefy guffaws, stepping back into view with a tangled mass of bungee cords, all in colors of coral snakes wearing a big chaw-stained smile on his bulldog face.

His lackeys all chuckle as if they'd been paid to. But Zilch can tell by their semi-worried glances that none of them besides Beefy really wants this, but Zilch has seen it before: cruelty is most effective when it comes in mobs.

As Beefy arranges the cords so that all of the hook ends are coming out of the top of his meat-slab fists, he asks Zilch, "You ever play Hood Ornament, pretty boy?"

"No, but I bet I can guess how it goes."

"It's *real* fun," Beefy says and gives the bungee cords a twang pulling them tight. "Hold him."

Zilch lays his head back on the truck hood and allows them do what they will, Beefy's barbwire bicep and big-ass belt buckle crew securing him to the pump truck's hood. The bungee cords snap tight around Zilch's wrists and ankles and it stings. Numbness settles in fast, blood being cut off as the cords are double and triple wrapped. He tries talking to the things inside him, his own microscopic construction crew: focus on the damage, not the pain receptors. Please. Sometimes this works, if his buggie-count is low and they've had to choose priorities.

Once he's belted across the waist, Beefy and his boys snicker and giggle at their handiwork, stepping back to admire Zilch mummified on the hood. Zilch was young and dumb(er) once. He remembers. Sure, this would seem like quite the knee-slapper if the person they were doing it to wasn't him.

Someone gets in the truck and Zilch cocks his head back, seeing Beef upside-down behind the wheel, still snickering, carefully taking a pinch of snuff out of a tin. He crams it in and meets Zilch's eyes and says through the windshield: "Hold on *tight.*"

And half of Beefy's head expands, like a puffed mass of pink bubblegum, then deflates back to normal. Some of that bufotoxin still in here, Zilch determines, rushing around his bloodstream again with his speeding heart rate.

Under Zilch's back, the pump truck's engine shakes him, makes all of the world before his eyes vibrate. He takes a deep breath and tells himself not to be scared but the drugs are putting cryptic and fatalistic ornaments all over for him: skulls and crossbones burn into focus in the very air like mystical glyphs, like his own burning bushes foretelling bad shit en route. An anaconda swirling through the air, cruising like a tape worm touring a gut, comes over the heads of the hard hat crew and says to Zilch, peaceful-like: "Better listen to the man."

"Huh?"

"Hold on."

The truck drops into gear and kicks some dirt, finding traction. The wind fills Zilch's ears and the snake is scattered away, nearly colliding with Zilch on the hood. The hard hat guys all let out semi-scared laughs, but the one laughing loudest and most genuine of all is Beefy. He's honking the horn—which is *really* fucking loud when you're bungee corded to the hood—and swerving left and right, left and right. Zilch pries his fingers into the gap where the quarter-panel and the hood meet, and tries to not give Beefy the benefit of hearing him scream.

He isn't successful.

EVENTUALLY THE KITCHEN CREW BEGINS TO ARRIVE AND Galavance is happy for it, even if it is some of the gossip-slinging high school chicks. *At least now there's someone else here with me and Patty*, she thinks. It was getting awkward enough there for a while, you could cut the weirdo vibes with a plastic knife.

Patty has the recipe card out for the stuffed peppers, and on a hotel pan sit eight of the halved vegetables. They try a bunch of combinations, from couscous and chopped garlic with a sprinkling of parmesan and a drizzle of extra-virgin, to a more Mediterranean-inspired mix of Kalamata olives, artichoke hearts, and feta cheese. But the sausage from Patty's cooler always has to go in, which immediately ruins every combination they come up. Nonetheless Galavance is still starting to have genuine fun with this; it's bringing back the mix-and-match cookies she used to make with her mother. A bit of this and a bit of that, just picking things at random her mother would set out for her. Sprinkles, raisins, walnuts, chocolate chips, *and* caramel? Why not!

"This is fine for today," Patty says as Galavance returns from the dry storage with a few more things for the next adventurous batch, "but I don't think the bigwigs will sign off on adding artichokes and olives onto the order lists. Those things are expensive."

Galavance sets the jars and plastic bags of ingredients down and in earnest asks, "What do you think we should do? I mean

. . . *I* don't think we gotta change anything, but not everybody might not feel that way." The lie bitters the back of her throat.

"I think we need to look at this recipe—the one the Inspiration Team originally came up with—take it apart, and see where it doesn't work. Let's ask ourselves: what makes these things taste like fishy ka-ka?"

"Ka-ka," Galavance echoes thoughtfully, thumbing her chin. Again, she's back in the kitchen with her mother, but this time she remembers that the sprinkle-smothered raisin walnut chocolate caramel cookies were like taste bud overload, something that only sounded good on paper. "What about the sausage? I think that's what's tripping us up. Does that *have* to go in?"

"The sausage has to stay," Patty says. "The ongoing order with the distributor is already signed by corporate, we can't back out. They'll be sending all sixty-two Frenchy's locations this sausage for the next three years. It has to stay."

"But I think that might be the problem," Galavance tries to delicately point out.

Patty's finger squeaks down the laminated recipe card to the handful of spices and herbs. She either doesn't hear Galavance, or chooses not to. Corporate has nailed the sausage to a tree. And Patty, Frenchy's most fervent follower, would follow that gospel until told otherwise.

Galavance wonders if upon promotion to corporate they ask you to deposit your soul in a box or if it's just forcibly yanked free without warning.

"Well, back to the drawing board," Patty says. "Any other ideas?"

To Galavance this sounds more like: *Well, girl, you best pull something outta yer ass right-quick or you can take it on the arches.* Under her work-issue polo, a line of sweat creeps down Galavance's side.

"HAD ENOUGH, ASSHOLE?" BEEFY BELLOWS OVER THE ENGINE noise, bringing the truck to a crawl.

Zilch says nothing, because this is the third time he's asked if he's had enough. Every time, Zilch says yes, and Beefy suggests "One more again!" and hammers the accelerator for another round down dirt paths among the tobacco fields. It's too early in the morning for this shit. Zilch sees flashes of the bufotoxin: more floating, laughing skulls, dancing devils, and other Old Testament imagery. Oh, and anaconda's still there, yukking it up. Prick. But they also pass a woman standing on the edge of the street in bare feet on the roll-out lawn. Dark hair and in a billowing white dress—tossed by the breeze of Beefy's fishtailing. Her hair momentarily covers her face but Zilch, for a brief second, sees her. Her gaze is full of pity, but tinged with anger and disappointment too.

When they turn the corner back into the Whispering Pines of Picturesque Bay neighborhood and tool down toward the cul-de-sac, Susanne is ripped from view—and Zilch can see that there's another altercation taking place, up ahead. A low-slung canary yellow car with a cartoonishly large whale tail is parked crookedly in front of 1330, as if the driver had leapt out before coming to a full-stop. Zilch spots the hard hat crew, all in white T-shirts and jeans—and another man. This one is tall, not only fat but legitimately big and bulky, with a head of blond spiked hair and wearing a gaudy, sequin-studded bowling shirt and a pair of either long shorts or short pants.

Strapped to the hood of the pump truck and rolling up fast, Zilch can hear the argument. The big guy with the spiked hair is yelling at the others, who have formed a semicircle around him, like they'd done with Zilch, but even more aggressively: teeth bared and holding tools that are about to become makeshift weapons.

"I didn't do a goddamn thing to Ben's truck, Darryl," the big blond guy is shouting. "Don't you think it'd be stupid as hell for me to steal the radio out of a truck I'm *renting* from someone? I just came down here to check on my fucking lot."

Beefy parks, leaving Zilch strapped to the hood.

Beefy and the guy with the spiky neon-blond hair get into it, shouting pretty much the same thing over each other again and again. Spiky's argument remains the same, while Beefy is simultaneously accusing Spiky of both stealing the radio out of the truck (which doesn't make a whole lot of sense, because if Beefy believed Spiky did it, why is Zilch tied to the hood?), and leaving it unlocked so it *could* be stolen in the night. And whichever Spiky actually did, he is very much going to be paying for it.

Zilch listens, since he doesn't really have much of a choice— he's still bungeed down tight.

Spiky says, "I'm fucking *telling* you, you guys, I locked that truck up good. I know you guys still think I'm full of shit, but—"

Beefy groans. "Your fucking Lizard Man story again. Here we go."

"I don't care what you say, Ben. The fucking thing is real," Spiky shouts. "I *seen* it. I mean, I'm sorry about your truck, but . . ." While gesturing at the pump truck Beefy just pulled up in, he now notices Zilch strapped to the hood.

As much as he can with bound wrist, Zilch waves. "Hello."

Beefy Ben, in Spiky's pause, takes over the argument. "Sure, sure, sure. Yeah, okay. You seen it. Okay, sure. Doesn't explain how my truck got all ripped up. Fuckin' stereo's missing—again, right after I replaced it last goddamn week."

"Whatever, Ben. Listen to me or don't. I didn't steal anything from you, man," Spiky says, back to the argument. Zilch tries to remember what the one with the goatee said this guy's name was. "But leave your trucks down here at night, unlocked, and see what happens."

"Is that a threat?"

"No, dumbass, I'm just *tellin'* you that you should fuckin' *listen* to me."

"I think that was a threat. I think you just threatened me, Chev."

Zilch snaps his swollen, blood-starved fingers. *That's* his name.

"Fuck you, Ben," Chev says, a slight tremor to his voice.

"Fuck *you*, Chev," Ben says, with no tremor whatsoever, and shoves him.

Chev swings, Beefy Ben ducks.

They square up again, dancing from foot to foot—Beefy Ben in his work boots, Chev in his Birkenstocks.

The young men are all screaming at each other, all in a tight pack with gnashing teeth, Chev in the middle. Forget a broken jaw, they're going to kill him.

Zilch needs to do something. Getting any information out of Chev after he gets his jaw broken is going to be difficult. A quick wriggle of his wrist—that he wouldn't have dared while the truck was in motion—and Zilch slips a hand free. He undoes the other bands and slides down off the hood. No one notices, they're all too preoccupied watching Beefy Ben and Chev repeatedly *almost* punch each other.

Every single one of them outweighs Zilch by a hundred pounds at least, and besides—what's he going to do? The last time he threw a punch was at Susanne's sister's wedding and he accidentally ended up punching the pastor instead of Susanne's cousin, his actual target. The reception was an otherwise very quiet affair.

"Guys? Could you maybe not murder him please?" Zilch says, hopping to look over the crowd's shoulder. Beefy Ben is side-stepping every one of Chev's slow throws, sinking jabs to Chev's soft middle. "Fellas. Can we play nice?"

Apparently not. Because the -ice of nice has barely left Zilch's mouth when one of Ben's buddies draws a utility knife, ratchets the blade out two inches, and angles the working man's dagger toward Chev.

Sometimes heroism shows up in stupid ways. Zilch had never met this goofy-looking kid before in his life, but for reasons that elude even him, he jumps in the path of the slashing blade. He could even hear it whistling, as it cuts the air, angling for Chev—and he could really hear when the whistling *stops*, slicing Zilch from the bottom of his rib cage to his belt in one butter-smooth motion.

"What the hell?" Zilch manages. But the attack goes unnoticed. He's shoved aside, bleeding and making the WTF face, immediately forgotten. Apparently, the smell of blood kicks something primal awake in the young men; they crowd Chev, far outnumbering him, and he's lost under a pile of hard hats and pit-stained tank tops.

Meanwhile, Zilch stands off to the side, bleeding from a gash in his belly that's deep enough he can see pink stuff inside. It's vaguely pornographic and, like the sting of being caught by your mother indulging in some blue film, the slice hurts almost as bad.

Blame the heat, blame the blood loss, but the mind ventures to weird places sometimes. Memories surface, and perhaps when you see your life flash before your eyes it starts with the freshest, most recent stuff. For Zilch: something he learned about Internet culture just yesterday morning. Did Galavance call it *scarfing*?

It stings—he doesn't have the means to numb himself up first, which he recalls correctly was part of the "challenge"—but he sinks a hand up to the wrist inside himself, and, well, who would ever expect guts to be so slippery?

Beefy Ben turns, jaw dropping, chew spit dribbling down his chin.

Blood swells behind the blade and dribbles out onto the ground, down the front of Zilch's pants, dotting the street at his feet. He's almost got the organic necklace ready for the runway.

Every single young man before him has turned to a dead-eyed statue. One runs away and gets in his truck—but doesn't drive off, just watches from behind the windshield holding the sides of his head. Darryl vomits. Chev's eyes are saucers above the hand he's clamped over his mouth.

"Am I doing this right?" Zilch says, chin to chest.

No one answers, but no one's fighting anymore either.

He curls a hand deeper into the wound—*Wow, it's really warm in here*—and grabs the squiggly loose noodle of guts and . . .

"Up and around like this and . . . ta-da! Scarfing!"

Zilch has a good length of purple intestine out of his guts and looped it over his shoulders like a drag queen's boa, a biological lei. He stands there, bleeding profusely, holding the knife in one hand, blood up to his elbow on the arm he used to dig inside himself with, a look on his face meant to ask: so, how do I look?

One of the young men has his phone out and it takes Zilch a second to realize the man isn't making a call, but is recording this display. Behind the lens of the camera phone, Darryl, puke on his shirt, has gone glassy-eyed.

Zilch wears his guts and with one step forward, the entire crowd shatters apart, everyone scampering away from the man wearing his own guts like a necklace. Chev backpedals until he's backed up against a truck and there's nowhere left to go. "You Chev?" Zilch asks.

Palms out. "Uh, yeah. Don't hurt me, man."

Zilch realizes he still has the utility knife in his hand. He zips the blade down and tucks it into his back pocket. He raises his empty hands to show them all he means no harm, but it seems that wasn't what was bothering Chev really. The flesh rope around his neck starts to slide and he catches it and nudges it back up into place. "So you saw the Lizard Man? Did I catch that right?"

"He looked . . . more like a big toad to me, but . . . yeah . . . I seen it."

He turns back to the other guys. "Anyone else got anything to tell me? Any of you guys see any other weird shit that I should know about?"

Darryl swallows before he speaks: "Besides you?"

Zilch picks his shirt and suit coat up off the dirt with his clean hand and points to the canary yellow Honda Civic with the coffee can muffler. "That yours?" he asks Chev.

"Yeah."

"Can we talk?"

"I was about to go fishing with my buddy, actually, and . . ."

"Has he seen the Lizard Man as well?"

"Yeah, he's like the local expert."

"Mind if I tag along?"

"Tag along?"

"You mentioned fishing."

"Oh, right. Sure, man. I guess." Chev looks him up and down. "But you're all bloody. I'm sorry, dude, but my car, she's just been cleaned and . . ."

Zilch sighs and unloops his intestine from his neck and starts to stuff it back into his abdominal cavity. As if on delay, another one of the construction guys vomits.

It takes a few pushes to get it all packed back in. When he's finished, Zilch reaches for a roll of duct tape left behind when everyone skedaddled. After wiping down his hands, he does some quick patchwork, then replaces the tape to the hook on his belt. "Thanks."

Zilch drops the bloody rag at Beefy Ben's feet and throws his shirt back on and buttons it, then examines himself to make sure there's nothing leaking through the white material. He puts his suit coat back on and buttons what remaining buttons can be buttoned. He looks up at Chev, who's holding his key cars limply—his eyes at half-mast and his bottom lip white as fresh cement.

Zilch gestures over his entire person with both arms. "No leaks. Happy?"

"Say, man, if you wanna go by the mental health clinic, I know where it is. My sister, she's a bit off her rocker—not saying you are, just that we all get weird sometimes—but I know where it is, if that's where you might . . . wanna go."

"I just wanted to get away from those fucking rednecks," Zilch says.

"You and me both, man. Make my life a living hell, those shit-heads." They speed down Kit Mitchell Road. Apparently everyone nowadays drives like they're outrunning something.

"So you had video of the Lizard Man, huh?"

"Yeah, ripping the hell out of Darryl's car. Is that what they were doing to you, messing with you because they thought you did it or something? I swear those dickheads would kill their own mothers if they thought someone had messed with their ride. I had that video, man, and then it was gone and now . . . of course, they don't believe me."

"Sorry about that."

"For getting me out of there? Hell, you don't have to apologize for that. I was just there to get my toolbox from the site before heading up to the lake."

"No, I meant the video."

"Say what?"

"Let's say that I wasn't directly involved, but I think I know who it was who erased it from your phone. If it caused you any trouble—on their behalf, I apologize."

"I don't get it . . . you some kind of hacker or something?" Chev says. His eyes go wide. "You one of the men in black? Government guy? I swear to Baby Jesus that those movies I downloaded—I had no idea they were pirated. I *like* paying for my shit, man. Fair and square. Honest, I do. Ask anyone."

Zilch laughs, shakes his hand to brush away the confusion. "Go ahead and download as many movies about pirates as you want. I'm after the Lizard Man. Frog Man. Whatever. The icky thing with a pension for ripping up cars, apparently."

"Back there, how'd you do that? That shit looked so fuckin' *real*." This happens. People twist themselves into pretzels trying to rationalize the unrationalizable. I didn't see that. I didn't. And if I did, it wasn't real. Haha, not real. *Not* real. Nope.

Zilch takes the reflector he found last night in the driveway out of his pocket. With the sun streaking into Chev's car, it creates geometric rainbows that dart around on the ceiling and across the console. Chev brings the car to a stop outside a gas station and before getting out to pump, he notices the lightshow and becomes mesmerized, eyeing his car's ceiling with the same captivation a cat would give a laser pointer's elusive red dot.

"Trippy," Chev says, playing his hands around in front of the reflections, letting the shapes shift and swell and collapse on his palms. He seems kind of unaware that Zilch is the one making this happen. He puts it away, Chev blinks, and Zilch can see the young man's brain click back on a moment later.

"Was your buddy with you the night you got the video?" Zilch asks. He slides a finger between the buttons of his shirt to make sure the duct tape is holding fast. Be a shame to get some "fake blood" all over his new friend's seats.

"Naw. He was the reason I was taking it," Chev says. "I knew he'd want to see something like that. He'd kill me if he knew I didn't try. I was just out there at the house—you know, where I was about to throw down with Ben a minute ago?—and cleaning up for the night. And this thing just comes right up out of the swamp right there and starts going to town on Darryl's tuner. Like, ripping the dubs right off and taking apart the hood. With its *bare hands*, like it was nothing. I've never seen anything like it. Busted out the phone to take a video to show Jolby and—"

"Wait. Your friend's name is Jolby?" There couldn't possibly be more than one idiot in the area with that same moronic name, could there?

Chev brightened. "You know Jolby, dude?"

"Through the grapevine."

"Huh," Chev says. "Small world."

"Yeah," Zilch agrees. It certainly fucking is.

Chev gets out to fill the Civic's tank and goes inside to pay. Zilch remains in the car and can actually feel the air warming up inside. Fighting with the uncooperative crank to lower the window, he notices his hand is shaking. Like he's strapped to a malfunctioning mechanical bull. He did some meditation stuff back in school—a hippie chick named Namaste briefly owned his heart—and while some of the *ohm*-ing helps, the pain cannot be tamped down completely.

Chev emerges from the gas station with a wildly colored can of energy drink and a prepackaged sandwich cradled against his barrel chest with one hand, while his other hand is holding a phone to his ear. He isn't good at being nonchalant, and since he's probably talking to Jolby about pot and a meeting place to get stoned, his eyes are darting around everywhere as if cops are going to rappel down from the gas station awning any second. He's also paying a lot eye-time to Zilch, trying to be cool about it. Zilch gets the clear impression Chev is talking about him, to Jolby.

Zilch wonders if Chev uses his Civic for a place to get high and perhaps, combining with the leftover bufotoxins and some marijuana fug permanently soaked into the Civic's interior, if he's not getting some kind of contact buzz by accident. He ignores it, and eventually Chev gets in and ends his call. The moment they drive out of the Texaco, the pain shifts from Zilch's new belly-slit back to the neighborhood of his skull; the compass has turned back on, and loud. Its needle settles between Zilch's eyes, dead ahead, pointing out over Chev's hood, in the direction they're heading at eighty-nine miles per hour.

Despite having just disemboweled himself not even half an hour prior and survived a clash with a giant amphibian just the night before, Zilch is still holding on for dear life and watching the world zoom toward him. Tick by tick, the hurt in his head swells.

They pass a wooden sign with inset letters painted yellow: *Cardinal Park.*

Chev parks in the lot overlooking a muddy beach littered with twigs and fallen leaves. There are some other vehicles, of the tree-hugger's variety—electric or hybrid with bike racks and dangling tie-downs for boats. Across the way, at the far end of the lot, is a shockingly green car that matches Chev's modification for modification: the mammoth whale tail, hood scoop, fire extinguisher proudly displayed in the rear passenger window. Familiar. Very familiar. In fact, it wouldn't look out of place parked in the garage of 1330 Whispering Pines Lane. The engine is running, exhaust seeping out of the tuba-sized exhaust pipe. For a moment Zilch can't see, a rush hits him that makes the world whiten to nothing around him. Just noise. Kids on the beach down the way, a motorboat buzzing past. The pain defies words.

"Over here, dude," Chev says, calling out of the static of agony crushing Zilch's brain.

Recovering, Zilch approaches the car as Chev doubles over at the waist, dodges left to right, trying to peer through the glare bouncing off of the heavily-tinted windows. Zilch, cradling his screaming brains, comes up beside him and he can't see if anyone is inside, either. Even when they're right up on the car, all he can see is his and Chev's reflections—side by side they look like the number 10.

Chev knocks on the driver's side window. "Anybody home?" The window zips down to reveal a young man with a shaggy head of hair plastered to his head. It suddenly smells like marijuana smoke mixed with peppermint car freshener.

"Hey, man," Jolby says, languidly. He smiles at Chev, nodding, as if some kind of unspoken inside joke had just been exchanged. He notices Zilch a half-beat later and his eyes dive down. There is a rustling of Ziploc bags, hollow glass, and the trademark *clink* of a Zippo lighter closing as Jolby scrambles to conceal his stash.

"Don't freak," Chev says, "He's cool, man. I told you about him. Remember?"

Jolby's eyes pinch to slits. "You didn't say nothing about him looking like a fed."

Zilch steps forward. "Hey, Jolby. Your buddy Chev here says that you're the go-to guy for anyone interested in the Lizard Man." *Don't say anything about knowing his girlfriend*, Zilch cautions himself, *it might spook him more than you already have.* "Maybe, if it'd be okay, I could ask you a few—"

"Dude, show him that thing you can do," Chev interjects. "Check this shit out, Jol, the dude's some kind of FX dude. He can make it look like he's scarfing. Do it, dude!"

"Ah, maybe not here." Zilch looks around. "There's families with kids around." There actually isn't, but he's not exactly into the idea of pulling his guts out twice in one day.

"You already messed up the prosthetic or whatever you call it, just take the tape off and do it."

"What do I get?" Zilch asks.

"Uh . . ." Chev stammers, ducks his head into the Accord, and confers with Jolby in a hushed murmur for a moment. When Chev pulls his head back out, he's smiling.

Jolby says: "You wanna know about the Lizard Man, man?"

Zilch nods.

"And you ain't a fed?"

Zilch shakes his head. He gets a tingle of something—paranoia, maybe. But this is the best lead he's got and pushes it aside. "Do we have a deal?"

"All right," Jolby says from the driver's seat window, "if you do whatever it is that Chev seems to think you can do and it's cool as fuck, I'll let you ask me anything you want."

"How much do you know?" Zilch asks.

Jolby gives him a crooked smile that doesn't make it to his eyes. "Quite a bit. Quite a bit."

"How about this?" Zilch asks. "You ever see this one?" He does the thumb-removing trick that used to get a real rise out of his nieces. "Whoa, look at *that*! I can pull my finger off! Now it's back on. And off again! Come on, nothing?"

Both guys chortle and wave a dismissive hand at him.

"If you got some kind of movie special effects under there, let me see it," Jolby says. "Quit clowning, dude."

Zilch sighs. "Fine."

He unbuttons his shirt and peels away the license plate-sized patch of duct tape. Underneath, the nanobugs have only gotten the two sides of the wound partly glued back together with tenuous strips of new pink muscle and flesh. He silently apologies for wrecking their work and takes a moment before shoving his hand through the fresh membrane in hopes that the nerve endings are still being ignored in favor of the wound and it won't hurt *too* bad. His fingers slip through, and it stings. With a sound like stirring a bowl of mac and cheese, Zilch pushes his hand inside himself to the wrist. Jolby gasps and Chev chuckles half-heartedly, acting as if he wasn't close to peeing his pants back at the house. Zilch's pain flares up as he digs. He knows doing this will kill off who-knows-how-many more scarabs, bugs he cannot spare, but if it buys him information, so be it. It has to be done.

Again, he scarfs. With the hot rope of guts around his neck, he puts his arms out and asks, "Ta-da. Satisfied?"

Jolby openly cackles like a braying donkey, shoving a balled fist to his mouth and howls with morbid delight. He swears, reclaims his dropped joint, and stares. Chev has seen this show before, but still watches with a smile, a soft toothless U on his face that says that he is really, *really* keeping his fingers crossed that the whole thing isn't real.

Jolby is now out of the car and extending his hand for Zilch to shake. He doesn't mind that Zilch's hand is smeared with blood, apparently, because he just takes it without even looking and gives it four solid snaps of the wrist. "That is fucking *epic*, man. Consider yourself part of the fucking crew from this point on, man. Jesus Christ. I've never seen anything like that." With an index finger, he pokes the guts hanging from Zilch's neck and Zilch, surprisingly, finds himself protective of it, as if Jolby had just prodded his bathing suit area. But he plays into it and allows Jolby to lean in close to examine the intestine, even going on to comment that it smells like what he'd imagine guts to smell like, like a deli.

The two of them seemingly satisfied, Zilch unwraps his guts from his neck and tucks them away. He replaces his silver duct tape patch. It's lost some of its tackiness and he has to really slap it on against his belly to get it to stick. He buttons up his shirt and coughs nastily into his fist. A final bubble of pain bursts.

"Come on, let's go take a cruise on the Bud Boat," Jolby suggests buoyantly as he locks his car. He and Chev start heading down the trail to the lakefront beach and nearby dock. When Chev looks back, Zilch waves a hand, bent at the waist and breathing heavily. Things feel . . . tingly and itchy all of a sudden.

"I'll catch up to ya," Zilch sputters. "Just need to reset the special effect blood pack thingy—just in case you guys make me do this again," he says.

Chev nods, reluctantly turns, and continues down the trail.

Once the boys are out of sight, Zilch steps into the aisle formed by a hybrid station wagon and Jolby's Accord. The guts are back in place, the duct tape replaced—but something still isn't quite right. He coughs again and again, and he can feel something moving when he does. His abdominal wall is torn, naturally, and coughing is more of a chore than it should be. Something feels broken deep inside, beyond repair.

All the while, he's wondering why Galavance didn't mention that Jolby was apparently the area's unofficial expert yesterday. Does she not know that besides keeping himself good and baked every hour of the day, he also dabbles in amateur cryptozoology? If she knew, she would've said something, he's sure. Jolby is not only lying to his girlfriend about looking for work, but keeping secrets about his hobbies, too?

Zilch sputters, wheezes, and the very moment he manages to drag a full breath into his lungs, he cough-cough-*coughs* it back out. His mouth loads with phlegm. Spitting it onto the gravel, he sees the loogie isn't foamy and white, but pink. He takes a knee to examine it. Dead scarabs. A *lot* of dead buggies. Great.

"You coming or what, dude?" either Chev or Jolby shouts for him—Zilch can't tell.

"Yeah," he says, hobbling in a crooked line along the trail after them. "I'm on my way." Adding, to himself: "But not in the way you mean."

The lake is quiet, aside from the battering wake of occasional passing speedboats that threaten to capsize them. Along the park, under the gazebos and shelters, there is a smattering of people on the beach, tanning or grilling out. The farther they row out from the shore, the more isolated it feels out on the murky water. Zilch rides in the middle, telling them he needs a minute to get his sea legs before rowing. In front of him is Jolby and behind him is Chev, both pulling in slow, splashy revolutions. They move crookedly through the water, Jolby's strokes much more powerful than Chev's.

Once out in the middle of the lake, and gliding along without either man paddling, Zilch feels the rocking sensation hit him. The wind kicks up and the boat moves in soft sways that make his head pound and he finds himself blinking slowly and staring at the water.

"Dude, are you gonna barf?" Jolby asks. "I mean, I've heard of some motherfuckers getting seasick real easy, but this is a *canoe*." Jolby and Chev have a good laugh about that one.

"No, nothing like that. Just got a bit of a bug," Zilch says. *Or a lack of them.* "Either of you holding? That'd probably smooth out the landlubber's queasies."

"Here, but don't light up until we drift out a bit further," Jolby says, taking his hand from one of the paddles long enough to hand Zilch the baggie and glass pipe. The glass is cold in Zilch's hands.

He takes a pinch of the green and has to fight to get it to settle in the bowl properly, it's so twiggy and loaded with seeds. The wind is blowing and some of the weed scatters along the middle bench and over the edge of the canoe.

"Dude, you're fucking *losing it!*" Chev cries, as if it's their air supply slipping away. Zilch slaps his hand down before one of the green tumbleweeds can scamper over the canoe's edge.

"Relax." He crams it into the soot-rimmed bowl of the pipe and looks back to shore. Another hot breeze comes by and the water becomes even choppier and nausea hits him again. He can feel a scarab needling his cheek—he accidentally crushes it between his molars. It snaps like a poppy seed and for a moment he has the taste of ozone in his mouth.

Jolby pulls the oars in, favoring his bandaged wrist. He's looking over his shoulder. "Okay, we're out far enough. But when you light up, turn that way. The life guard has binoculars; Rick Coogan got busted out here last summer that way."

"Coogan," Chev snorts. "What a stooge. Stoogin' Coogan."

Zilch sparks the lighter and takes a long pull. The weed tastes just as bad as the crushed nanobug.

Jolby kicks on a ghetto blaster lashed to his bench. Some radio station that plays strictly electronica comes over the speakers. It sounds like fire engine screams and random prepubescent shouts. Both boys nod their head to it, seemingly moved by a frantic rhythm that eludes Zilch.

Ignoring it, Zilch takes his second hit, momentarily fearing what might come out besides smoke when he exhales, and passes the lighter and pipe over his shoulder to Chev, seated behind him. He speaks in that stifled, corked voice of someone holding their breath, asking Jolby, "So, what do you know about the Lizard Man of Old Man Weatherly Bog? A deal's a deal, right?"

Jolby sits splay-legged, twin lengths of pale, hairy thigh uncovered by his cargo shorts. He's a pudgy guy, kind of turtle-like in posture, with a heavy face and small, inset eyes. If he smiled after saving someone's life, it would probably still look like he was scheming. It's just that kind of face.

Jolby says: "You mean Picturesque Bay?"

"Sure."

He seems to mull the question before looking away and chortling, going with something else other than what he had thought first. "Can't believe they call that fucking shit-pond a *bay*. That place is and always will be a goddamn swamp. Can't imagine living there. Mosquito Central, once everything settles."

"I thought you guys were draining it," says Zilch.

"We be trying," Chev says, holding his toke. "Speaking of which," he adds, speaking over Zilch's head to Jolby on the other end of the canoe, "Beefy Ben might need to get a talking to as well, bro."

Jolby looks startled for a moment, sees Zilch scrutinizing him, then shoots a withering glare at Chev. Chev shuts up. Zilch caught it too: *As well? As well as who? Me?*

"Guys, I sorta feel like I missed something," Zilch says. "Did you bring me out here on this boat to give me the Sonny treatment?"

"What?"

"*The Godfather*."

"Oh, yeah. Sonny was a bitch." Jolby recovers for Chev's slip. "But naw, dude. We're trying to get the property drained so we can put up some retaining walls on that side of the lot," Jolby says, side-stepping talk of Beefy Ben altogether like it never even came up. He sighs, glares at Chev for a beat, then stares out into the water. "But once they decide to expand the neighborhood and drain the *whole* thing . . . it's *really* going to cause some problems, then."

"It hasn't killed anybody," Chev answers and again, Jolby gives him another shut-your-stupid-face scowl.

"You mean the Lizard Man?" Zilch asks.

Jolby sits up straighter. "It's like this," he begins, and exhales his hit. "Those dudes that all work down there—Ben, Darryl, all them—they're what you'd call morons. If they knew what we knew, they'd leave Whispering Pines right quick."

"Yeah," Chev contributes, "like in the cartoons when some dude bolts and there's just a smoke outline of where they were standing, dude. Zoom!"

"Exactly right, dude," Jolby says, eyes still on Zilch.

"Because of the Lizard Man?" Zilch asks.

Jolby drops the boombox's volume knob to a whisper. Somewhere, "Pour Some Sugar on Me" is suddenly playing, quiet and tinny. Zilch wonders if it's the last twinkle of his earlier hallucinations, but out of the recesses of Jolby's short pockets comes a cellular phone.

"It's my bitch. Hold on." He points to an alcove in the distance where the shore makes a bent S-shape, with plenty of wild growth forming a cave of foliage over the water. "Get us over there," he instructs Chev and answers the call. "Hey, babe."

Since there is nowhere to go for privacy, Jolby subjects Zilch to the entire conversation he has with Galavance. Zilch is sitting close enough that he can hear her voice faintly through the phone's earpiece. She sounds worried.

He covers the mouthpiece. "Dude," he calls over Zilch's head to a panting Chev, rowing, "what covers up a fishy taste?"

"Summer's Eve. My mom swears by it, dude," Chev says.

"What? Nasty. No, for *food*, stupid."

"Lemon juice," Zilch says. "Fresh squeezed, preferably."

Jolby looks at Zilch a moment, before uncovering the mouthpiece. "Chev says lemon juice, babe. Fresh squeezed."

Galavance says something Zilch can't make out. Maybe "I'll suggest that" or "Let's ingest fat," he isn't sure. Jolby puts his phone away, and stares at Zilch as Chev rows on, humming to himself. They move into the alcove, the shade not unwelcome.

Thumping a paddle against the bank crawling with tree roots, they sit in the half-dark, Jolby lit from behind in the foliage cave's mouth. He reaches into his pocket and produces, pinched between finger and thumb, a black button. He flicks it at Zilch, where it ricochets off his nose and lands on the canoe floor among the dead soldiers and blackened, sundried bait. Zilch picks it up, and puts it to his coat approximately where it once had been attached, where the broken threads are still hanging.

"Missing something?" Jolby says.

Zilch tosses the button overboard. *Plunk.* "Quit jerking me around. If you know where it lives, spit it out." Then it hits him. He tries to not let his face betray it. *Play dumb, let them join you in stumbling, and make your move, Zilchy.*

Jolby looks Zilch up and down, sneering. "I can only assume you tried some shit with my girl and she ran you down. I can smell it on you—that's not fake blood. The fuck *are* you, man?"

"Just some guy," Zilch says.

"So, what, you couldn't get nothing out of her so you decided to press your luck, dupe Chev's dumb ass into bringing you straight to me?"

"Hey," Chev whines. "Not cool."

"Do you know when it takes over?" Zilch says. "I'd appreciate some answers—because so far it's just been shitty music and even worse weed."

Jolby shakes his head, eyes closed. "It ain't bothering nobody, man. There ain't *nothing* down here for you to find. I'll give you one chance to say you'll leave it alone or your ass is grass, dude."

Chev says: "Dude, he knows. He knows, dude."

"Shut *up*," Jolby says, leaning past Zilch to scold his friend. He resettles his eyes on Zilch. "But yeah, you're right. Chev. The shit's blown."

"Do you want me to . . . you know . . . clonk him?"

Twisting in his seat, Zilch sees Chev going through a travel cooler, taking out an ice pack and brushing some frost off of one end for a better grip. Chev's eyes catch Zilch watching him and the galoot moves to stand, leaning forward with one hand bracing the aluminum edge of the canoe, the other raising the frozen-solid freeze pack to brain him.

Zilch goes for the utility knife in his back pocket but for a big guy, Chev is quick with the ice pack and bats the thing right out of Zilch's hand. It drops into the dark lake water and vanishes. On the backswing, Zilch catches Chev's wrist and pulls him off of his seat, smacking his arm against the rim of the canoe until the ice pack falls into the water, too. Chev twists around like he probably could've gone to state in wrestling, and before Zilch can snag a wrist or take a handful of Chev's spiky coif, he finds himself in a full-nelson.

Caught, Zilch doesn't struggle. "Okay, okay," he says. "You win."

Jolby, at the other end of the long canoe, waits for the canoe to stop rocking. He looks above Zilch's head and nods to Chev. "You got him?"

"Got him."

Jolby looks at the palm of his open hand. When he turns it to look at the reverse side, Zilch can see what he was eyeing: a discoloration, like a bruise taking color but fast—yellow rapidly darkening to a dark green.

"Do you at least know what's going on when you're . . . it?" Wriggling against Chev is no use; the guy must have some serious muscle under all of that padding. "I'm just a special effects guy . . . a location scout," Zilch attempts.

"Let him go, he ain't going to put up any fight now," Jolby says. When Chev releases him, Zilch sinks down off the bench between the front and back and gives it one last go at getting to his feet, but nothing is cooperating. His lungs burn like he's just done a line of dish detergent and he's not sure if he's actually hallucinating, but Jolby's head is changing shape, making bone-cracking sounds as his flesh squeaks like rubber while it's stretching.

"You can't know about this," Jolby says, his voice sounding pained. He puts on a sweatshirt and brings up the hood, struggling it to slip it over his rapidly broadening cranium. He's growing greener by the second. His eyes swell, their whites turning speckled and brown. His skin becomes a forest of tiny raised lumps, bumpy like a pickle. Finally, the green young man turns, grips the side of the canoe, and contributes a bellyful of stringy, pale yellow bile to the lake.

"A were-amphibian," Zilch says, every stationary thing in his line of sight dancing, wiggling, singing. "Does Galavance know?"

"Why are you so interested in my goddamn girl, man?" Jolby sprays. He has his head turned over his shoulder, spraying yellow strings from green lips with each shout. "She's mine, dude. She can't know I'm like this. Just *look* at me, man."

Zilch looks and says, "I see it, Jolby. And she's a good chick and I know you want to do right by her. For her benefit, you should work with me and we can let her move on with her life."

"Yeah, that's exactly what you'd want, isn't it?" Jolby tries to get the zipper to cooperate, but with clumsy, thick webbed fingers it proves too tricky a task and he gives up. "I mean, what are you here for—you gonna put me in some zoo or something?"

"My bosses, they'll get you a good story," Zilch says. "They'll say you saved somebody from drowning. Right here, you can be the Champion of Cardinal Park. They might even put your picture on the sign, or rename the park altogether. Jolby Park."

"What are you talking about, man? You gonna put me in some witness relocation thing? Fuck that. I like my life." He pauses after the last part, speckled eyes cutting away from Zilch briefly, doubting his own claim. "Is that what you wanna do? Take me away from her?"

"No," Zilch says. "I'm supposed to kill you."

Jolby laughs a phlegm sound. "Is that supposed to make me feel better?"

"No, it's not. But think about Galavance."

"Don't fucking say her name, man. She's mine. We're *together*."

"But you're a were-amphibian."

"Don't you fucking think I know that?"

"If you know it," Zilch says, "then that means it's far enough along that you're starting to remember when you turn, right? Do you remember what you do when you're . . . like this?"

"Sometimes."

"It's taking over, Jolby. I think it's too late. Do this, for Galavance, man. Let her get on with her life."

"You just wanna steal her. I take one look at you, with your fucking suit and . . . I can just *see* it, man. Plain as motherfucking day. I got your number. Oh I got it."

"It doesn't matter what I want," Zilch says. "This is what has to happen. I'll make it quick. You get found out by the public and you get a bunch of guys like Ben who're *really* itching to kill something—they'll take their time. They'll hunt you down, trap you, drag you back to wherever, and keep poking at you and siccing the dogs on you . . ."

"Dude, stop. Fuck." Jolby, perhaps picturing that, is unable to look up. Zilch watches him peer out over the water, at the people grilling and sunbathing in the distance. "I believe you," he says finally, quiet. "I bet Ben *would* do that if he knew what I was. Especially since it's me. We've never gotten along. Why are people like that?"

"Because as a species, we like to point fingers and say, 'Them. They're not like me.' We like having enemies maybe even more than having friends." Zilch struggles to sit up. "So let's just get back to the beach and we'll zip over somewhere nice and peaceful. Either of you own a gun? Or a really thick pillow, like goose down maybe? I'll be Chief and you can be Jack Nicholson."

"I can't tell her about this."

"I'm not asking you to," Zilch says, his patience waning. *Just let me kill you so I can have those couple of minutes without a fucking skull-splitter before I'm sent onto the next one. Please.*

"Because if I do," Jolby says, "then all the other shit, man . . . it'll . . . I can't, once I start talking, I know it'll *all* fall out. I know it. She's all I got and I can't lose her and if I tell her about *this*," he stares at his own slimy palms, "I'll have to tell her about everything else." Desperation makes his already-large, froggy eyes even bigger. "But that's how it should be, right? Get it all out at once."

Zilch asks, "What do you mean?" Jolby coughs. "Talk to me, man. What do you mean you'll end up telling her everything? Did you kill somebody?"

"No. What? Come on, dude. No, all the chicks."

"Chicks . . . you killed?"

"No, man! Listen to me. I haven't killed anybody. I . . . fucked some other women." He pauses. "Eleven other women." Jolby's head is in his webbed hands. "Fuck, what am I gonna *do*?"

"Let's take this thing back to the beach," Zilch says. "One quick second it can all be—"

"You're not killing me!" Jolby cries. "I can't, not before she knows everything. I've been *cheating* on her, dude. All the time. Not with just a couple of chicks, but . . . eleven. Eleven different chicks, man." He sobs. "Before we moved in together. Sarah Le Croix, Bobbi-Jo Lumley, Tara Harwood . . ."

"Tara was hot," Chev adds.

"Dude, not helping!"

"Before this started happening to you?" Zilch asks.

Jolby can only manage to nod. "Yeah." He clears his throat. "Chev?"

"Yeah, buddy?"

"Do him."

"Hold on a second, fellas," Zilch says.

"But dude," Chev says, "that's . . . murder."

"Do him, Chev," Jolby says. "Off your fat ass and *do it*, dude."

"I don't wanna kill anybody." Chev looks down at Zilch like he's a half-squashed bug. "I don't think I can do it."

"Let's talk about this," Zilch says, knowing he's in no shape for a fight. Negotiation is all he has.

"Do him or I do you both," Jolby says.

"All right, Jol. All right. I'll do it."

Zilch manages to turn halfway around to look at Chev only to catch the flat part of an oar rushing at his face. He sees stars and feels hands cupping under his armpits. He doesn't put up a struggle. He can't. Every part of him feels heavy, as if he's had lead shot into his bloodstream and now it's collecting at the ends of his limbs. He sees the undulating glimmer of the sun on the lake water and watches helplessly as it rushes up at him.

Some of the tightness comes out of his limbs now that drowning is imminent, muscles relaxing, relenting. Zilch bobs to the surface and gasps for air. He looks at Jolby peering over the edge of the canoe at him. He actually looks apologetic, momentarily, until the oars come sliding back out and hit the water. The first stroke comes and Zilch can feel the soft push of the water moving past him, brushing his belly—the lake water is doing his gaping wound no favors, the duct tape keeping no water out whatsoever. Bubbles come up around his chin and he feels the cold water rush in, filling him. The *S.S. Zilch* is sinking.

Zilch reaches up and grabs the canoe edge. He can feel himself filling up more and more. "Jolby. Wait a second. Just wait. Hey."

Chev slides an oar down between Zilch's chest and the canoe, ready to peel him off.

The oar flashes in front of the sun—*clonk*, again. A whoosh of cosmos dashes his vision a second time. All sound snaps away as he goes back under the water. Raking his hands, he draws himself back to the surface—gasps—and sinks again.

Trying to pull yourself to the surface when you have a giant hole in you is about as easy as climbing out of a grave. Zilch manages it, barely. He surfaces, gasps, doggy-paddling to the muddy bank. Mud sucking at his shoes, he stands, turns, and sees the back of Chev's spiky blond head. A pinprick, distant, already at the beach. Jolby, hood low, hops out of the canoe before it's even at the shore and goes bounding up over the sand to the parking lot, Chev right behind him. They get looks by people passing in bathing suits, raising sunglasses in disbelief at what they'd just seen. Two candy-colored cars start up and peel out of the lot, one after the other.

Zilch takes off his jacket and wrings a gallon of brown water out of it. "That could've gone better."

A jet-ski comes growling near, piloted by an aggressively mulleted man in a brightly colored life preserver. Fish-tailing to a stop, white water crashes against Zilch's legs, who stands wondering what fresh hell this dickhead might bring. The man straddles his gurgling watercraft and drops his wraparound shades, showing Zilch the violet glimmer in his eyes. "Hello, employee."

"Eliphas?"

"Indeed."

"Fine time for you to show up." Zilch struggles to get his sodden jacket back on. "I really could've used a hand about five minutes ago."

"You know I cannot interfere."

"I know."

"It'd seem you've become ill-equipped to handle this mission."

The employee delivery module in Zilch's pocket weighs heavily. "I can do it. I just wanted to give him a chance to volunteer for it." Zilch meets Eliphas Dungaree's gaze. "To go into it willingly, not against his will, like something that happened to *somebody* I know."

"Jolby Dawes does not deserve your mercy, Saelig. He is a selfish and contemptible monster. Kill him and end the mission." Eliphas studies the sky. "My brothers are already preparing another employee. They don't have much faith in you completing this to any degree of success in the time allotted."

"Look," Zilch says. "Galavance didn't seem like somebody who could take having a dead boyfriend, piled onto everything else, in stride. He might be a piece of shit, but it'd ruin her."

"Is this about the present situation," Eliphas says, dropping his gaze to look at Zilch again, "or are you towing personal feelings into this—as we cautioned you against doing, at the beginning of your employment with us? Because one young woman's emotional status does not mean risking the lives of countless others, should the parasite take over Jolby Dawes entirely."

"Exactly my point," Zilch says. "It's a parasite. So can't we just dispatch the thing making him act like an asshole and leave him alone?"

"That's not the mission. The mission is to eliminate the Lizard Man."

"Technically," Zilch interrupts, "not to be *that* guy about it, but Jolby is more of an Amphibian Man, actually. Lizards don't spend a lot of time in the water. And our guy is pretty froggy-looking."

"Why do you care, Saelig?"

"What?"

"About the well-being of that girl's emotion-part. You are unlikely to ever see her again."

"I just think if we can do this with as little collateral damage as possible, it might be good. *He's* a shit, sure, but *she* seemed nice enough."

"None of that matters," Eliphas says. "Without the parasite there is no *lusus naturae*, and the objective of your mission is the *lusus naturae*, not its cause, or surrounding elements such as Galavance Petersen. Besides, severance between host and parasite, at this late stage, is unlikely. It would likely kill them both anyway, if you attempt. So, end your mission as you wish."

Eliphas scoots forward on the jet-ski's padded seat to free up the back. "Would you like a ride across the lake so you can continue with your task?"

Zilch doesn't climb aboard. "She doesn't deserve to go through that."

"Are you letting your own experiences color your expectations for the outcome of this mission? Because I'd advise against that."

"You want me to keep fucking up."

"Pardon?"

"Because then, stripped of everything that I remember, I'll be a perfect little employee then, wouldn't I?"

"I don't follow your logic, Saelig. There has to be a penalty system to keep everyone working at peak performance."

"Why not an award system? People *like* working if they get treated well now and again."

Eliphas gives Zilch a blank look. "That just wouldn't work. Let's return to a more pressing issue; you're not swimming in time, especially given your somewhat haggard state—which I see has gotten worse since we last spoke."

Zilch tries to find ammunition to add to his argument but comes up dry. He sighs, and splashes out to the jet-ski. "Just get me across, man."

Eliphas rockets them across the lake and burbles up to the muddy beach's banks. Zilch starts to climb off, having thought of something cutting to use as parting words, but before he can manage any, the jet-ski whips around, recoats Zilch in a wash of lake, and speeds off. Zilch runs a hand down his face to get the water out of his eyes, watching the agent—behaving very un-agent-like—pull some sick jumps from a passing boat's wake.

Zilch turns and moves up the beach, feet squishing in his water-logged burial loafers, and begins the walk back to the highway, coughing occasionally. The pain swiveling around in his head, the thing marking Jolby's growing distance from him, is once again Zilch's only companion.

His shaking hand moves into his pocket, feeling across the cold metal of the employee delivery module. *No. Not yet.*

"What about lemon juice?" Galavance says, pulling open the walk-in cooler by its giant industrial handle. There's a gallon jug of the stuff next to a few enormous cans of sauce and a salt shaker as big as her head.

Patty steps in, wrapping her arms around herself against the chill.

"It might cut the flavors we keep getting from the sausage," Galavance explains.

Patty is skeptical. "Lemon juice?"

"It's worth a shot," Galavance says. "The order form says this is one of our cheaper ingredients. It's not fresh-squeezed, but maybe it'll work."

Patty shrugs, but Galavance can tell she, too, is excited at the prospect of this possible citrus savior—even if she's playing it down in a very regional manager kind of way. "Who knows, let's try it."

The entire kitchen staff for that morning's pre-open meeting are test subjects again. When they see the pan come out of the combi-oven and the tin foil peeled away to reveal three containers loaded with green peppers—the color falls from everyone's faces so quickly you can practically hear it.

Using tongs to put one pepper each on a paper napkin for everyone present, Patty says: "Now, give 'em a chance. These are different. Miss Petersen and I started working very early this morning to get these things just right, so please bear with us and lend us your taste buds one more time. They *have* to be better than yesterday."

Everyone exchanges looks. The dread is palpable.

"Just *try* them," Patty urges. "A couple bites aren't going to kill you."

Since it's clear no one has a choice, everyone steps forward and, with no shortage of disinclination, accepts a pepper.

Galavance stands by and watches as everyone takes the first bite. It's quiet for a while, but no one's face twists up, no one rushes off to the bathroom. She watches hesitation dissolve into intrigue, then mild pleasure. *Huh*, each face seems to say, *these aren't the worst thing in the world.* Galavance tries hers, and the pepper is cooked to perfection—it's soft but still has a bit of a crunch, and the sausage isn't awful anymore. There's a real faint aquatic tinge in there, but it's hidden, a subtle hint in the back of her mouth. Who would've thought Chev knew how to cook?

"Could I speak to you a moment?" Patty asks Galavance. Everyone else gets the hint that they're off the hook and can go back to work.

Patty takes her into the area just outside the kitchen, in the narrow hallway adjoining the dining area to the bathrooms, and customers as well as employees are brushing past. It's the lunch rush. "I just wanted to tell you, Galavance, that I'm *really* pleased with what I saw today."

"Can I . . . say something, quick?" Galavance says. "My friend told me to use lemon juice."

"I figured, but I thought I'd let you have that one," Patty says.

"I'm sorry I lied. I wasn't raised to steal credit."

"You didn't steal it. You never said 'I thought of the most amazing idea, Ms. Patty, let's use lemon juice!' You reached out to someone, they knew the answer, and you used your resource. Like a leader would. We only flounder alone." That last line is in the company handbook somewhere, Galavance recalls, some sort of a bad fish pun.

"My colleagues often draw conclusions based on what they've seen in just one day," Patty continues. "But after today, I'm glad I took the time to let you shine. I'm going to put a word in with corporate to move you up into the next pay bracket— provided your punctuality remains reliable. You'll technically be on probation, as you were when you started, but I think you have a lot of potential."

"Patty, I don't know what to say," Galavance gushes. She could let her fakeness drop aside now. This joy she feels is genuine. "I mean, I guess after what you said to me yesterday, I kinda sunk in and I just—wow, thank you so much. I—"

"Hold your ponies, girl," Patty says, chuckling. "This deal comes with a caveat. Today, you were given a task, a problem, and stuck with it until it was solved. Those peppers were—I'll admit—were dreadful. And I'd appreciate it if you didn't pass that around, me saying that. But every one of your coworkers actually swallowed this time. You fixed one problem. But I need to see that it wasn't a fluke, that you'd be willing to do this every day. I need your help with another menu item that has sausage as an ingredient. Unfortunately, I don't think this one can be fixed with lemon juice."

"Okay, I understand," Galavance says, but her mind is racing, she's imagining taking the trip with Patty back to corporate in New Orleans, maybe even getting a job at headquarters, moving out of Raleigh and living somewhere else for the rest of her life. Mardi Gras! Bourbon Street! The thought is almost overwhelming.

"Today was *work*," Patty points out. "And so will this next project, too. We'll have to meet at my hotel, because not even the cooks making this secret recipe are allowed to know it."

"What about Cheryl? She went to cooking school."

"She did. But because of that, our head cook here is trained in one very specific way. I need someone who can still think outside the box, who'll be willing to try anything even if it goes against 'the rules.' Look, Galavance. Frenchy's wants this next item perfected, photographed, and under the menu lamination for all thirty-five Frenchy's locations across the American South in less than two weeks. And I know I can't trust my taste buds. I need yours." They pause and step apart as a customer passes, heading to the restroom. Patty's got a smile on her face. "Well? What do you say? Do you have time to make Frenchy's next hit?"

It's not quite dusk but the moon is already out. Zilch looks at it as he wanders along, thumb out. An eighteen-wheeler blasts past, knocking him into a stumble with only its wind.

A carload of drunk twenty-somethings veers off the road to give him a scare.

A mile on, his thumb is still only yielding middle fingers. He feels like something that's been skinned—a lone creature without its protective metal mobile shell. He passes a flattened raccoon wearing a pink dog collar. Odd.

The pain compass start to ring, but it's dull. Vaguely *thataway*, it's pointing. Zilch keeps moving, shuffling backward, thumb out. No one stops for the sorry, soggy fuck on the side of the road. The clouds are lit from beneath up ahead, something bright on the ground blocked from his view by a thicket of pines. He lowers his thumb and stops walking backwards and meanders towards it.

Black Top Oasis is one of those super gas stations with three dozen pumps and a full restaurant inside. He crosses through the lot, and the folks in their minivans all clunk their door locks as they notice him.

Inside, it's frigid with air conditioning and he's so damp, every inch of his flesh goes goosepimply. The skin across his cheeks is tight and when he catches himself on a CCTV monitor bracketed to the ceiling, he sees a so-pale-he-looks-monochrome asshole in a soggy suit clunking around in ill-fitting shoes—an undead Charlie Chaplin. He can smell the roller dogs and liquefied "cheese." He stares at the crushed ice drinks being churned, mesmerizingly, by a machine.

"Can I help you?" someone says, the real question ("Buy something or beat it, weirdo.") barely disguised.

"You guys got a phone?" Zilch asks the cashier. He hears his own voice, croaky as Jolby. He coughs into his hand, looks at it, and wipes it on his pant leg.

The cashier, who's not even trying to hide his disgust, points toward the doors, back outside. "Pay phone, out there."

Out in the humid twilight again, Zilch picks up the receiver and mashes the zero, hard.

"Operator."

"Yeah, hi, I'd like to get connected with Galavance . . ." He stops. "Shit."

"Galavance Shit? Seriously? At least *try* to make it funny if you're gonna do this crap."

"No, sorry, it just hit me I never got her last name."

"Sir, I need a full listing—first *and* last name—if you'd like to be connected."

"Could you just look up 'Galavance'? There can't be that many."

"This isn't the White Pages, sir. If you look under the phone at the booth you're at—"

"There isn't one here. Who the hell steals a phone book?"

The operator sighs. "The name again, sir?"

"*Galavance.* Youngsville, Wake Forest, Franklinton, somewhere in there."

"I have one Galavance, a Galavance Petersen. There's no landline listed, only an address."

"What about a cell phone number? I kind of need to talk to her pronto."

"We don't have those records, sir. I suggest if you and this Galavance Petersen are acquaintances, perhaps when you get in touch with her again you can request that she jot down her number so that you two can remain in contact whenever an occasion such as this may arise and—"

"Just the address, then. Holy hell, lady."

"I can't give you that."

"Would that be information that would be in the stolen White Pages?" Zilch asks, wringing the ribbed metal cord where the phonebook used to be attached.

"Yes."

"Then what difference does it make if you give it to me or I read it from the phonebook?"

"I already said that I am not the White Pages, sir."

Zilch clutches his head. It's not the pain compass, but that ache that comes from dealing with bureaucrats. "Please, lady. Help me out here. I'm begging."

A trailer court: Focal Point Fields, she tells him.

Off of Kit Mitchell, roughly where Galavance ran him over Friday morning. He repeats the address to himself until it hardens, memorized.

Next, he asks for the number to the local Frenchy's franchise. He's counting on her still being at work, not only because that means she's away from Jolby, but also that she might be available to take his call before she sees him again. The operator patches him through, glad to be rid of him, but the girl who answers at the restaurant says she's not allowed to say if Galavance is there or not. Company policy. "Stalkers and whatnot, creep," she elaborates and hangs up.

Zilch stands holding the receiver in his hand. In the glass front of the Black Top Oasis, he can see the reflection of not only himself but the several well-lit awnings over the pumps behind him. Stepping out from between pumps three and four, he sees a vague smudge of a silhouette—its cut is familiar to him, the trace of a hip and a long arm hanging to one side, nails painted black. Her hair is long and tied back, a raven length of it reaching nearly to the waist of her dark jeans. In the window's reflection she is an approximation of her beauty—and he's not even sure if she is actually her (A gift? A promise from his employers to keep doing a good job?)—but he savors the moment, not wanting to interfere but only, for this snippet of wonderfulness, to behold her.

She turns and the harsh light from the awnings above the pumps makes dark shallows where her eyes should be. Below them, her lips curl into a smile. She speaks, and it's her voice, as he remembers it.

Do you remember our first date?

Zilch's hand begins to shake. He can only muster a nod.

It rained the entire time. And you, of course, didn't have an umbrella. So we shared a copy of Rolling Stone, *back when they used to be huge. It covered us both. Cindy Crawford was on the cover. I wanted sushi for dinner and you said you knew a great place.*

Zilch wants to tell her he remembers but knows if he opens his mouth right now it'll only be a choked squeak. He still cannot turn to face her. She can't be more than ten steps behind him, keeping her distance.

And it was a good place, she continues. *I used too much wasabi and you ran to the kitchen asking them for a glass of milk. But it only made it worse. You said when you kissed me later that night you liked your kisses spicy and that I should always have wasabi before we kiss. We were barely old enough to drink yet were blissfully, stupidly in love. We used to sit and talk for hours, just talk. We'd sit in your car and listen to your awful tape collection. We used to make love four times a night and dream out loud lying around in your crappy apartment, expanding walls into new rooms of our someday dream home in our heads. We'd never get there. You'd fuck it all up long before then.*

She's wearing the same wine-colored lipstick she used to, back when he knew her, back before he left her—and later left her again. He isn't sure if lake water is still running out of his ear or if those are tears on his cheek.

The wasabi kisses will be the next memory they bleach out of your head if you fuck this one up, babe. I only exist as this, now. I know you want to come see my grave in Wilmington, where I'm buried next to my parents, but you know if you wander too far they'll pull you out—and maybe you won't even remember where you were running off to in the first place. Word to the wise: don't bother going. There's nothing to see there.

Zilch wonders, for a fraction of a second, if it's not them doing this, some kind of mind fuck or a hateful motivation technique—but she looks so much like she did, and sounds so much like she did, that he really doesn't care.

You're not built for this. You know that and I know that. But you have to keep trying.

He tries not to blink, wants to see as much of her as he can. He knows it's a mistake, but he's unable to resist turning around to look at her—to *really* see her—and when he does, there's nothing there.

I'd tell you I love you, that I'd forgiven you, but it'd go against the last thing I said to you, her voice continues, completely disembodied. *My feelings haven't changed. They will never change. And this is all you'll have of me now. Go do what you're here for— she needs your help.*

Then her voice spreads out into one long unbroken tone and raises in pitch until the droning in Zilch's ear returns as it was. With it, the compass also jumps back to full, skull-popping agony; belligerently, as if making up for lost time, punishing him for the few seconds he was allowed with her.

He'd rather have his gut opened again than have her stolen away from him, over and over. He doesn't know who to blame— his waterlogged brain, the bufotoxins courtesy of Jolby, or the agents—but right now anger isn't rising inside him, only loss. He's still holding the receiver—it's now just a droning dial tone in his ear—and he looks at where she should've been standing, between pumps three and four. There, on the oil-spotty ground, is a set of wet footprints in the shape of a woman's size six sneaker. Zilch hangs up the payphone with enough force to crack its plastic. He still feels heavy—there's lake water sloshing around inside him as well as self-hate. One he can get rid of, and he goes around back of the gas station where he finds the automated carwash and an air-pump with a bright red sign reading FREE AIR.

At the end of the building there's a coiled green hose and a spigot that looks like it's for Oasis-use only. But since it's not marked, Zilch assumes the water is free too. In the dark behind the gas station, with eighteen-wheelers grunting on the interstate nearby and crickets in the field the station buts up against,

Zilch removes the duct tape patch from his belly and leans back, prying open the slit in his stomach. He turns on the hose and sprays inside real good, angling himself toward the highway so that, when cars pass, he can actually see what he's doing. Not that he's concerned about lake debris so much; he's just curious, really.

He regrets it immediately.

Most people go the whole run, birth to death, without ever seeing any part of their internal organs unless it's a CAT scan or X-ray. But here's Zilch, peering in and seeing scraps of seaweed amongst the vein-covered sack of his stomach, the coiled mass of intestine, and whatever the hell *that* thing is. Zilch reaches in and pinches the seaweed out before dousing everything with the hose. It stings like someone's tattooing his insides. When it starts to bleed, he knows it's clean, or clean enough; it's something you learn in culinary school when it comes to cutting yourself. If it bleeds, the debris is out—if it doesn't, well, you should probably make a trip to the doctor. He only sees a couple of scarabs, floating dead. They slide out of the wound and onto the ground. He watches them ride the red trickle toward the gas station's storm drain. It hurts, but not as much as it should. He only feels cold, numb and waxy.

The sagging edges of the wound aren't mending. Pinching them together, they don't take. They flap apart, wide and loose, pornographically. He buttons his damp shirt over the whole mess. Maybe he should've used a different method to get those idiots' attention, he considers. But then, the phrase 'a different path probably would've been wiser' could be stapled onto every square of the calendar of his stupid life.

He gets his suit coat—which has lapped the definition of 'filthy' a few times now—back on, sits, and tries emptying his shoes, but trying to scrape the sand out is pointless. He puts them back on, even though they're so full of lake floor grit his soles feel like sandpaper when he walks.

Back around front, under the glare of the fluorescent lights of the pumps again, more car doors thump-lock as the soggy ex-corpse passes, pale and cold and miles from where he needs to be. Humming Willy Nelson, Zilch continues along the roadside, thumbing for a ride he knows he won't get, back on the road again, hesitating only momentarily between pumps two and three—where her two wet footprints are already evaporating.

♂

"Do you know where the Hilton is?" Patty asks, steering her rolling file-folder up to her rental car.

Galavance nods. "I'll follow you."

They get split up at a red light Galavance doesn't dare running—not with her boss's boss's boss's boss right there.

Patty's car continues on, down to the next intersection, then the next, then out of sight. Galavance arrives as the sun is setting, the parking lot full of minivans and other rentals as remarkably unremarkable as Patty's. Typically, Galavance hates walking around in her work clothes; she feels like a drone. But it feels like a business meeting as she enters the hotel lobby and notices the bad art on the walls and potted fake plants. Upstairs, passing identical doors—some leaking the sound of TVs, others of people screwing—Galavance gets turned around more than once in the identical hallways. She has always found hotels to be spooky places. The rooms that might be empty behind those doors are scarier than the ones that might be occupied. She imagines beds with no heads on the pillows, chairs sitting empty, each room with crowds of anti-people in muted, watching congress.

She finds Patty's room and knocks.

"One moment," Patty says. Inside, her TV is on—some talk show—and Galavance can hear her zipping up suitcases hastily and thumping things around. Finally the door opens and Patty is in a tie-dyed T-shirt with a ring of the Grateful Dead bears dancing on it, and some jean shorts. It's weird seeing her boss in something other than the super-starched Hillary Clinton attire. For once, Galavance feels like the better dressed of the two.

There's a pile of take-out containers on the dresser. Of the two beds in the room, the one Patty clearly hasn't been sleeping in has a massive load of luggage on it, all matching in old lady floral print. Galavance catches the scent of something akin to fried onions, and the stale whiff of recent vacuuming.

Patty closes the door behind them. It's awkward immediately.

"Do you want something to drink?" Patty asks.

"Uh, sure."

Patty opens the mini-fridge and from a six-pack of Bud Light that's already missing three, hands Galavance a can. Not what she was expecting.

"This way," Patty says, gesturing to the bathroom. "We'll get started right away."

Inside there are two folding tables, cutting boards. The shower curtain has been repurposed as a hanging rack for a knife set and to suspend the box of sausage labeled SAUSAGE. One end has been cut open and it's draining a pink gunk into the tub. Galavance can smell the fishy reek they'll have to, again, find a way to cover up. There are numerous dry and canned ingredients on the fold-out tables. A small army of tiny seasoning bottles, tinned stewed tomatoes and carrots, and some economy-sized boxes of dry pasta. She's moved the microwave in here as well, and it's plugged in alongside a hot plate. Some pots and pans, scrubbed and ready, sit stacked inside one another.

The light in the hotel room bathroom, like all hotel bathrooms, chases away any trace of shadow. The mirror is broad, taking up the entire far wall. Galavance can't help but notice how small she looks next to Patty, and how much taller. Both of them appear washed out and tired. Red eyes, red knuckles. Kitchen scars.

They wash their hands at the two sinks, framed side by side in the mirror. "I know this is kind of unconventional," Patty says, working the soap foam hard between her small hands. "And I'm sorry I can't put this down as overtime for you. But I do appreciate the assistance."

Galavance was kind of hoping that it *would* count as overtime, but still, showing this bit of dedication—one night away from home—has been promised to secure a pay bump. It's worth it. "It's totally fine," she says, rinsing her hands of soap. She washed them for the full length of time, singing "Happy Birthday" to herself as she was trained, first thing, first day, at Frenchy's.

"I don't know how long this will take," Patty says. "Do you need to call anyone to let them know you're here?" She dries her hands and offers Galavance a clean towel from the pile housekeeping has left, all scratchy and bleached of any puke or blood the previous guests had wiped on them.

"No, my boyfriend probably won't even notice," she says and chuckles—the bathroom's acoustics lets her know how fake her laughter is. "He works late a lot."

"What does he do?" Patty asks, dull and unabashedly disinterested, tying an apron on. She offers Galavance her own.

"He and his friend are building a house," Galavance says, tying it on, "with plans to sell it."

Patty moves to the folding table, grunts to pull down the hanging box of sausage, and pops open the lid. The fish smell leaps out, stronger than it was at the restaurant. It's nearly over-powering, but Galavance swallows down a gag.

"Where abouts?" Patty asks, pulling open the plastic liner inside the box, unleashing more of the stink—which she seems unbothered by entirely. "Near where you two live, or somewhere else?"

"A few miles from our place," Galavance says. Because it's just her and Patty, just like earlier that morning at the kitchen, she feels the need to fill the silence. Plus the more talking she does, the less, she hopes, she'll have to deal with that smell. "It's this new-development neighborhood," she adds. "Kind of rough for them right now, since it floods there a lot. It's basically built on a swamp."

"Is this in Franklin County, by chance?"

"Yeah. How'd you know?"

Patty's small hands hold a load of the tiny pink cubes of diced sausage, fuzzy with white frost, ready to move over into a mixing bowl. She pours the diced meat out, after a moment, and goes to fetch a plastic spoon from the rack of tools hanging from the shower curtain. "Does he like working there?" she asks, after a very long delay, her broad back to Galavance.

"I guess, yeah," Galavance says. "Say, should I . . . be doing something?"

"We need to let the sausage get to room temperature. It was frozen—I had it thawing in here all day," Patty explains. "But it's clearly not quite there yet."

"Why does it smell that way?"

"We don't know," Patty says, facing the unrolled knife kit lying open across the toilet tank. Big knives, tiny cruel knifes.

Knives with serrated edges. Knives with big, broad chopping blades. Twenty in all, arranged in descending size.

"I was thinking on the way over here," Galavance says, and accidentally stammers, "if the sausage smells like fish, should we really be serving it? It might be bad. I mean, to be honest, this stuff here smells even worse than the stuff from this morning."

Patty turns. The fluorescent light of the bathroom buzzes, on and on. There are no windows in here. "I should probably be clear about something."

"Okay . . ." Galavance says, trying to sound as chipper like she normally acts around Patty. But she's a little freaked out. There's an air here, now. Something changed.

"I don't want to have you sign anything, Galavance, but none of what we do here can leave this hotel room," Patty says. She doesn't blink behind her glasses. "Understand?"

"Sure, yeah."

"Sending the Culinary Inspiration Team to Los Angeles was Corporate's last ditch effort to save the company, to get our name out there. We can't afford to market on TV or the Internet anymore—the ads are too expensive. Frenchy's has been slowly dying since late last year. They've had to close a few locations, I'm sure you've heard."

She had. "I kind of thought that's why you were visiting, to see if ours was worth keeping around."

"It is *definitely* worth keeping around," Patty says, her face brightening slightly. "It's rapidly become the apple of Corporate's eye, in fact. It's a very good location in two ways. One, being so close to the mall and movie theater is ideal real estate—good flow there. And it's also placed quite helpfully near something else."

"What's that?" Galavance says.

"I've been entrusted by corporate to see this menu item through," Patty says vaguely, gesturing at the bowl of pink cubes. "I've worked for Frenchy's since I graduated high school—a long time, you don't need to tell me. I'd do anything for them. They paid for my ingrate son to go to school. They helped me when my cheating husband needed back surgery. They let me take two weeks off when my banshee of a mother was in the hospital. And I've paid them back every chance I could. Long hours. Long-distance trips away from home, like this one. I'm here because I'm dedicated—like I know you can be too, Galavance."

"I'm happy you like your job," Galavance says, but isn't really sure why.

"I do like my job," Patty says. The TV in the other room has some action movie on and there's sudden gunfire, loud pops, and screaming. "And I know that for a young person to like their job, they need to be shown they're something more than an easily replaceable cog. Nowadays, they need to be shown that they're cared for and cared about and will be looked after, their natural skills put to good use. I see a lot of potential in you. Creativity and an open mind. Thus, speaking on behalf of Frenchy's, I'd like to ask if you, Galavance, if you would like to be part of something most Frenchy's employees never get to be. Not even Cheryl, who went to cooking school."

"I'm not sure I understand," Galavance says.

"If you say no," Patty says, "that unfortunately means I'll have to sever you from the Frenchy's family. Immediate termination."

"You'll fire me? Just because I don't help you with this menu item?" Galavance knows there's something else going on, but she's playing it slowly, trying not to let things escalate. Not with so many knives presently scattered about the room.

"It's harsh, I know. But turning down an invitation to the big leagues is a slap in the face, and Frenchy's, despite its problems, still has a lot of pride. It can be great again. Like we were in the 90s. The local rival to invading foreign invaders such as McDonald's and Burger King and Wendy's. To get here, to spread beyond the Southern United States, we just need help. I know that, corporate knows that, and that's why I was put in charge of spearheading this. Openminded hard workers, specifically. Like the kind I've discovered in you, today."

"Can I have some time to think about it?"

"The work on this menu item needs to start soon, whether or not you choose to be a part of it."

"Okay, all right, just give me a second."

Galavance steps out of the tiny bathroom and into the main part of the hotel room, though it's not any less claustrophobic in there either. She goes over to the glow of the TV, passing the second bed to the closed curtains. Parting them, she can see Raleigh in the distance: the airport and the few skyscrapers the town has. She can see the university from here, where her dad went. Not Asshole Amos, but her real dad.

With the room so bright and it being so dark outside, the window is a mirror. Galavance can see Patty behind her, standing in the bathroom doorway. She has a plastic spoon in her hand, low, at her side, staring at Galavance's back, the tiny eyes behind her glasses huge and frog-like.

"Does your boyfriend tell you about how his work day was when he gets home?" Patty asks—not *nearly* far enough away for Galavance's comfort, talking loudly to be heard over the TV.

"Sometimes, yeah."

"Any anecdotes about working on a house in a flood-zone you might want to share?"

"Putting up drywall is a pain because the humidity wrecks it. Tile is expensive. Plumbing is complicated."

"Nothing about the location itself?"

"There's lots of mosquitoes," Galavance says. "Why are you asking me about—?"

"I'm sorry. I get nosy sometimes. I've only ever worked for Frenchy's, so other people's jobs are really interesting to me. Do they own the plot the house is on, your boyfriend and his business partner?"

"They do, yeah." Galavance's pulse is racing.

"So there's no money coming from the house until they sell it, right?"

"Yeah."

"You're basically the sole breadwinner, then."

"I guess."

"You guess?"

"I am. I mean, yeah. It's just me."

"Must be tough. There aren't many alternatives outside of food service for girls who only have a high school education."

Galavance is about to snap, "How do you know that?" until she realizes anyone in an assistant manager's position or higher can look up how much Galavance makes, or see a copy of her driver's license, her address, her work history, her social security number, everything. Galavance's entire tiny life probably wouldn't fill a whole page.

"I want you to succeed," Patty says. "I want Frenchy's to be the means by which you attain it. I don't want to fire you." Galavance watches as Patty's reflection moves away from the bathroom door, into the room. She sits on the corner of the bed, the springs squeaking under her. She sits in profile, watching the carnage on TV. A man's head gets a bullet through it and because it's *that* kind of action movie, brains splatter the camera.

Patty doesn't so much as blink at the make-believe murder. She turns the big wooden spoon in her hands, sitting forward, the gunfire opening another man's arm, taking off his hand and sending it flopping across the movie set warehouse floor. Patty's face creases, a tiny smile hitching up.

Letting the curtains fall back, Galavance faces her. "If it means keeping my job, I'll do it. I agree. I still don't understand why it means I'd get fired if I didn't—"

"Glad to hear it," Patty cuts in. She remains on the bed, watching a henchman getting hit with a rocket-propelled grenade. "Now let's make some stroganoff." Patty gets up and turns off the TV as she passes it. Now the room is silent, and there's only the hum of the city, just outside the hotel's walls—but so far away.

Galavance makes herself follow Patty back into the bathroom-turned-kitchen. The low-tide smell hits her again like a wall. Patty puts a hand on Galavance's shoulder and gently guides her around, turning them both in a circle, until Galavance is the one farther away from the door. Patty closes it behind them, standing in front of the door, that big wooden spoon in her hand, still, fluorescent lights buzzing angrily overhead.

"I'm glad you agreed," Patty says. "It feels good to know I'm no longer alone on this. It's been hard, keeping this secret."

"That the recipe for stroganoff comes on the side of Hamburger Helper?" Galavance says, hoping to diffuse the tension.

"Not this kind. I asked so many questions about where your boyfriend and his business partner have their house and whether or not he's told you about the location because it's crucial to keeping this recipe available to Frenchy's. See, food company distributors give a discount to their bigger clients. The major fast food chains can ask for a lower rate because they give the distributors so much money. Frenchy's used to be one of those, like I said. Now, since we're closed so many locations, the snake at the distributor—the same we've had for *decades*—has decided to hike up the price."

"That sucks," Galavance says for a lack of anything better to add—while eyeing the knife roll and trying to decide on which one, if she has to, she could use to defend herself against Patty.

"It does suck," Patty says. "And since success relies on innovation, I've been appointed by corporate to find a new means of acquiring meat."

Galavance can feel her face drain. The tips of her ears, her lips, and fingers all go numb. "Uh, what?"

"I used to hunt muskrat with my father. I don't know if I ever mentioned that in my initial interview, but like I knew you only had a high school diploma, corporate knew I knew my way around a rifle. That or they just knew I'd do anything it took to get the job done—that I'd *learn* to use a hunting rifle, if need be. Either way, I was the right woman for the job. I've been making many trips to South Carolina and, now, North Carolina. I thought it was crazy, at first, taking boat-rides out into the swamps looking for something I was sure was made-up. But frog legs are expensive, and our distributor, like I said, decided to jack up our price even more than it already was. I had to do something."

"They sent you here to find the Lizard Man?" Galavance's heart was throwing itself against her ribs like it was trying to escape a burning building.

"Not the Lizard Man, Miss Petersen. A six-foot frog-man, or frog-*men*, seen all over North and South Carolina. I've bagged forty-three so far. And while the meat's been a hundred percent free, we still can't chase the reek out of it. It was a small miracle what you did with the stuffed peppers, but that's just one item on the menu, and with something like stroganoff, where the use of lemon juice is impossible—"

Galavance's eyes move to the mixing bowl on the counter. Then the small pile of pink dice, thawing, a pink puddle under them. Then the tub. The red slime crawling toward the drain. Then, in her mind, all the sausage she had seen the cooks fry up over the past few months, putting it over salads, over rice. All those greasy, empty plates Galavance had taken back to the dishwasher. Then, hitting her like a second ton of bricks, she recalls what she snuck out of the leftover fridge and took home to Jolby. And what she'd eaten, *herself*, so many times, by the forkful from Jolby's Styrofoam plate. What she'd eaten earlier that morning, all those samples yesterday. "We ate that. I ate that . . . and it was . . . ?"

"When they've fully turned, there's nothing human to the meat."

"But it was human *once*. Meaning if it was, it still sorta is." Nausea explodes deep in Galavance's belly. "Oh, God."

"It's called total physiological transmogrification. The Culinary Inspiration Team brought in a genealogist to test it, then an occultist, and finally one of the nine wizards from the Chattanooga branch of the Unholy Union Coven. And they all agreed. It's 100 percent amphibian. I have to kill them fully changed into their frog-man state, of course, but if I do, any trace of human goes away, Galavance."

He wasn't lying. That crazy asshole she hit with her car *wasn't lying!* Galavance laughs, despite herself. Of all the things that pop into her mind, of course Saelig Zilch would be what rises to the top. Clarity, or total denial, shoves aside her mounting nausea. "So are you working with him? Is he like the location scout or something?"

Patty's face twists. "Who are you talking about?"

"The other guy looking for the Lizard Man."

Patty's eyes widen. "Who's looking for the Lizard Man?"

Shit. "Nobody. I mean, I heard someone at the gas station the other day saying that someone was asking—"

Patty stomps forward over the cold tile floor. "Who was it? Did he speak to you?" Patty snaps, and Galavance can feel her hot breath on her face. "Who's he with? McDonald's? Burger King? They've got spies everywhere."

Galavance tries backing up, but the back of her legs hit the rim of the tub. She does not want to fall into that muck and tries to push Patty off.

"Who was it?" Patty roars, shaking Galavance. "Who was it? What was his *name*? Was that the son of a bitch at Whispering Pines? Is he there *now*?" Galavance's ear rings as Patty smacks her upside the head with the wooden spoon. "Speak, you uneducated little skank, speak!"

"Let me go!"

"Tell me, tell me! *Everything* is riding on this meat staying a Frenchy's-exclusive source! If we get it tasting better, we can refresh the brand and get some real buzz going—but *none* of that will happen if the King or the Clown or that freckled-faced cunt beats us to it first!"

Even if Galavance did know where Zilch was and wanted to say, she couldn't—not with Patty's hands closing around her throat. She feels the trapped blood swelling in her cheeks, numbing her tongue. She reaches to the side—knocking over the hotplate, the set of skewers, grabbing up the first thing in reach.

Bringing it up in a swing, the pot collides with the side of Patty's head. Her short fingers soften their iron grip. Free, Galavance pushes Patty and the regional manager slumps aside, hitting her head a second time—this time on the toilet rim, en route to the floor. She lays still, on her side, and a line of blood begins to trickle out of her hairline.

Galavance is still holding the cook pot by its handle, expecting Patty to spring back to her feet at any moment. But sticking around to see if and when she wakes up would definitely be a bad idea.

I have to find Jolby. If Patty were to show up at the house, likely with that rifle she was going on about, demanding to know about Saelig Zilch, and Jolby got lippy with her, there would no saying she wouldn't use the same excessive force again. Galavance saw Jolby get in a fistfight once, after school. He's no fighter. Whereas Patty, Galavance just learned the hard way, was one scrappy little shit.

Galavance steps over her boss's unconscious form and out of the bathroom. She uses the wall to find the door, and falls out into the hotel hallway, the carpet burning her knees. Getting up, she runs the labyrinth of the Hilton's carpeted corridors, passing door after identical door, taking the stairs instead of the elevator when she finds them, and out to the lot. With her khakis so tight, she struggles to free her car keys.

Following the sound of breaking glass, some of it raining down on her, Galavance looks up—above, Patty, in the gap of smashed window, leans out, blood running down her face, bringing the rifle scope up to her eye.

Galavance gets her car unlocked and pulls the door shut just as a bullet sparks off the asphalt where she'd been standing. She fumbles and screams at herself trying to stick her key in the ignition. A second bullet thwaps through the roof of her car, piercing the passenger seat's cushion—a small puff of free foam rising from the smoking bullet hole. Dropping her pink getaway into gear, Galavance floors, tearing it over the curb and across the Hilton's manicured lawn, out onto the street—and is nearly bowled over by an approaching pickup truck. The traffic scatters. She rips through the next red-light—who cares anymore if Patty sees her do it—and hits the interstate, never letting her foot off the gas.

At 110, she flies through traffic, jinking from one lane to the next, dodging even the most daringly lead-footed. Dialing Jolby, she pinches the phone between her shoulder and ear to keep both hands on the wheel. She nearly rear-ends a motorcycle who, unlike her, wants to obey the traffic laws. She barely missing splattering him across the pavement, just as the phone rings for the fourth time in her ear.

"This is J-Boy. Leave yo message, ho. Peace."

"Jolby, it's Gal. Are you at the house? I need you to go home immediately. Bring Chev if you have to—it's not safe there for either of you."

Zilch wasn't lying. He wasn't lying. He wasn't crazy and he wasn't lying. Galavance's hands slide to ten and two on the wheel. "Holy shit, holy shit, holy shit."

Her bowels, on the drive, have turned to liquid. She's so scared and so panicked that she wonders if she hasn't already gone in her work pants. Parking in the yard instead of the driveway, she hops out, bursts in through the front door. "Jolby?" She didn't even think to check for his car in the driveway—she just wants to see him, his face, her boyfriend. Not in the kitchen. Not in the living room. Nothing, nobody. She pushes open the bathroom door, finds it empty, and stands before the commode unsure of which end to point toward the bowl. She pulls down her pants and sits. It's awful. All she can think about are all the stuffed peppers she's eaten. All of those leftovers. Then, all of those customers who'd eaten it, too. She gets up off the toilet seat, turns, and throws up.

After, she takes off her sick-spattered clothes and washes her hands and face and brushes her teeth three times. She can barely keep eye contact with herself in the toothpaste-spotty mirror. *I'm a cannibal. I didn't know it until twenty minutes ago—so does that excuse it? Is it okay that I didn't know?* When she balls up her ruined clothes and goes to toss them in the wastebasket, she steps on the pedal to lift the lid and sees something, inside the trash, move. She recoils, drops the clothes on the floor, and nearly sends herself out the bathroom window. But she has to see. In her underwear, ready with her hairbrush to bludgeon whatever may be inside, she reaches from as far away as she can to press her big toe on down the trashcan pedal that will flip up the lid again. Galavance cranes her chin out, peeking down inside the plastic bag, looking for whatever it was amongst the greasy, yellowed Q-tips and balled tissues . . .

She spots a tangle of medical tape and sullied cheesecloth. The bandage Jolby had wrapped around his wrist earlier, maybe. She reaches in with her brush, gives it a bump. Nothing. Angling some of the bristles under the bandage's edge, she flips the mess of gauze and tape over. *Please just be mice.* If they had mice it would be no big surprise. Jolby eats in bed constantly and—Galavance is sad to admit to herself as she suddenly remembers—her first step onto the bedroom floor after waking that morning had been right into an unfinished plate of congealed SpaghettiOs.

The bandage is bloody inside, and it's not just blood, but these clumps of things like dark stringy scabs. She peers down closer, leaning and feeling the veins jump out in her forehead and neck. She looks into the bandage, the loose weave of the cheesecloth. And there, among the dried red and brown flakes of her boyfriend's blood from an injury he said he got at the job site, are tiny strings, squirming. Galavance moves her head to one side so the bathroom's naked lightbulb can shine directly on them.

Galavance stands up and gives a whole-body quake, unable to control herself, then heads back down the hall, still shivering. She was already shaking from the ordeal with Patty. She checks the trailer's deadbolt, twice, before going up the hall to the bedroom to get changed. She has to pass the bathroom to do so and peers in as she passes. The tiny worms have not escaped the trash can. After putting on jeans and a T-shirt, whatever's within reach, it's on her trip back to the kitchen—giving the bathroom wide berth—when she pauses in the living room, and that's when it hits her—*bam.*

If those heartworms at the vet's office in the jar came from a dog, then what if the worms in the trashcan came from Jolby? What if he's got some kind of intestinal . . . weirdness going on? What if it's from the sausage? *What if I have those in me, too?* She tries to tell herself she hasn't eaten nearly as much as Jolby has over the time she's worked at Frenchy's. On her lunch breaks, she would often opt for a protein bar and a soda. Very seldom, other than this morning of course, did she eat that much Frenchy's. But all those taste-tests they did. Fuck. Nausea hits her in a foamy orange wave. She can't help remembering how the squeaky bits of sausage felt as she chewed them. How it tasted as she swallowed.

What if that was how the Lizard People were made? Patty did say something about them transforming. So unless it was a curse, some family blood-thing, that meant . . . Jolby has it. And maybe that's why Patty, like Saelig Zilch, were both so interested in the wetlands near Whispering Pines of Picaresque Bay. She has to sit on their hand-me-down sofa. She holds her head in her hands and stares saucer-eyed at nothing, her mind practically smoking. This isn't good.

She flinches when she hears, up the hall, the metallic clatter of something falling over. She's left the bathroom light on and from the couch she can see the waste basket, rolling on its side, peeking out of the bathroom at her.

When she heads back up the hall, she's prepared, with two hair ties and a paper towel made into a filtration mask. She has on big rubber dishwashing gloves and has wrapped herself in Saran wrap. She keeps her eye on the trash can—which is still, for now—and snatches up her can of hairspray from the counter. Then, from her pocket, her Bic. She shakes the can, stepping forward, spraying a tongue of fire into the mouth of the trash-can. The plastic bag liner melts, and the Q-tips burst into double-headed torches. Jolby's bandage takes the fire, the old blood inside bubbling and turning thick and black. The worms inside twist and curl, go crispy, and finally still once they're curls of ash.

Proud of herself, Galavance steps back, the hairspray can still in her hand. It's hot. The nozzle, she notices, still has a finger of a flame going. The push-down part is melting and the flame, suddenly, grows a little bigger—and makes a soft, agitated pop.

Fearing she'll lose her hand if it explodes, she tosses it into the tub and starts the shower. Pulling the shower curtain aside, she realizes, is stupid, because if the can detonates it's not like a millimeter of vinyl is going to stop aerosol can shrapnel. The can lets off a soft thud and she peeks behind the shower curtain, squinting against the showerhead's back-spray. The can is still burning and now part of the shower wall is black. The flames are small but they grow quickly, up the shower wall, to the drop ceiling. Trying to adjust the showerhead does nothing. Something whooshes next to her and suddenly the bathroom wallpaper is on fire—and rapidly spreading.

"Shit. Stop," she tells the fire, snapping a towel at it. "Stop."
It doesn't listen.

Backing out into the hallway, Galavance stares as the bathroom fills with white smoke and the fire takes the rack of towels, then the shower rug and the toilet paper still on its roll. The garbage can, on the other side of the room, is still burning and contributing to the blaze from the other side. The flames meet in the middle and the room is engulfed. Galavance jumps as the smoke alarm starts screaming, telling her something she already knows. She feels in her pockets for her phone. Then, from the burning trash can, she hears her ringtone go off. She'd forgotten her stupid piece of shit flip-phone in her work pants. Great.

Chased out by a whoosh of smoke, Galavance shoulders her way out onto the Astroturf-carpeted patio and takes a few long strides across the driveway and into the yard in her bare feet. She moves her car down to the end of the driveway, away from the house. There's no use in yelling for help, so she just stands, leaning on her car, watching, waiting for the people on the side of the street to call the fire department. Not that there'll be anything to save once they arrive. A friend of hers used to call double-wides matchboxes. Once a fire reaches that cheap insulation they're all made with, you can say goodbye to anything inside. Fifteen minutes and they're down to their metal frame. Seems accurate so far. Not that Galavance is particularly interested in timing her home's destruction right now.

The thermometer fixed to the siding rapidly rises, reaching a hundred and thirty before sputtering red all over the inside of the foggy, plastic dial. The windows alive like jack-o-lanterns, and inside is the sound of things inside bursting and crashing—that's all of her stuff that's in there, making those sounds. The photo albums, her DVDs, makeup and jewelry, her clothes. Too late now. So much for being like Ripley.

Ϙ
ˌ

Out of the dark behind him, Zilch hears sirens. Red and white lights flash across him and he watches a set of fire trucks scream past. Their destination is obvious: the underside of the low clouds, not far from here, are splashed with an undulating orange—the smell of smoke is on the air when the wind turns, the reek of melted plastic and burning foam-stuffed furniture.

He's running before fully arriving at the logical conclusion.

Zilch moves toward the column of smoke in the distance as fast as he can, cutting through people's yards, slapping aside the hanging, prickly arms of pine trees. He goes down into a ditch and then through a lumpy field. He cuts through some heavy brush, nettles and the skeletal fingers of dead trees clawing at him. Then he's on a dirt road, running blind with no street light or moon to guide him—just keeping his attention trained on the glowing sky ahead. He's in the trailer court now, making the bend to the far lot. He comes into view of it, a double-wide burning like some biblical thing in the dark, people standing around outside in their sleeping attire, faces lit, mesmerized. The firemen have beaten him there. The ropes of white water they're shooting in through the windows do nothing; the fire is hungry and will not be told when it's had its fill.

Coming up closer, among the confusion and parked emergency responder vehicles and fellow trailer-court resident gawkers, Zilch finds Galavance sitting cross-legged on the hood of her bubblegum pink Cavalier, staring at the brick-shaped blob of flame that was once, apparently, where she lived.

"Galavance," Zilch says.

She turns and looks at him with glassy eyes, then slides off the car, looking at Zilch as if she's not sure if he's real. Surprising him—and herself, it seems—she hugs him.

"Are you okay? What happened?"

"The Lizard Man is real," she says in his ear. "I think Jolby's one."

"Where is he?" Zilch asks. "Have you seen him?"

"No. I don't know where he is. I called and he's not answering. I thought he might be here. My boss, she's . . ." She presses her hands to the sides of her face, holding them there, wide-eyed, mouth open. Too much has been going on, he can tell.

"I need to find him," Zilch says. "Is he at the house, you think? Wait, what did you say?"

"There were these little worms in his bandage. And my boss—well, technically my boss's boss's boss—she's lost her mind. The sausage at work isn't sausage. It's . . . I ate some of it."

"Slow down. What about sausage?"

"And I don't know if he's okay, or if . . ." She shakes her head, realigning reality. "She knows about you, too."

"Who's this we're talking about?"

"The regional manager for Frenchy's. Patty LeDoux."

"Okay, she knows about me? How?"

"I told her you were looking for the Lizard Man at the swamp, near where Jolby's house is."

"All right, and what about worms? Never mind, explain on the way. I thought I was gonna have to break some bad news to you, but apparently you already know."

"Know about what?"

Zilch is moving toward Galavance's pink car, looking almost yellow with the flames lighting up its clear coat. He stops. "We just need to find Jolby," Zilch says. "If I could beg one more ride off you, I swear it'll be the last."

"But the fireman guy, he said I need to stick around and file a report when they're through. He actually just went to the truck over there to get the form so I can fill it—"

"We don't have time for that," Zilch says, and stifles a cough, his chest burning. Whether it's smoke or dead buggies, he can't say. "*I* don't have time."

"So this Patty person has been tasked by this dying chain restaurant to hunt down mythological creatures because the meat will be free?"

"Yeah, and then she shot at me."

Zilch nods up at the hole in the car's ceiling, then at the one between his legs in the seat. "I was gonna ask—I don't remember your car being so . . . perforated before." He recalls the ghillie-suited individual with the rifle. "I think maybe she and I have met, actually."

Galavance doesn't respond. He watches her driving with both hands, ten and two on the wheel. It's dark and the car's one headlight keeps flickering out and back on with each bump they hit. She says, barely above a whisper, "We have to find him."

"We will. You think the worms you found mean . . . ?"

"That Jolby's sick and he might turn into a whatever you called it."

"A were-amphibian." Zilch grimaces. "Well, uh, the thing about Jolby *maybe* turning into a were-amphibian is . . ."

"What?" She looks between Zilch and the road, twice, fast. "Tell me!"

"Look. Steel yourself, but I'm afraid he's already a were-amphibian. And *has* been for a while."

"How do you know that?"

"He told me."

"*What?*"

"Galavance, you mentioned bringing home leftovers from work. How long have you been doing that?"

"For about as long as I worked there."

"Sausage, huh? Smart. Grind the bits and bobs down to unrecognizable mush and—"

Galavance gives him a glare. "Could you maybe not admire the people turning the people I love into menu items? *I* ate that shit. Fucking Psycho Patty says that when they turn, they're no longer themselves—not people at all—but it doesn't make me feel any better." She's somewhat green right now, Zilch notices, but not Jolby-green.

"You said she's been hunting them. She's gotten a lot of them before?"

"That's what she said."

"Does she think Jolby is the last one?"

"Last one that's . . . alive." She looks over at him again. Briefly, but he can see the sadness piled in her eyes. "Can you fix him?"

"No. Actually, I sort of have to kill him."

"What? Why?"

"Because that's how it works." Zilch holds the side of his head to combat a dash of pain that fades quickly. His left ear starts ringing. "I'm sorry. We can certainly *try*, but separating the parasite from him now, after its gotten comfortable in him, will probably kill him anyway."

"But we can't kill him. It's not his fault. He's not the amphibian-thing all the time."

"Would you prefer I do it or your gun-toting regional manager?"

"Neither! He's my boyfriend! He may not be perfect, but . . ." She has nothing to finish that sentence with.

She's all over the road, and he can't help but say something. "Maybe we should slow down."

"If I don't take you to the house then you can't find him—and if you can't find him, you can't kill him!"

Zilch scratches his chin. "Listen. All right, so if this thing is spread through some kind of parasite, maybe that's what I'm actually after. My bosses say the Lizard Man—host and parasite—are one and the same, but they also told me they'd leave it up to my discretion. Again, we'll *try* to get it out of him. Clearly he's full of the things if you found some in that bandage of his. Maybe we get out the right one, the mama worm."

"What if I have one? Will you kill me too, if I turn into a monster?"

"Probably. Kidding. I'm *kidding*. We'll get it figured out. Let's just focus on the were-amphibian we know for sure." He adds: "Just so you know, if we find him, he's not all there upstairs."

"What do you mean?"

"It's making him steal car parts."

"Why?"

"I don't know. It's just what the parasite has him doing. Some kind of compulsion, I think, crossed wires."

They reach the Whispering Pines' muddy entryway, and continue driving until they pull up along the front of 1330. It's like all the other halfway-finished homes on the block, each empty, glassless window dark. Galavance shuts off the car but makes no move to get out. Zilch watches her eyes moving over the interior of the car—the chrome-plated vent-covers, the jewel-eyed skull shifter knob, the rear-view mirror in the shape of a supine woman.

"I always just figured he was getting money from his mom or buying the parts used online or something. I never thought he'd be *stealing* these things." Her eyes switch from all of the various modifications to her Cavalier's interior, back onto Zilch. "And that's enough for your people to think Jolby is a threat? That he's stealing car parts?"

"He was seen. Before Chev knew it was Jolby, he got a video of him and put it online. It wouldn't be such a problem if he wasn't a were-amphibian stealing car parts," he says. "If he was just some regular guy doing it, sure, no problem—not their jurisdiction. But because he is what he is, then that becomes their problem, apparently. Does Jolby like the Frenchy's stuff you bring home?"

"He seemed to, yeah. Why?" She's already referring to him in the past tense, Zilch notices.

"Never know—it might be useful. What was that thing Sun Tzu said, that knowing is half the battle or whatever?"

"I thought that was GI Joe."

"Either way, it's sound advice."

Galavance looks out the windshield, points. "Was that light on when we pulled up?"

Zilch bends forward to peer up through the windshield at the house. The plastic over one of the front windows is now lit from within. A shadow streaks past going one way, then back, person-shaped, pacing.

"No, it wasn't," Zilch says. Coughing suddenly, he looks at his hand. It's sprayed with red dots. "Look, this might get ugly."

"Say, uh, could I tell you something quick?"

Zilch looks at her sidelong. "Sure . . ."

"So, I said you were crazy a whole bunch of times, before. Right after I hit you with my car. And that was . . . pretty rude."

Zilch looks like he's fighting down a grin.

"And, well, you're not crazy. And I guess what I mean is: I'm sorry. For saying that," she says. "Oh, and for hitting you with my car. I don't think I apologized for that. Which, obviously, is something you should do after doing to somebody."

"Don't sweat it," Zilch says. "Let's go figure this thing out."

Zilch wonders how much time he'll have to do so. The dashboard clock reads 11:59. Just as he looks at it, Saturday marches onward to—

SUNDAY.

"Keep him calm," Zilch says as he leads the way across the muddy lawn. "Besides, I don't really think I stand much of a chance against him, anyway."

The single light inside goes out.

The sound of the swamp is too loud to listen for footfalls or whispers. Zilch stops in the driveway with Galavance and they stare up at the split-level ranch that is 1330 Whispering Pines Lane, waiting for someone to make the first move.

"What should we do?" she whispers.

"Maybe you should say something," Zilch suggests. "Let him know you're here to help him."

Galavance takes a deep breath and shouts at the front of the house: "Jolby, it's Gal. I didn't really like how we ended that last fight so I thought I'd come out here so we could talk to face to face. This is my friend, Saelig Zilch."

"Keep going," Zilch tells Galavance. "That's good."

"Come on, Jolby. Let's talk about this. Saelig doesn't want to hurt you, it's just that you're sick and you need help and—oh, come *on*, Jolby. Do you have any idea how much crap I've been through today? I've been shot at. There was a fire at the house.

Actually, there is no more house. Then I hear all this trouble with you stealing stuff and . . . I'm not having a real good time tonight, is my point."

"Nicer stuff, if you can," Zilch whispers out of the corner of his mouth. "Think of him like a scared cat that ran up a tree and can't get down."

"Right, sorry." Cupping her hands around her mouth, Galavance shouts, "Jolby, I don't want to, like, talk down to you here like this is some kind of intervention, but you're sick. You got some kind of bug and Saelig and me really want to help you. Is Chev in there with you? I'm sure he wants you to feel better too. Chev? Are you in there? Jolby?"

The plastic covering one of the second story windows rustles. There is an audible slap as something heavy is thrown down into the mud in front of them.

Zilch doesn't approach it, whatever it is, but Galavance rushes forward, moving as if Jolby had pitched himself out the window to his death. But Zilch saw it move, just a twitch, whatever it was. And anyways, it's too small to be a person.

"What is that?" Galavance says, reluctantly stepping closer. She blanches and practically jumps away from it. "*God . . . oh . . . oh, my God.*"

Zilch steps around her and recoils once the shapes start to make sense. It's a torso wrapped in paint-spattered plastic sheeting. Underneath the several layers of it, he can just make out Chev's lifeless face, eyes rolled, his tongue swollen and purple. His arms are ripped off at the shoulders, chewy and jagged cuts—and his bottom half is truncated at the navel, his guts unspooling inside the plastic packaging. Blood pools where the sheet is bound with colored insulated wire and rubbery fan belts made into improvised twist-ties.

"What the *fuck*, Jolby?" Zilch shouts at the house. "Now I have no fucking choice but to kill you. If you didn't do this shit, we could've maybe talked about options—but now—fuck, do you have any idea what you've put your girlfriend through? You're lucky she's even stuck around this long, you piece of shit."

There is the sound of splashing from around the back of the house. Zilch leaps over Chev's corpse, skidding and slipping as he tries to charge across the muddy yard. He nearly runs into the swamp, the water rising up to his knees before he stops. All he can do is stare out at the disturbed wake, a stretching V marking Jolby's progress across the bog, moving swiftly just under the water's surface. It's too dark to see where he's intending to go or if there's even a shoreline out there at all he's heading for.

Before long the wake has disappeared completely. All Zilch can see are some twisty trees, a few pathetic meter-wide islands of mud. Galavance tiptoes her way through the soggy yard to stand next to him.

"Did he go out there?" she says.

Zilch nods.

She screams suddenly, startling Zilch. "*Jolby Dawes! Stop being a dumbass! Get out of that water right now!*"

There is no reply. The scratching sensation in Zilch's head fades, stops—Jolby is falling out of range. The crickets, non-murderous frogs, and other swamp life go quiet for a moment, then return at full volume when Galavance doesn't shout again.

"I've never seen a dead person up close before," Galavance says, following Zilch as he drags what's left of Chev through the front door of 1330 Whispering Pines. She deliberately keeps her eyes off of the corpse in his transparent plastic wrapper, closes the door—a makeshift slab of plywood on hinges—behind them, and stares at the wall to avoid looking at what her boyfriend has turned his own best friend into.

Zilch drops Chev with a wet smack to the unfinished floor. "Not to be crass, but you get used to it."

Galavance rarely ever visited Jolby at work. The house made her see red, so she mostly avoided it. So it's with fresh eyes that she surveys exactly what her boyfriend's been up to. To describe the house half-finished would be a lie, it's not even remotely that far along; and most of it looks like it's been done out of order. Some rooms have their hardwood flooring down with a nice dark stain applied, while others are just rows of studs. Drywall has been put up here and there, some of the panels crooked or measured incorrectly, insulation peeking out of a gap at the top. The living room seems to have been abandoned some time ago and has, since, become something of a squatter's den, a couple of lawn chairs aimed at a TV and a videogame console set on a stack of two-by-fours. A toppled ice chest lies nearby, its contents spilled across the floor, a few roll-away beers and a water-logged sandwich. Baggies with pot crumbs have settled in the corners, there are overflowing ashtrays everywhere, and an elaborate resin-stained hookah is set high on a bucket of drywall mud like it's a relic to be worshipped.

Among the mess, there are red smears all over the fiberboard floor. If they'd been just a few minutes early, they would've walked in on Jolby dismantling his best friend. Stepping into the kitchen, Galavance sees that this is where the fight must've shifted from a struggle to something worse, ending in murder.

She sees Zilch is also piecing it all together, righting a lawn chair and picking up a video camera where it had fallen over, still screwed into its tripod. The thing is still on, and the flip-open display on its side is aglow, a blue screen reading END OF TAPE.

Galavance turns the camera in her hands, finds the rewind button, and backs the tape up. She sees, in the tilted view, Zilch dragging in Chev's body a few minutes earlier. She rewinds some more and hits play again.

"We're gonna put this high score on the internet, man," Chev says, "and everyone will bust their asses trying to top it. Tonight's the night, I can feel it."

Jolby and Chev play a video game for a while, the room filled with bleeps and bloops and the clatter of controllers being worked feverishly. Galavance fast-forwards some and when she hits play again, there's a lot of shouting and the sound of feet shuffling back and forth. One voice is pleading. "Dude, stop, please."

"You can't tell anybody," another voice says, no one she recognizes. It sounds like they've been gargling nails. "I can't let you."

"But we killed that dude."

"It doesn't matter. It was like self-defense. He wanted to kill me. He *said* so, dude." Hearing the slight shrill tone to that, the same as when Jolby gets defensive, Galavance's scalp goes numb. He sounds horrible, but it's definitely him.

"Stop trying to touch me, man." Chev sounds scared.

"I just wanna talk to you. You're being crazy."

"*I'm* being crazy?"

"Quit walking away."

"You need to tell Gal what's going on."

"No. She can't know. I can fix this. You have to help me."

"I'm trying to, dude, but you're not making it easy, freaking me out like you are. Dude, what are we gonna do? What's the plan?"

"You gotta help me with the monster. So we can sell it when we're through."

Chev's reply is heavy with doubt. "I'm trying my best, dude." He is placating Jolby.

"You can help me another way, if you don't wanna help me get parts anymore."

"Sure, dude, anything."

"Will you contribute?"

"Contribute what? I told you I only make so much at the Pizza Shack. I've signed over the last three paychecks to you, whole."

"Not that. Contribute in another way. You can help more than with just money."

"What? Why are you looking at me like that? Quit it, dude."

"I'm not looking at you like nothing, dude. Just come here, talk to me."

The figures pass in front of the camera. And, bringing the camera close to study its tiny pixilated screen, Galavance sees Jolby. One side of his face is stained green, like he's been smeared with Halloween makeup. When he speaks again, harsh and guttural tones, only now can she pick out her boyfriend's voice. And she can't believe it. The thing on camera is growing greener before her eyes, following Chev around the living room in slow circles—passing in front of the camera once, then again. Her heart is in her throat.

"I said *come here*," Jolby says, with a snarl, leaping out of frame. Galavance hears—but doesn't see—Chev make a strangled sound, the sound of begging. The work lights throw their shadows onto the wall, and she watches as Jolby's silhouette, in the middle of strangling Chev's, changes. The head grows large and bumpy, hissing down at Chev in his grasp, who is gurgling and pleading for Jolby to stop. Galavance shuts the video off, unable to take anymore. Looking away, she makes accidental eye contact with Chev's corpse, just across the room, staring at her.

God. To think dirty underwear used to be her biggest concern. Her boyfriend is a murderer. This truth does not go down easily.

Zilch slides over one of the lawn chairs. "Sit. You look like you might pass out."

"I can't sit. I can't. My fucking boyfriend killed his best friend."

"I know. We have to find him," Zilch says. "He might hurt someone else. He could be doggy-paddling across the swamp right now, on the hunt for his next victim."

"Stop," Galavance says. "I don't want to think about that."

"Do you think the guy or gal he might *currently* be murdering wants to be thinking about it?"

"This isn't my fault."

"I didn't say it was. But we need to find him."

"I know," she says. "What do you think he meant, that whole thing about making Chev 'contribute'?"

"Again, I've got nothing." Zilch desperately wants a cigarette. "We need to find him. So let's just sit tight, wait until I get a ping on the compass again, and try to talk some sense into him."

"I don't want to be in here," she says. "It's hot and I think I just want to go . . ."

"Weird, isn't it? Suddenly not having a home."

She nods, solemn. "Yeah."

"You get used to that too," he says. "Just like anything else. But it really is like a phantom limb, isn't it? Well, I suppose you wouldn't know that—you got all your parts, it seems. But, trust me, that's what it's like."

"Is this you trying to make me feel better?" She keeps glancing at Chev's body. It's like his eyes are tracking her. "God, do we have to keep him in here? I mean, I feel sorry for what happened, but . . . it's like he's looking at me."

"I'll move him." Zilch steps past her, crossing the living room, his shoes clunking on the bare plywood floor. He bends and takes a solid grip of the plastic encasing Chev and hoists him up into his arms. Galavance turns away just as the corpse's head loosely lolls on the gimbal of his neck, facing her with dead eyes. He pauses in the doorway and turns, holding Chev like he's carrying his dismembered bride over the threshold, and turns to face Galavance.

"Want some good news?" he says.

"That would actually be pretty great right now," Galavance says.

"Far as I can tell," he says, "the change isn't permanent yet. He's still going back and forth. I saw him once as the creature, then as himself the next day, before he changed again right in front of me. There might be a chance we can still get that thing out of him."

She doesn't know why but it seems like Zilch has something more to say. The look he is making—pitying, apologetic—makes Galavance wonder. But right then she isn't sure if she can take any more bad news. Chev was a sweet guy. He didn't deserve to be murdered, especially not like that.

"I'll do everything I can," Zilch adds, and steps out into the garage. She watches as he eases Chev to the cement floor of the garage. There are a few tools scattered around, and some kind of glitter on the floor everywhere. She bends and presses her thumb to one of the flakes. It's red on the other side—some paint that'd been chipped off of something. She looks up and notices the shelves bolted to the garage wall; among the tools on them, hidden poorly, are car parts. A headlight, a hub cap lying half under a rag, a chromed gear-shift knob.

"Seems Jolby was operating a one-man chop shop out of this place," Zilch says, looking around. "Kind of stupid, seeing as how they were trying to sell this place, weren't they?"

Galavance holds up a hand toward Chev's body to block it from view. "They couldn't even show the property before the house itself was complete. No one besides Jolby and Chev ever set foot in this place. Sometimes he'd get mad when I dropped by to surprise him and wouldn't let me in. He said it was fumes one time, other times I thought maybe he . . . had a girl in there or something. Guess that would've been better, huh?" She chuckles, then feels sick about it.

She watches as he scans the wall of the garage, staring at the various car parts. He seems to be focusing on one headlight in particular and its dangling wires—like his thoughts are actually elsewhere. "He was hoarding parts. Taking more than he'd ever have any use for." He faces Galavance. "It's pretty common with were-folk; came across a guy once that made what looked like a beaver's dam in the attic of his own house made out of nothing but shredded newspaper and his own hair."

As much as Galavance tries *not* to picture that, she fails. "So, what does that mean?"

"There should be more here. If he's had this thing in him for as long as we think, then he's probably been stealing car parts for just about as long. There'd be more here. That or Chev was cleaning up after him. Or maybe Chev found his trove of automobile-related treasure, and that's when Jolby told him what he was. My point is: Where is it all now?"

"I don't think my car could have another mod put on it. Same for his car."

"Then maybe he's got another project somewhere," Zilch says.

"What kind of project?"

Zilch shrugs. "A spaceship to take him—and the parasite— back to home to Planet Ick? Dunno."

"Where would he keep it, though? I mean, he only has this one property and our trailer lot was tiny. He doesn't have any friends besides Chev, and Chev lives—lived—with his mom. Her garage is packed close to bursting with antique dolls." Galavance takes a step closer to Zilch. "Level with me. Have you ever been able to avoid killing a person who's a were-thing? Can you just take the bad part of him?"

❧

SHE'S STANDING VERY CLOSE TO HIM. ZILCH FEELS THE NEWS swell in his throat, like any second his Adam's apple is just going to pop and all of this awfulness he's been carrying around, like Jolby cheating on her with eleven different women and hiding it for years, is just going to come gushing out.

It's on the tip of Zilch's tongue, but he doesn't say it, partly because it's not his place; it should be Jolby's responsibility to air out his dirty laundry. And who's to say that the cheating wasn't caused by the same thing making him transform and tear his best friends to shreds, too? Sex and violence are base behaviors, things most monsters can't get enough of.

He has to look away from the face she's making. She really believes he's a good guy, deep down.

"I haven't before," Zilch says finally. "but that doesn't mean I won't try. Look, let's go back inside and sit down for a minute. I think you're probably running on fumes by this point." He escorts her back into the door and once she's inside, starts to pull it closed behind her, staying out in the garage.

"You're not going to come in?" she asks, like she's afraid to be left alone in the house.

"I'll just be a minute." He nods at one of the Budweisers lying on the floor. "Crack one of those and take a load off."

"What are you going to do?"

"Check the evidence."

"Do you really need to call it that? He was a person."

"Well, you just called Chev *it*, didn't you?"

"I meant his body. That's an it, isn't it? If there's no person inside of a body, they're kind of just like . . . furniture, aren't they?"

"Stay with me," Zilch says. "Pinch yourself if you have to. All I'm saying is: I phrased it that way for your benefit, calling Chev's body evidence."

"I'm all right. I'm not a delicate flower." She nods to herself, mostly convinced. "I mean, can't you just leave Chev alone? He suffered enough, I think."

"Can't. I have to know what we're up against. Did you see any other parts around?"

"Car parts?"

Zilch says nothing, grim-faced.

"No," Galavance says finally. "I didn't. You don't think Jolby . . . ate his best friend?"

"Maybe. He clearly didn't eat all of him, if that helps."

"Not really."

"Anyway, I think Jolby's condition has changed since our previous encounter. He certainly wasn't powerful enough to rip a person limb from limb last time. And not only are there no parts lying around, but I didn't see anything he may've used to cut Chev up with either."

"You think he did that to Chev with his bare hands?"

"Can't say until I check."

"Need me for that?" Galavance is frowning.

"No, but you can watch if you like."

"If it's all the same," she says, taking a seat in the lawn chair, "I'll just stay in here I think."

"That'd probably be wise. Come get me if you hear anything. Maybe try to get some sleep."

He can hear her scoff through the door after he pulls it closed. "Sleep. Yeah, fat fucking chance of *that*."

Zilch prepares a makeshift operating theater in the garage. He hoists Chev up with a grunt and drops him onto a sheet of plywood set across two sawhorses—only a small spurt of Chev goo shoots out in the process. There's a toolbox in a corner of the garage, and he goes over the meager assortment at his disposal. Most of it's for cars—socket wrenches, oil filter wrenches, and only one blade. Turning it toward the naked bulb above him, Zilch can see the knife is dinged to hell and it's sticky with some acrid-smelling black gunk. Apparently, before realizing that tooth and claw could come in handy when stealing car parts, Jolby had used the knife for jimmying loose whatever he was after.

Zilch decides the knife, even dirty, will suffice for what he needs it for and doesn't bother to clean it. Chev, by this point, is well past worrying about infections.

First, the plastic. With one slice down the length of the sheet, blood gushes out and over the edge of the plywood operating table. Zilch hops back, trying to avoid getting any on himself, and he's only partly successful. It's still somewhat warm, and to make matters worse, a powerful odor quickly hits him with the power of a slap to the face.

Zilch latches a hand over his nose. "Jesus, Chev. What did you eat?"

But it's not decomposition he's smelling. Chev has been dead less than a few hours. Nor is it the smelled of torn guts, either.

Unfortunately, Zilch knows that smell too. No, this a different brand of stink altogether. Swampy, almost sweet in a way, but concentrated.

He takes the plastic off, rolling Chev out of it. Guts come loose and uncoil, tumbling over the edge of the table, dripping some mustard yellow substance onto the cement floor. Zilch rolls Chev onto his back again, and his head swings loosely around using the momentum to look up at him. And the eyes roll towards Zilch, too. Using two fingers, he closes Chev's staring dead eyes.

It's pretty gross, admittedly, but Zilch can't help but snap back to culinary school right now, butchery class to be specific. The first few weeks were learning the charts of different cuts. The animals were drawn up on charts like mapped territories. He and his fellow students had to be able to name each part as the chef instructor slapped the end of his pointer at them. Then, one day, Zilch walked in with his class to see a dead cow lying in the middle of the room, ready for the knife.

"Jolby did a real number on you, didn't he?" Zilch says, leaning in close to study what remains of the young man's arms—they look torn, yanked off, the shoulder muscles shredded. The spine is twisted, snapped like a twig, rendering Chev half the man he used to be. It doesn't surprise Zilch that Jolby is capable of this feat of strength—just the other night Zilch got flung, bodily, like a Frisbee. But the fact he did it to his best friend is the worrying part. Why?

Jolby could very well be past help, Zilch considers. Finding a pack of smokes on the workbench with one gift-from-the-gods cancer stick inside, Zilch desperately wants to fire it up, thinking it'll help him process, but he's without a lighter. He heads back into the house, keeping quiet because he suspects Galavance may've taken his advice and found someplace to lie down a while. Instead, he finds her in the living room with the TV on and a videogame controller in her hands.

"Hey," she says, half-engaged. "Was I being loud?" She's piloting a fishnet-clad heroine on the TV, pummeling bad guys.

"No." Zilch finds himself partly hypnotized by the video game's manic speed and flashing colors for a moment. "You're fine. Got a lighter?"

Galavance snatches the barbecue lighter from the floor and tosses it to him, hands springing back onto the controller before her on-screen heroine on her mission of revenge is overtaken by street toughs. "Jolby plays video games when he's stressed. He says it helps. Thought I might give it a try."

"How's it treating you?" he says, lighting his smoke.

"I'm still thinking about everything. Numb. I guess this is probably how people become alcoholics, huh? Personally I'd rather have booze but I hate beer and that's all they have. So, video games it is. What'd you find out?"

"Good news is I don't think your boyfriend's gone cannibal. *Think* being the operative word there."

"Bully for him, if you're right. Too bad me and a few hundred thousand Frenchy's customers can't say the same."

Zilch chooses not to remark on that.

In his silence, Galavance, hammering buttons, says: "Do you think he's going to be all right?"

"That's hard to say," Zilch says. "It's out of my hands now that a human life has been taken. Unless I get word to approach things differently, I'm going to have to, you know, put a stop to him—to use a tired expression."

Galavance, on screen, loses a life when three chainsaw-wielding ninjas efficiently chum her character. "Kill him, you mean?"

"We've gone over this."

"Can you ask them to change their minds?" she says, restarting the level.

"Who?"

"Your people."

"It doesn't work that way. I can't negotiate; I have nothing to barter with. It's either I follow the rules or . . ."

"Or what?"

"I'll get an F and it'll hurt my self-esteem," he says, because right now he really doesn't want to get into the specifics. He was just at his folks' place for Chrissakes.

On-screen, Galavance double-jumps with a katana in hand and slices a Medusa-like thing in two, mid-air. "So? I got all kinds of bad grades in school."

"I don't actually get graded," Zilch says. "Think you could turn that noisy-ass thing off and actually look at me?" She doesn't. "I have no choice here. I have to put Jolby down. And, you know, I'm kind of surprised you're as bothered by that as you are, given what kind of guy he is."

She keeps playing, making it to the next level. "He didn't kill Chev. The thing *inside* used Jolby to kill Chev."

"Tell me something. Do you love him? Like *actually* love him? Do you miss him when he's not around? Do you dream about him, other than to drive a lawnmower over him? After a long day, do you look forward to spend some time with—?"

"What are you trying to say?"

"I'm saying . . . maybe give it some evaluation. Maybe he's not such a great guy, and if, you know, he happens to take a permanent vacation, perhaps that's not the worst thing in the world."

"That's fucked up. We've been together for a really long time. Like a *really* long time."

"I apologize." *He cheated on you.* "I'm just trying to soften the blow, should the worst become unavoidable." *He cheated on you, a lot.* "Only trying to help."

"I need your *help* to make him better. Not kill him. Did examining Chev's body—or whatever you were doing out there—help you in any way?"

"Not yet."

Zilch watches her character take a few punches before she fights back. Galavance beats the ninja to death, then moves onto the next one. "Of course I love him. What kind of question is that? And all I meant about not listening to your bosses is: you're in the South, so where's your rebel spirit?"

"Don't bring any of that The South Will Rise Again bullshit into it," Zilch says. "A hundred and fifty years, guys, time to let it go. And . . . I can't do anything about it, all right? They more or less own me."

"So? What happens if you say no? What if you just *say* you killed Jolby or *say* he got away?"

"One, they'll know if I don't kill him. Two, I'm not going to risk that," Zilch says.

"But *why*?"

Zilch draws a deep breath. "They'll keep sending me until he's dead. I get one go with this body. If this one gets too screwed up, or if they need to replace it before I finish the job, I'll just get sent back in another one, with less in my head than I had the time before."

"Meaning you get stupider each time? That explains a few things."

"They leave the basics but they take more of . . . more of her, each time."

"Her who?"

"That doesn't matter right now. It has to happen, Galavance. He's a killer."

"He's not though. It's what's *in* him that's making—"

She's interrupted by deep moaning coming from the garage. Galavance and Zilch stare at each other. She says what they're both thinking: "What the shit was *that*?"

"Chev, I think."

"What? How? He's dead."

"He is," Zilch says. "He was." He moves to the door leading out to the garage, pushing his ear close to listen. He can hear flopping around, the leg of a sawhorse grating across cement.

"Then how is he making sounds?"

"I don't know. This is a new one for me, too."

"Go out there," Galavance cries. "Do your job."

"Do I have your permission to get mean if I have to?"

"Stop. That's different. Chev is . . . *was* dead."

"And your boyfriend, a murderous frog-boy, killed him."

"Just go. Stop it from making that sound anymore, please."

Zilch steps out into the garage, closing the door behind him. "Chev?"

The work light lies overturned, and the plywood operating table is knocked askew. Chev, on the floor, swivels his head around loosely so he is roughly facing the intruder with eyes looking off in different directions. "Dude, I thought you were dead."

"You took the words right out of my mouth," Zilch says, keeping his distance.

"What a load off, man. Your death was weighing on my conscious, big time."

"Well, I'm still kicking. Gonna have to try harder than that," Zilch says and tries to laugh and it comes out a shaky *hee-hee*. "Say, Chev, if you don't mind, could I ask you question?"

The torso on the floor nods. "Sure, dude. What's up?"

Zilch spreads his hands. "Uh, *how*?"

"How what?" Chev blinks, his features clouding. He looks around. "Why am I in the garage? And why is it so cold in here?"

"I'm not really sure how to put this, Chev, but you've gotten a bit of a boo-boo."

"Sunday, Sunday, Sunday!" Chev's gurgles cheerfully, going cross-eyed.

"What's that, buddy?" Zilch leans in close. "What's that about Sunday?"

Chev coughs. "I feel funny."

"I bet you do. Focus, Chev. What was that about Sunday?"

"Huh? Shit, is today Sunday? I gotta get home. Mom's probably waiting on me to drive her to church." Chev wriggles, like he trying to sit up, but can't, and finally his head knocks back on the cement floor, defeated. "Did we take some shrooms or something, bro? I feel *super* weird."

"Where's Jolby, Chev? I need to talk to him."

"Last time I saw him . . ." Chev starts. His features flatten. "*Dude.*"

"Things got heated and you guys got into somewhat of a tiff."

"Was that real?" Chev says. "It feels like a dream. Because it was like we were talking then he . . . dude, I'm starting to freak out here. Am I dead? Are you God?"

"I'm definitely not God. But you need to tell me if Jolby has another hideout besides this one, some place he might go if things got too nuts here. Across the swamp somewhere, maybe? Someplace out in the woods? Anything you can tell me would be—"

"Sunday, Sunday, Sunday!"

"Yes, it's Sunday, well done. Anything else?"

Chev makes penetrating eye contact with Zilch. "The monster." The exposed bone in his shoulder swivels, as if Chev is reaching out to take Zilch's arm to ensure his words sink in. "On *Sunday, Sunday, Sunday* is when the monster will be complete."

"What monster? Jolby?"

"No, dude. *The* monster. I'm part of the monster, too, now. That's what Jolby said. He said . . . I could help *contribute* . . ." Chev goes even more ashen, maybe hearing himself. He tries sitting up again to look down at himself. He gasps. "Oh, *fuck*. Dude, what the fuck . . . why am I . . . ?"

"It's okay. It's okay. Tell me where he is."

"He kept saying incubator. Incubator and the monster. Am I gonna die, dude?"

"Chev, tell me where he is." Zilch is getting nothing on the pain compass. Chev is his only lead. "Help me find him."

Chev's head drops back and his pupils dilate wide at the same time that he lets out a long sigh. He's gone.

Zilch thinks for a minute, then starts to turn around to return back inside when he notices Chev's chest start to move again—rising and falling, but not with any rhythm. He isn't breathing. There's something inside him, squirming around. Keeping his eyes on the writhing half-corpse, Zilch reaches out next to him and takes up the first thing he finds within reach: a socket wrench. Better than nothing. He raises the tool overhead, ready.

The young man's chest continues to push up in outward shoves, swelling the skin around his throat, then higher up, his jaw starting to drop open, lips parting with a soft peeling sound. A pale yellow strand flops out onto Chev's chin, then another, draping itself across his nose. Another strand finds his spiky hair and wraps around a strand for purchase. It tugs, and Chev's jaw is pushed wider as a mass of pale tentacles swell between his lips, more and more spilling free. His head is erupting with new, squiggly life and Zilch stares, wide-eyed and frowning, socket wrench forgotten in his hand for a moment.

Until the thing splits open its underside and reveals a circular mouth full of tiny barbed teeth.

Zilch, with a shriek that's so shrill it hurts even his ears, swats at Chev's face with the wrench—he hears teeth break and an annoyed whine from the creature trying to bloom itself to completion from the dead man's mouth. Zilch whacks at it again but the creature is relentless, it's boneless body absorbing the blows as it continues to emerge. Some of its wax-yellow tentacles feel around along Chev's cheek, then his ear, as it reaches for the garage's cement floor. Thinking it might try to escape, Zilch stomps near it, and it shirks back but it keeps slithering, determined, pulling its wriggling mass behind it until a final dead push of air escapes Chev's lips—as if the corpse is relieved that the painful process of mouth birth is over.

The sentient mop head of tentacles scuttles toward the garage door. Zilch stomps on its slippery trailing strands and it shrieks again, but doesn't slow. Zilch, as much as he doesn't want to touch the thing, grabs what he can of it—but it feels like cooked spaghetti and it keeps slipping out of his grasp, some of it breaking apart in his hands. It bleeds yellow, sap-like blood on him.

More than halfway under the closed overhead door, it cannot be effectively grabbed, so Zilch presses one shoe on the rim of the garage door and pushes down with all his weight. The creature underneath, pinned, screams again in agony, its tentacles flailing around, snapping and slapping in desperation. Zilch stomps on the aluminum rim of the door until he hears something like the sound of a balloon wrapped in a towel popping from under the door and the tentacles go still.

Panting, Zilch counts to three, watching for movement. He lifts the garage door an inch and sees the splatted creature, a pale yellow asterisk on the garage floor, lying motionless. He fetches a snow shovel down from the wall, scrapes the thing up, looks around, and drops it with a plop onto the workbench, finally stepping back to stare at the dead amorphous thing. It hadn't given him any hits on the compass. No, it's some kind of off-spring. Jolby got Chev pregnant, it would seem. Zilch picks it up nervously by one of its limp tentacles and carries it inside.

Galavance has her hands over her ears, still seated in the lawn chair with knees to chest, and looks over at him out of the corner of her eye when he enters. "Do I want to know?" She notices he has his hands behind his back. "What was it?"

"Before I show you this thing, I feel I should preface what I've learned. I think there was some Darwinism going on in this house. Jolby used Chev as an incubator of sorts," Zilch says, bringing the dead creature out ahead of him as Galavance goes wide-eyed, "for his new bun in the oven."

She nearly topples the lawn chair. "What the *fuck* is that thing?"

"Chev was infected too. But Jolby killed him so he wouldn't turn, I think, to spare him. But he still got infected."

"Don't bring it *closer* to me! Stay over there with it. I can see it fine from here."

Zilch looks down at the thing lying in his hands. Some of its tentacles are thick as fingers, others are papillae, like drooping skin tags. "I think he wanted to grow one in Chev and then take it out, plant it somewhere else. I'm not sure."

"Plant it in what?"

"You, maybe."

"So that's what Jolby has in him?" Galavance gives a full-body shudder, then another, an aftershock. "Jesus."

"I think this is how it spreads. And I think Jolby's the only one that makes . . . these delightful things. If I'm right, Patty doesn't know about this aspect of their evolution. She thinks its spreading through the sausage—and maybe that *is* how Jolby got it in the first place—but it's really coming from these things. Jolby is host to the impregnator."

Galavance's mouth turns down. "Do you *seriously* have to put it in terms like that?"

Zilch takes one hand out from under the squiggly critter to scratch his belly. "He might have a nest out there," he adds, jutting his chin in the direction of the bog. "We need to find it before any more of these bundles of joy get introduced to the good people of North Carolina."

"You still think we have to kill him?"

"If I'm right about him being patient zero," Zilch says, "I'm afraid that's a yep. Anything else on the video camera?"

"Just them recording themselves playing video games," she says, absent, knees still pulled to her chest.

"Why?"

"It's popular online."

"You watch other people play video games?"

"Yeah." She looks at him, pleading with her eyes. "Is there seriously nothing I can say to make you not kill him? I know he's not perfect. But we've been together for such a long time I . . . I don't know what I'd do if he wasn't around anymore. My house is gone, my folks are about through wanting to help me out. He's a turd, but he's *my* turd."

Zilch lets the dead critter slide off his hands and into the beer cooler. He kicks the lid closed over it and sets a couple paint cans on top of it, just in case it's playing possum. "I think if you have somewhere to go, you should. I'm sorry, but this is how it has to be."

"Fuck that." She stood from the lawn chair. "That's bullshit. I think you know there's something you could do—you're just too goddamn lazy to try."

"*I'm* lazy? I'm not the one who's been with some jobless, cheater piece of shit for half her life refusing to give up on him just because it's comfortable."

The fury sloughs from Galavance's features. "Cheater? Why did you say he's a cheater? He's never cheated on me. He wouldn't."

"I just assumed," Zilch says quickly, backtracking. "I was projecting. I stepped out on my wife and . . . well, I was just talking out of my ass. I take it back. He's not a cheater, I'm sure Jolby, current circumstances aside, is a perfectly upstanding young man who'd never—"

"You know something. Stop bullshitting. You know something. Tell me."

Zilch pauses. The cat's out of the bag—there's no use in trying to put it back in. "It's why he never told you what's going on with him. Because he's afraid if he lets that one secret slip, it'll *all* come out."

"What secret? That he's sick?"

"That, yeah, and the other thing . . . the women."

"He flirted some, sure, but . . . when would he have time? Between working here and all the time he spends at home, with me . . ."

"Galavance, I heard him say—"

Galavance rushes out outside, down the front steps, and is charging across the lawn. Zilch follows, calls for her to stop, but she's already out into the swamp, the water up to her knees after only a couple strides.

"*Jolby!*" she shouts. "*Jolby!*" She doubles over, pitching her shouts out over the dark water. "*Jolby!*"

Zilch watches as she takes another step out, then decides to follow.

Galavance's voice is getting reedy with each scream. "Jolby, come back, I wanna *help you!*"

"Hey," Zilch says, sinking up to his knees as he catches up. "Stop, before we both drown."

"But I need to help him. He's not okay right now, but I can help."

"He isn't worth it."

"You don't know him."

"I know enough. And you'll be no good to anybody dead, Galavance," Zilch says, daring to advance further out. The water is surprisingly warm. "Come on, we need to go get some supplies if we're going to do this."

"Supplies? For what?"

Zilch presses his lips together, sighs out through his nose.

"If you took that thing out of Chev, maybe you can take it out of Jolby, too."

"He's too far gone," Zilch says. "He's killing people. That and I'm telling you: he *isn't worth* all of this."

Galavance turns away from Zilch and shouts again: "Jolby!" Another step. "Jolby, come out of there!"

Zilch stays behind, watching. She's up to her waist, then her ribs. She hits a sudden deep spot hidden under the cloudy water and sinks to her chin. Zilch feels the secret boil out of him, hot and awful: "He cheated on you."

She stops walking and stops screaming, just bobbing, her golden hair floating on the water the only bright spot out on the moonlit swamp. Whether she's actually listening, he doesn't know, but at least she's quiet and not walking out any further for the moment.

"How many?" she says after a long moment, only the crickets and frogs filling the silence.

"Eleven."

She spins around again, nearly losing her balance in the water, then comes out toward him, water falling away, her tank top and pants soaked through with swamp. She has tears in her eyes. "Lying to me isn't gonna make me give you permission to kill him."

"I'm not lying."

She shoves him, actually shoves him, hard, with both hands. The impact of her palms on his chest hurts, and he stumbles backwards, not expecting it. Suddenly there's a memory of Susanne, but he remembers that she never actually shoved him or slapped him, just raised her hands as if she was going to. He remembered how self-hate would redden her cheeks, how she'd grind out a growling kind of sigh and leave him wishing she had just hit him and gotten it over with.

Galavance shoves him again and again, all the way until they're on a drier portion of the muddy lawn. But apparently not dry enough—she slips and he catches her by the arm. She tears herself away with too much oomph and slips again, this time actually falling with a quiet *splorch*. She stays down, sitting on her knees, cursing under her breath, and flings some mud off of her hands with jerks of her wrist. "Were they girls I know?" she finally asks, looking up at Zilch, embarrassed.

"He didn't say." He offers her a hand.

She shakes her head and stands as nimbly as someone new to roller-skates. "I feel really stupid."

"Love will do that. Look, I'm sorry it's going to have to come to this, with him. And if you want to just head somewhere, stay with a friend while I deal with this, I'd understand. I'll try my best to make sure I sneak in a punch or two on the guy for you when I catch him."

She smiles faintly. "I'll stay."

"We can *try* to make him better," Zilch says, "but we'll need his cooperation. He has to want it."

He can see there's an ember of care for Jolby she's still nur-turing, coaxing it with soft, careful breaths even as it's doing its best to go out for good. "Maybe if this thing's got a hold of him," she says, "maybe it's not him that's doing the cheating, maybe it's the thing, you know, his other side, controlling *him*, making him . . . cheat." She doesn't look at Zilch when she says this, focusing on her hands, scraping the mud away. She's filthy from her toes to her neck.

"Maybe," he says, trying to sound hopeful.

"I'm gonna go inside, take a shower. Then we can go get stuff you need. What were you thinking?"

"Guns," Zilch says. "Maybe a net too. Might need to borrow your credit card, if that's okay."

Saying nothing, Galavance gives him an unreadable look before turning away to slap her wet feet up the front porch stairs and inside. Zilch remains out in the yard, watching the sun rise. When the cicadas start their ratcheting riot of noise in the surrounding trees, singing this early, he thinks, you know it's going to be one hellishly hot day.

THE ONLY AVAILABLE CHANGE OF CLOTHES IN THE HOUSE IS A pair of Jolby's smaller shorts, destroyed Chuck Taylors, and one of Chev's shirts. It's only after she'd put them on that she pauses, realizing she's wearing a dead person's clothes. Could a T-shirt be haunted? But, out of a lack for anything else, it will have to suffice, haunted or not.

Galavance glances at herself in the mirror; she looks like she just got home from camping: sunburnt and filthy. She meets Zilch outside, and he gives her an odd look but says nothing. She feels bad about having shoved him, and when she apologizes for it as they walk toward her car, he cuts her off halfway and dismisses the whole thing, mumbling something about having had it coming.

On the two-lane heading up out of the sticks, their bearing trained on the interstate, Galavance notices Zilch looking out the window as they fly past a house with an overgrown lawn. She knows the place; it was a frequent stop for her friends when she was in high school. Rumor went it was haunted. They'd visited a few times, late at night, but never saw anything—spent most of the time breaking what little furniture was left in the house or using someone's dad's old spray paint to write things on the wall. Galavance never contributed, but also hadn't protested when Jolby wrote some gross thing or drew a giant dick on the wall. Back then, she'd probably found it funny.

"Something wrong?" Galavance says.

They shoot past the house. "No," Zilch says.

"What's her name?"

"What *was* her name, and I'd rather not discuss that, if it's all the same," he says.

"Come on, you know all the sordid details of my relationship. Share."

Zilch pauses. "Susanne."

"Was she your girlfriend?"

"Wife," he says, looking down at his left hand. She glances from the road to look, too, and notices a pale indent around the base of his ring finger.

"Is she still . . . ?"

He shakes his head, uses his left hand to scratch his belly. She kind of wishes he'd changed clothes too, since he's got so much of Chev's blood on him, but she figures her car will have to be burned, same as her house, when all's said and done. "A few months before me," Zilch adds, finally.

"What was she like?"

"Patient."

"What do you mean?"

"Let's just say Jolby and I aren't exactly cut from a *different* cloth."

"You said you cheated on her, huh? Real nice."

"Among other things." Zilch takes a smoke from Galavance's pack sitting in the cup-holder without asking. "Not to sound like I feel sorry for myself but I think once I'm done they'll still press the button marked for the basement."

"Wait, I thought you said they take away memories of your wife each time you mess up."

"They do. I'm sure she and I had some good times, but at this point, the bad memories are the only ones still crystal clear. Sometimes it feels like they want me to give up, if I'm being honest, that they'll keep taking memories from me until I look back and all I can ever remembering was living in misery. And once that happens, when these jobs are the only things I have left, I'll have successfully been beaten into submission."

"I'm sorry."

"I wouldn't be," Zilch says. "Not to get all woe-is-me about it, but it's really not worth the energy."

They drive for a while in silence. Coming into the suburbs surrounding Raleigh, it's all strip malls and big box stores. Even though it's early Sunday morning, they still get stuck in traffic, waiting three rotations at an intersection. Zilch takes another cigarette from Galavance's pack—she doesn't protest—and he smokes, scratches his belly occasionally, and stares out the window at nothing.

Every other car they're sharing the road with, to Galavance, looks like Patty's rental.

They park and go up to the front of the Mega Deluxo Super Store, only to nearly walk face-first into the front doors. The place hasn't opened yet, so they stand out in the sun, Galavance's skin feeling weird and tight from having used the Lava soap in the shower back at the house, because that's all Jolby had. Zilch watches the traffic across the parking lot, eyes squinting into the searing dawn sun, hands in his pockets.

The doors unlock, automatically clunking open at eight o'clock.

In the sporting goods aisle, Galavance watches Zilch pick up an item from the shelf. "A harpoon gun? Seriously?"

"Best we'll be able to do without a waiting period," he explains, then takes down some fishing nets, explaining they might be able to cut them apart and stitch them together into one big net with some fishing line, which he also throws into their cart. "I thought you'd be happy. A harpoon gun might only give him an ouchie."

"It's a harpoon gun. They kill sharks with those things."

"I know you haven't seen Jolby lately," Zilch says, "so trust me when I say I believe this is the tool for the job. I'll aim low, at his legs. Scout's honor."

Galavance turns and looks over her shoulder. A few shoppers are now milling around the Mega Deluxo now. Mostly everyone's still at church, she suspects. But for the few a.m. bargain-hunters that are here, and with each one she sees, she worries it could be Patty. All her boss would have to do is look up Galavance's employee records to find her address. Of course, there isn't a trailer there in that lot anymore. But she does know about 1330 Whispering Pines—Zilch said he'd seen her. And if she's already been hunting Lizard Men, bloodhounding a regular person wouldn't prove much of a challenge.

"You should feel great right now," Zilch says, steering the cart down the aisle, hopping on and riding it to the corner, fishtailing around the end-cap. "You learn your boyfriend cheats on you and now you have a perfectly good reason to kill him, carte blanche. And nobody will ever know you had anything to do with it; he'll just disappear. Imagine if that offer was opened to every woman suffering while some idiot drains her soul to E. There'd be a line around the block."

"I'm not his number one fan," Galavance says, "if what you said he said is true, but it might be good to be prepared for other things we might need a weapon for."

Zilch turns sharply around the next aisle. "Meaning your gun-totin' regional manager?"

"Exactly." They make another turn and down an aisle they've already traversed. "It's like the Bermuda Triangle in these big box stores," she says. "Maybe this way?"

"Listen, we'll get Jolby fixed, if we can. So whatever plan we end up using, there won't be any reason for your boss to bug you anymore."

"Bug me? More like kill me."

"Poor choice of words. I admit it. But if Jolby's unable to turn froggy, he'll be dead to her, no pun intended. If that happens, we're clear. I can go on my way, you can go about yours—with Jolby, without Jolby, your call—and that'll be that."

Galavance hasn't considered how this whole thing might end. She kept imagining there'd be no other way out other than killing Jolby. She knew she could argue against it with Zilch, but deep down, she never thought it might actually work out in a way that Jolby would survive. And if his cheating turns out to be exactly like what Zilch says. . . then she really didn't know how things would look after this was all said and done. Would she stay with him? Would they take whatever their bargain insurance would fetch from the house fire and go shopping for a new home? Would they move into Raleigh, rent an apartment?

Would she, despite this whole cluster-fuck they'd been through together, stick with him just because of what they'd both survived, to honor the ordeal and let everything before he got sick be bygone? She couldn't say.

They pile their purchases onto the conveyer checkout belt: a harpoon gun and the extra packs of aluminum bolts, four fishing nets, two rolls of high-test line. And from the shelf of candy right by the lane, a pack of Big Red gum. The cashier swipes everything over the scanner and doesn't bat an eye.

Rolling the cart back out into the heat, Galavance folds a stick of gum into her mouth. She swallowed some swamp water and the burning cinnamon in her mouth quickly takes care of it. Big Red's is what her mother used to chew after she quit smoking, always popping it when in deep thought. Galavance, though she's tried, could never get it to make that loud *snap* like her mom could.

They're back speeding along the interstate in short time. "You know, it's weird," she says to Zilch. "You see those real mystery shows on TV about women who murder their boyfriends or husbands and do all this work to bury them or hide their bodies, and it makes you wonder: if they were the sort of women that'd do such a thing, do you think they used coupons if they had them? How deep do you suppose that psychosis goes? Like, 'Well, I've got to remove all trace evidence of Jim-Bob's blood from the bathroom, so should I get *two* bottles of bleach or just one? After all, I *am* going to need it for Jimmy's grass-stained football uniform.'"

"And here I thought *I* had a dark sense of humor," Zilch says. He laughs, but it soon becomes a cough and then degrades even further into a full-bodied hack that pitches him forward in the seat as he thumps a fist against his chest.

"It wasn't that funny," she says, freeing one hand from the wheel to slap him on the back, though it does nothing.

The coughing eventually subsides on its own, and Zilch rolls back in the eight-point harness, clutching his belly. He's shaking his head side to side with his eyes scrunched closed, plainly in some sort of terrible torment, sweating profusely.

"What is it?" Galavance asks between glances at the road. "Is it your nano-bites or whatever?"

Zilch manages to say: "Pull over, please. Please. Pull over. I do not want to do this in your car."

"Do *what* in my car?" She cuts off a SUV to take the upcoming exit.

"When I was doing Chev's autopsy," Zilch says between shallow huffs, "some of his goo got on me. It must've found a way in."

She pulls into a McDonald's and throws on her four ways. Zilch has his door open before they're even at a full stop. His shoe drags on the rocky ground, pebbles flying everywhere. She jams the brake, and he stumbles out, nearly falling, and begins jogging up to the front doors when he stops, still bent at the waist, turns, and goes running through the line of cars piled up at the drive-thru window, to the back of the lot.

Even from where she's parked the car, she can hear him getting violently ill. She kills the engine and steps out to check on him.

Around the fenced-in Dumpster shed, Zilch is bent forward, his shirt pulled halfway up his back, and he appears to be either jamming his hand down the front of his pants or vigorously rubbing his stomach, Galavance can't tell which. She moves off the trash-strewn road and onto the grass.

"Saelig? You okay?"

His head twists around, looking at her over his shoulder. His hair hangs in a soggy, sweaty mess over his forehead. Something black dribbles out of his nose. She sees something spilling out from between his legs—*is he* peeing *that out? What is that?*

Zilch wheezes: "I think your boyfriend knocked me up. But it's okay. Just stay back there for a minute. I've almost got it," he says. Is it just her, or does his skin look a touch green?

"Is there something I can do to help?"

"Are you actually offering or just being nice?" he says. "Because I'd be careful doing that—someone might take you up on it one day."

"Do you need a stick or something?"

"No, I think I've . . . almost . . . got it . . . *there you are!*"

Zilch stiffens up straight and pulls with both arms above his head. He twists around, losing his balance on the dew-slick grass—and that's when she sees it, when he's spun by the thing fighting to crawl back inside him. It looks just like the thing Zilch pulled out of Chev, except very much alive, clinging to him, wrapping around Zilch's arms to the elbow—it's either going to strangle him to death or crawl back inside his warm innards. Maybe both.

Galavance's wad of Big Red tumbles out of her mouth. She hears, on the nearby street, tires screech and the crunch of a fiberglass bumper. So she hasn't snapped. She's *not* the only one seeing this. That's good, I guess.

"OH, FOR THE LOVE OF PETE," ZILCH MOANS, TAKING A STEP forward and then two back. The thing erupting out of his torn belly is as thick as her arm. It looks like one, too, except instead of just having fingers at the end, it has them all over. Like a tree, except made of a soft membranous flesh the color of whipped butter. It stretches up and out of his belly, seemingly turning on its host. Zilch throws a hand up in front of his face as the thing tries to throw itself down his throat, any port in the storm. It only manages to paste him with a damp kiss of sorts, leaving him with the tastes of low tide.

He stumbles and thrashes, ramming himself into the enclosure surrounding the dumpsters, trying to crush the thing to death. He falls out into view of the patrons waiting in line at the drive-thru. The minivans disperse quickly, tires squealing. Zilch fumbles and rolls around on the hot asphalt of the parking lot.

Galavance stands by, hands out, and he can tell she wants to help him but can't bring herself to do it, scared that the thing growing out of his belly might actually win. It's putting up one hell of a fight, that much is for certain.

Zilch lurches to his feet, his hands embrangled with tentacles. The creature backs up, then shoots itself forward, causing Zilch to take a few involuntary steps in retreat—colliding with glass. The window of the McDonald's spider-webs. The creature spins itself around in the socket of Zilch's gaping abdomen, and works like a leg to kick off the ground, propelling Zilch all the way through the cracked glass. He tumbles into the restaurant, his back crunching against the broken glass all over the floor. There are screams, overturned soft drinks, and trampled Big Macs as the customers flee for the exits.

"What do I do?" Galavance screams at him, having run in through one of the doors.

"*Salt!*" Zilch roars, pointing at one of the tables still littered with burgers and soft drinks. The creature has opened itself up, pinning him against the condiment stand, sending out tentacles to the edges of the table and pulling itself down, crushing him. The back of his head knocks the ketchup dispenser pump, and red goo spurts out onto his eye—not helpful.

Galavance slaps a salt shaker into his palm. Zilch begins shaking it like he's frantically dispersing holy ashes. Even just a few granules sprinkled onto the creature make it twitch horribly

in pain. Zilch takes this opening to push himself off the condiment stand but he uses too much force and launches himself
toward the counter. The visor-topped employees in the back
scatter as he comes hurtling across the barrier.

Galavance follows behind him, shouldering aside the pim-
ply-faced line cooks. She's worked in fast food long enough, and
has contemplated murdering her wait-staff enough times, to
know exactly what in a kitchen could easily double as a weapon.
There are many options.

She lifts the basket of uncooked fries from the fryer and sends
it clattering across the tiled no-slip floor. She grabs Zilch by the
nape of his jacket—one of the few places the tentacles haven't
enveloped him—and turns him around. "Here," she says, offering up the open, burbling maw of the deep fryer.

"Uh, I think *not*," he grunts.

"What? Why not?"

"I'll get cooked too."

"Over here then," she says, pulling Zilch by the shoulder
of his coat to the griddle. She takes the spatula and flings aside
a few of the greasy meat patties, giving Zilch a clear space to
work. He turns, wrestling the thing as it slowly comprehends
what's in store, and before it has a chance to launch any sort
of coordinated defense, flings himself chest-first onto the greasy
metal, body slamming the creature as it flails and slaps at him in
a scrambling, panicked flurry of its tentacles.

A couple of punches and jabbing elbows help to stun the
thing. Its hold on Zilch seems to weaken, and taking immediate advantage, Zilch—with a two-handed grab, balled fistfuls of
squiggy awfulness—presses with his whole weight, kneeing occasionally just for the trouble it's put him through, the sizzling and
crackling like eggs cracking over an overheated pan. It takes a
moment, but soon the thing is blackened, its membranous flesh

charred, and only when it lies still does Zilch slide himself off, dragging the thing off the griddle with him, letting it hang from the socket in his gut like an extra appendage, smoking and limp.

With a knife from the prep area, Zilch saws the creature loose from his belly, then reaches in and with one quick jerk, pulls loose its roots, gathering up all of the dangling strands and flaccid, steaming lengths of the thing, then doffs the whole balled mass under his arm.

"Thanks," he says. His gaze shifts around to the stunned, silent diners at the McDonald's all staring at him, some with their phones out. "Think we could get back on the road?"

Galavance apologizes to every set of eyes they meet on the way out, Zilch leading the way with the limp, dead thing still under his arm. They go out to the car, get in, and drive off. She watches him free up a place to deposit the creature by moving all their purchases from one bag to another. Despite it being dead, he still ties it up with double-knots.

GALAVANCE, ONCE SHE COULD TAKE A FULL BREATH WITHOUT receiving a full-body quake, asks, "Did it make that hole? In your stomach. Did it do that?"

"Actually, I did that," Zilch says, matter-of-factly.

"*You* did that? Why?"

"I scarfed. To break up a fight. I had to talk to Chev, and some rednecks were gonna beat him to death any second unless I did something."

"So you decided to scarf. Right there. Why not just yell 'Hey!' or 'Please stop'?"

"I had to get their attention. By the way, thanks for the bringing me up to date on trending youth pastimes. It really helped."

"Glad to be of service," Galavance says, pale-faced.

He has his shirt open, chin to chest, looking down into the sagging gash in his belly and picking out flecks of the parasite like a chimp inspecting itself for fleas. Galavance shivers again, then again. She has to look away. Her butt always goes numb when looking at unsettling things. She never understood why—a physiological reaction to mental trauma she never really could grasp the usefulness of.

"Should we be worried people were taking pictures in there?"

"They'll take care of that," Zilch says, unconcerned. "How're you holding up?"

"I feel like I'll never be able to take enough showers. But all things considered, pretty okay." She nods to herself. "Hanging in there."

"Sure, but . . . no sudden compulsion to steal car parts?"

"No." She looks over at him. "Should I?"

"Dunno. Maybe yours is taking longer to take root."

"I think I'd know if I was turning into a were-amphibian," she says. *At least I hope I'd know*, she thinks.

"We should do a test when we get back to the house. Old wives method I remember my mother using on me when she thought I'd gotten worms," Zilch says. "I wasn't what you'd call big on washing hands. Not until I went to cooking school, where they practically cane you for forgetting."

"What kind of test?"

"I'll explain when we get back to the house." He bums another smoke.

Galavance sparks one up too. "Do you ever think that maybe forgetting about her entirely might be for the better?"

"Who?"

"Your wife."

Zilch sits looking at the cigarette burning between his fingers. "I've considered fucking up on purpose to just let them take the rest of her, but isn't that just giving them what they want? Without needing to dangle anything anymore—and I'd just be a robot doing a job, to them—then I'd be the perfect employee. But believe it or not, I liked my wife. Even if I can't remember everything, I'm willing to go through hell to hang on to what I still have."

"Even though you cheated on her."

"I wasn't doing so hot at that time. Made a lot of bad decisions."

"And that forgives your cheating? If anything, that makes it worse."

"Are we still talking about me here? Or someone else?"

Galavance sighs.

"Because," Zilch continues, "if you're trying to find excuses to let me kill Jolby, I can give you one. And this saying applies the same as it did back in my day, same as it does now, same as it did a thousand generations ago: once a cheater, always a cheater. We fix him this time, he'll probably be really thankful. He'll think you hung the moon. But give him enough time to get comfortable again, he'll repeat his mistakes."

"Stop," Galavance says, "I don't want my boyfriend to die. Until I hear it from him *directly*, until he looks me right in the eyes and I hear him say he cheated on me with eleven different women, I can't make any decisions. And you telling me he's 'not worth it' and I'm better off without him and all that horseshit is just you trying to make yourself feel better. Play the martyr in someone else's car, not mine. I don't give up on people that easy."

"Funny," Zilch says, "my wife said the same thing in her vows when we got married. Then look at what happened. She died rushing to get to the hospital where I was recovering from an OD—with my mistress in tow."

"That's completely different."

"How?"

"Jolby's a good guy."

"Gee, thanks."

"No, sorry, I meant . . . I meant Jolby's mixed up now, fine, yes, agreed, and I won't break my neck trying to save him if what you say is true. I still have to know. I still have to hear it from him, if what he did is true. Maybe the parasite makes him lie, makes him screw up his relationships so it can have him all to itself. Ever think of that? Well?"

Zilch, in the passenger seat, says nothing for a moment. "No, I didn't think of that. I just know what he told me and I remember it clear as day, he said—"

"I don't care," Galavance says. "I won't make your job easier. I'm sorry if that annoys you, but I can't give up on him."

"Because you've put too many eggs in that basket, is that why? It's never too late to have an egg withdrawal. Cash out, while you still have a shirt on your back."

"Let's not talk for a little while, okay? Let's just get to the house and figure out how to fix him." She glances down at the shopping bags in the floorboards, one containing the offspring borne of her boyfriend's mutation, and the other, a harpoon gun. "Hopefully nobody will have to get hurt."

"I think it's too late for that. Chev's no longer with us, remember?"

"Anybody *else* get hurt, I meant. Can we just be quiet now, please?"

Traffic thickens as they continue along. Churches have let out all over, and cars full of well-dressed people are pouring out onto the highway. Zilch does a good job not saying anything until they leave the interstate for the two-lanes, then the dirt roads. 1330 Whispering Pines Lane, now under a cloudless early afternoon sun, is as they left it.

The deck behind the house could very well be considered a dock. The bog is almost even with the planks, one corner dipping under. A tiny brown lizard skitters along the railing. Out in the farther-off reaches of the swamp, obscured by a hanging gray haze, Galavance watches one of the closer mud islands for any indication of movement, any jiggling tree limb, but there's nothing but birds and the occasional ripple in the water as a snake or a frog—the smaller, regular kind—goes under. She turns to see how Zilch is coming along.

"Try not and shoot yourself with that thing," she says, noticing he has the harpoon gun out of its package.

Attempting to load the gun—referencing the user's manual spread out on the porch railing next to him—Zilch works a small winch on its side to draw back the cable, each turn more difficult than the one before. He's sweating again. He's even paler than the day she hit him with her car, licking his lips a lot, his blinks are slow.

"You all right?"

"Yeah. It's just hot is all. Are we talking again?"

Galavance nods. "I just needed some time to think."

"Completely understandable." Zilch, with the harpoon loaded, takes aim across the bog, down the plastic gun's sights. "I've been told I'm not good at shutting up. But spend as much time alone as I do, and the minute you get within range of another person with working ears, it tends to become a challenge not talking them deaf." He lowers the harpoon gun and sets the safety on and off with his thumb, getting used to doing it until it becomes second nature.

"So you said we were going to test me, see if I have one," Galavance says.

"Right," Zilch says. "Go inside and see if you can find some bread."

Inside the house, the air has grown stuffy and stale. She opens the beer cooler to find not one but two dead parasites, both bagged and still, among the few remaining ice cubes that haven't melted. She can't help but look at them and think, *Those are kind of like Chev and Zilch's babies*, and it makes her stomach twist. Finding no bread, she drops the lid, replacing the paint can to weigh the lid down, then steps into the kitchen. There's nothing but stoner food in the cabinets. Cheddar-flavored this and bacon-flavored that. She doesn't find any bread but decides on the closest thing: a bag of fried corn puffs dusted with nuclear orange cheese powder. She brings the bag back out onto the deck where Zilch is standing, hands cupped around his eyes, looking out into the bog.

"Feels like we're being watched," he murmurs. "Think he has a pair of binoculars out there?" Zilch waves and hollers out over the water. "Jolby, come out to play-ay."

"So it's not bread," Galavance says, presenting the bag of cheese curls, "but will these work?"

Zilch tucks the harpoon gun through one of his belt loops. "Worth a shot. Put your head back and open your mouth."

"Why?"

"Because this is how Mom did it."

He didn't ask her to, but she closes her eyes when she tips her head back, because otherwise she'd be staring up into the noon sun. She lets him place one of the cheese curls on her tongue. "Just let it sit there. If there's anything inside, it'll come up to get it."

"This will actually work?" she tries to say, tongue out. She can feel the cheese dust swirling down her throat every time she breathes, but fights down the desire to cough.

"Apparently."

She can still feel the sun, even with her eyes closed, can feel the rays baking her cheeks and forehead and bridge of her nose. She can feel the cheese curl getting sodden by her saliva, collapsing slowly into a soggy, gross mass on her tongue. She doesn't feel anything slither up her throat but the longer she holds the position the more she struggles not to gag.

"Okay," he says after what feels like an hour. "I think you're in the clear."

She spits the saliva-soaked cheese curl off the side of the deck, into the swamp water. It floats for a second, then a dozen small fish dart up out of the brown murk to pick it apart. She has spots in her eyes and she's mildly dizzy from having her head back for so long. The fish nibble and devour the Cheeto until there's nothing left.

"I still think I have one," she says.

"Are you feeling like you're gonna go froggy on me?" Zilch says, hand slowly curling around the grip of the harpoon gun.

"No," she says. "I think Jolby's my parasite. Feels shitty to talk about him like that when he's not here, and going through what he is right now—" she puts up a hand to cut Zilch off before he can even respond to that "—but for the longest time it felt like we had a partnership. Like if I ever needed him to pick up the slack, if I got sick or was fired out of the blue or something, he'd do everything he'd need to so we'd stay afloat. But I think he was just saying all that.

"Honestly, I think he'd probably just bolt the minute he had to do for me what I've been doing for him. I mean, look at this house. This place should've been done months ago. And the parts of it that *are* done are all fucked up and wrong. He can't do anything right. I blame my dad for being like this."

"I blame my dad for just about everything wrong with me," Zilch says, "I think we all do. But what do you mean?"

"I can't give up on anything. I've been trying to finish reading the same book for two years. If there's a stain on the carpet, I'll scrub it until the rag I'm using has disintegrated in my hand. Back when I was little, anytime Mom did something Dad didn't like—before she eventually left him, I mean—you know what he'd do? He'd make me and Mom stand on chairs in the living room and he'd put that song 'Stand By Your Man' on the stereo, on repeat, and make us sing along with it until he was satisfied. It was usually sometime after the fifth beer. It was like that fucking *programmed* me, I think. Didn't even hit me until now, but here I am, despite everything Jolby's done, and I'm still standing by my man." She knuckles her forehead. "Jesus, I'm such a fucking cliché."

"When you love someone," Zilch says, "you hope—even if they aren't at that moment—they'll eventually become the person you need them to be. Or that they'll see what you need and learn, when you need it, to be that person for a while. But sometimes it's hard to notice when someone's in trouble. And men—not to talk shit about my own gender—can be pretty goddamn thick sometimes. Present company included."

Galavance turns to look at Zilch, unable to keep the look of shock from her face. "What, do they make you listen to self-help tapes when you're not hunting monsters?"

"Like I said, I spend a lot of time alone."

Hours pass. Zilch goes in and pulls out two chairs from inside, and they both sit. He tries to angle himself under the awning, chasing the elusive shade. Soon, he's reduced to standing, since sitting won't get the sun off his face. And ten minutes after that, the sun has moved west far enough that he's left with no shade on the deck at all.

"Should we have gotten some kind of bait?" Galavance says.

"I was kind of thinking that's what you're here for."

Galavance smacks him. Zilch laughs.

"Seriously, though. He can probably see us, or hear us," she says. "And he's probably got more than one way out of the swamp than through the cul-de-sac." She takes off her sunglasses to peer out at the mud islands and beaver dams and gnarled twists of drowned trees. "He may not even be out there."

"Or maybe he's sleeping off a food coma, still full of Chev." Zilch winces having suggested it, and changes the subject. "You said Jolby really likes the stuff you bring home from the restaurant?"

"Yeah, but now that we know what that sausage really is, there's no way in hell I'm ever going back there."

"Do they deliver?"

"You really think Jolby wants Frenchy's? I mean, that sausage is . . . his other were-amphibians, right? Isn't that fucked up that he'd be hungry for his own were-people?"

Zilch shrugs. "He liked it before, right? The stomach wants what the stomach wants."

"Frenchy's. May I take your order?" It's her boss. Not Patty—her everyday boss. Galavance realizes now she hasn't actually seen him in months.

"Yes, hello my good sir," Galavance says into the cordless phone, trying to mask her voice but ending up sounding like Marvin the Martian, "I'd like to place an order for delivery."

"Galavance?"

Shit. "Yeah."

"What the fuck? You were on the grid to open today."

"I know, but I had a family emergency."

"You didn't call," he says, and mouth-breathes, fast. "I could write you up, you know."

"Is Patty there?"

"Yeah, she's right here. She told me you two had a heart-to-heart and she saw a lot of potential in you. Before you pulled a no-call no-show, that is. She might make me fire you."

"But she's there? In the restaurant?"

"Either she is or I'm looking at a really good impersonator. Do you wanna talk to her about this? If you can't respect me, maybe she can straighten you out."

"Nate, look. You're two years younger than me. Don't act like some big-dick hotshot just because the regional manager's there. You know what? Fuck this. Here's a message. And you can CC this to Patty as well. Fuck Frenchy's, fuck the both of you, I'm done."

She breaks the cradle slamming the cordless phone back onto it, a few numbered keys spraying out from under the receiver.

Zilch folds his arm. "So when can we expect the order?"

"Sorry."

"We still need bait. And we know Jolby likes Frenchy's."

"I know. But Patty's alive. That should be our main concern right now. She can probably trace the call back—"

The phone rings. Zilch and Galavance hold their breath, saying nothing, as if Patty can hear them even if they don't pick up.

"She's caught others," Zilch says at a whisper. "Maybe if we asked real nicely, she might offer a few tips . . ."

"She tried to *kill me*."

It rings again.

"I can't say for sure they'll send me back. They've hinted they're prepping another employee to take my place." Zilch had been coughing the entire trip back to the house. Raising his hand, he shows Galavance all the dead pinhead-sized scarabs, dried to his palm in a black scattershot. "I'm pretty sure the next guy won't be so patient to hear out your Plan B."

The phone rings again.

"I don't want her anywhere near here," Galavance says.

"I don't think there's much we can do to stop that. She knows this place. I saw her, in her shrub costume, just across the street. *You* know she knows this place. *I* know she knows this place. So you either answer that phone and tell her we need her help, or she's just gonna come by on her own."

"I can't do that. She's cooking people."

"Were-amphibians, but I get your point."

A fourth ring.

"Do you? I ate some of that. People, Saelig. I ate people—because of her. I may not have one of those . . . things in me, but I'm still a fucking cannibal."

"You're not a cannibal. You didn't do it on purpose."

"Is that what defines a cannibal—actually *knowing* you're eating people? Because I feel like a cannibal."

He hikes up his shoulders, drops them. "Then you're a cannibal. What do you want me to say? But, regarding your homicidal regional manager: what other fucking options do we really have? Waiting for Jolby to come to us isn't exactly working like gangbusters."

Beep. "Hey, this is Jolby and Chev," Chev says from beyond the grave via the voicemail greeting. "If you're interested in the property, please contact the realtor."

"*Galavance, it's Patty,*" sounds from the tinny answering machine speaker. Patty's speaking low, barely audible over some droning machinery. Galavance recognizes the rumble of the Hobart dishwasher going and she can picture her, in the far back portion of the restaurant's kitchen, huddled around her phone, far from being overheard by the others. *"I apologize for our misunderstanding last night—"*

"Misunderstanding?" Galavance says to the answering machine. "Bitch, you tried to shoot me."

"—but I think perhaps we can come to a middle ground, if you'd be willing. See, in full disclosure, I would really appreciate it if you keep what you and I spoke about last night at the hotel under your hat. I'd even be willing to tell Nate to forgive your little no-call no-show slipup today. We're only human, as imperfect as God made us. Please pick up. I know you're still there—you only called a moment ago, sugar. Please. Let's talk. I need your help and you need mine, I reckon. Otherwise, why would you have been trying to place an order for delivery? You must need it, right? Please pick up, sweetheart."

Galavance leans back from the phone, as if the barrel of Patty's thirty-ought-six might spring from the answering machine.

"—I completely understand if you were the one who called the police. Or if it was one of the other people staying in the hotel, or the management. Either way, you really put a bee in my bonnet, making me have to hide my rifle and try to make it seem like the shot came into my room's window, not out of it. Got me so frazzled I barely slept a wink, and I was nearly late for work this blessed morning! Imagine, me, late! Please pick up, Galavance. Let's talk this mess out."

"What do we do?" Galavance says. "She's going to come here."

Zilch hits the button to end the recording, cutting Patty off mid-sentence. "Let her."

§

AFTER GIVING THE HARPOON GUN TO GALAVANCE IN CASE Jolby shows up before Patty does, Zilch heads back out to the garage and rolls up the overhead door. In the early afternoon light, Chev's dead eyes have developed a milky cataract. His mouth hangs open. Zilch pulls a drop cloth off one of the shelves and covers the wreck Jolby made into his best friend, feeling a bit bad for the guy. Chev had trying to be a good friend, and look where that got him.

He faces the garage wall. The inside isn't finished. Between the studs are exposed nail heads keeping the plywood sheets in place. He imagines head-butting the nails, driving one into his brain, killing that particular portion of gray matter where all his self-doubt is stored. Or maybe he'll aim for the part storing all the times he screwed up in crystal clear high fidelity. Or the little cottage in his mind where Susanne lives.

A shadow forms next to his on the cement floor, not drawing itself long as if someone just outside the garage has come up the driveway, but forming from the chest-out, growing arms and legs and finally a head. It's a silhouette he recognizes but he can't bear to look up and see nothing there, so he keeps staring down at his feet. He can almost smell her standing behind him.

"What do you want?" he says.

I like what you told Galavance before. Didn't really sound, at first, like something you'd say. Color me shocked—you sound like a real-life adult-like person now.

"I do try," Zilch says, looking at the many nail-points jutting out at him. "Forgive me if I don't turn around, hon, but I don't really think that's you."

Believe what you want, babe.

He puts his palm up to one of the nails and presses until he can feel the tip nearly pierce his skin. "I'd ask you if you'll forgive me," he says, "but I figure we're way past that."

Sorry to disappoint, but no, I don't forgive you. But that shouldn't matter. Right now, you need to forgive yourself. And quit trying to give yourself the stigmata, that's not how it works.

"Is that the lesson?" He stops pushing the heel of his palm against the nail. He looks at the tiny red shallow indent he made and rubs with his thumb until it vanishes. "Is that the goal of working off my moral bankruptcy, then? Self-forgiveness? If so, I gotta call bullshit."

The shadow moves closer until its head begins to slide up the wall next to him, among the nail-tips, wooden studs, and the mosaic grain of the particle board. He holds his breath. He can hear the swish of her loose clothing as she moves, the soft padding of her bare feet on the cold cement floor. One small intake of breath through his nose and he can smell Susanne's shampoo. But despite all the small details screaming at his brain, telling him that it's really her, he still won't turn around.

Fix this for her, Susanne says, *and move on to the next. You're much easier to like when you're busy. You can't stand to be bored. Keep your hands full.*

"I'm sorry for what happened," he says, throat tight. "I really am."

I know you are. Help her. Stay busy. This can end.

Suddenly he hears music playing somewhere—and getting louder—and he turns around to look and Susanne's gone, her shadow vanished.

Heavy bass punches the air in slightly delayed harmony with the rattle of a loose bumper. Patty, based on Galavance's description of her, didn't sound much like a hip-hop fan. Zilch stands in the open garage, hands in pockets, and watches.

Coming up Whispering Pines Lane, a single car approaches at a crawl. It's painted candy apple red and the windows are tinted black. The driver threads between mud puddles and bumps that might make the vehicle bottom-out. When it turns into the driveway, Zilch can see through the windshield; behind the wheel is Beefy Ben, and he has his boys with him.

"Great," Zilch grunts to himself.

The music, muffled to a tooth-loosening rumble with the windows up, dies. Every occupant in the car is looking straight ahead, right at him—so he moves out into the orange afternoon sun, regretting that the harpoon gun is with Galavance.

Beefy Ben steps out of the car but doesn't approach, yet. "Fuck are you doing out here again, crackhead?" he calls. "Chev musta got you to the hospital right quick."

Six other occupants exit the vehicle. They're all carrying paper bags from a recent fast food run, and set them on the roof and hood of the car. They're dressed pretty much the same as before, except their jeans aren't ripped from work but ripped for fashion and their yellow hard hats are all replaced with matching white baseball caps, all uniformly backwards. Ben, burning holes into Zilch, is crushing French fries by the wadded handful, fried potato crumbs tumbling down the front of his shirt.

"You chuckleheads should piss off," Zilch says. "I'm not in the mood."

"Do et ageen," one of Ben's cronies say with a drawl so thick and his mouth so full of takeout he's nearly incomprehensible. "That thing ya deed, bo. Scarf. I toll these other guys and they dun be-leeb me."

"I'm from the South," Zilch says, "but still I have to ask. *What*?"

Beefy Ben plays translator. "Rip your guts out, dickhead."

The wind turns and on it, Zilch smells the booze on them. "Seriously, guys. Fuck off. I'm sure there's a Klan rally somewhere you could attend."

Beefy Ben sets his most-likely-spiked orange soda aside and snaps open a pocket knife. He moves forward and Zilch forbids his feet from shuffling back in a slow retreat. The extended blade trained at Zilch's chest, its tip hovering an inch away.

"Do it. Or I'll do it for you."

Suddenly, it sounds like a huge rubber band has been pulled back and released. There's a whistling buzz and then a solid *thunk*. Everyone pauses—Beefy Ben, Goatee Darryl, the remaining idiots, even Zilch. They turn and see a tiny silver harpoon buried into the front tire of Beefy Ben's car.

Galavance stands on the front porch of the house with the harpoon gun held in both hands, still trained on Beefy Ben, the single-shot weapon reloaded.

Zilch can see it in Beefy Ben's eyes that he's not the type to be shown up in front of his buddies—especially by a woman.

"Sugar, you really should not be pointing that at people," Beefy Ben says, approaching her slowly but steadily. Galavance remains still, standing on the top step of the front porch. She keeps the business end of the harpoon gun trained on Ben. Her hand doesn't shake.

"Why are you always being so ugly to Jolby?" she says.

"He told you about that, huh? Came crying to his girlfriend to fight his battles? I give him shit 'cause he ain't a real man."

"And *you* are, peckerhead?" Galavance says. "That's a laugh."

"I ain't seen Jolby around in a while—maybe he's hiding someplace? Call me your secret admirer," Beefy Ben says, all butter, now within arms' reach of her. "I seen you, girl, bunch a times, coming by here to call on your boy. I seen them itty bitty shorts you wear. Ain't for his eyes only, I reckon. I've been with girls like you," he says. "Tell you what. Gimme a kiss and I'll forget you did that to my car."

"Leave," Galavance says, but Beefy Ben, quick as lightning, snatches the harpoon gun away from her. The trigger guard snags her finger and bends it at an unnatural angle. She yelps and Zilch moves to help, but Ben's gang of hayseeds swarm to block his path.

With one more twist, Ben wrenches the harpoon pistol from her. "Shoulda just let go of the damn thing. Only got yourself to thank for that broken fanger."

"Ben," Zilch shouts. "Leave her alone."

Beefy Ben turns and with one quick jerk, pulls the pistol's cable back without needing the winch, and loads another bolt. He storms across the yard and angels the readied bolt at Zilch's face.

"What you gonna do if I don't?" Ben says, grinning.

"Put it down and get the fuck out of here, now."

"Oh? Is that a demand? Scarf Boy's making demands?" Beefy Ben turns over his shoulder to Galavance. "Some friend you got here. Not even your boyfriend and yet, here he is doing what Jolby never fucking did—taking a stand."

"This is between you and me, you hillbilly piece of shit," Zilch shouts at the back of Beefy Ben's beefy head. "And unless you want a bullet in you, I'd suggest getting back in that ridiculous thing you call a car and going, now, while you're still able."

Ben turns slowly back to face Zilch, his massive head rotating as if it's on a rusty lazy susan.

"Now, I *know* you didn't just fucking call me a hillbilly."

Zilch groans. "Enough of this chest-thumping alpha male crap," he says, reaching out to both pull himself free from Ben's goons and grab the harpoon gun. Ben, startled, pulls the trigger.

Zilch feels the wind come off the rubber bands as they contract, snapping against the air. The harpoon moves so fast he doesn't even have time to flinch. He can see Beefy Ben, and Galavance, both gasp, their eyes turning enormous. Galavance gasps so hard that it takes her a moment to gather the wind necessary to actually scream. Zilch turns and Beefy Ben's friends all go, "*Damn!*" in a collective sympathetic wince so synchronized it looks practiced.

Zilch reaches up and feels that the harpoon has been driven into the corner of his left eye. He can see it, like one can see their own nose by crossing their eyes.

"You shot me in the face," Zilch says, genuinely insulted.

Galavance slaps Beefy Ben's shoulders, the back of his head, the side of his neck. "What the hell is wrong with you?"

One of Ben's buddies say: "Goddamn, bo. That thing's probably in yer goddamn brain. Ben, we probably oughta scoot."

"Give me that fucking thing," Zilch says and grabs the gun out of Ben's startled hands. "Go."

"Okay, man. I mean, you're not going to press charges or nothing? We're cool? You can still see out of that eye, right?" Ben is saying, walking backwards to his car across the yard. "I don't really got much money. I mean, I could give you a few bucks now if you want, we were just about to go down for a beer run—hey, yeah, let's do that. You like beer? We could drink this over, nothing like booze under the bridge, right?"

"*Get lost*," Zilch shouts, pointing the harpoon gun at him. The back of his head starts to ache—a small pinching sensation that swells to a throbbing, blinding pounding in half a breath.

Cradling his head with his free hand, still pointing the harpoon gun with the other, Zilch watches Beefy Ben and his friends all pile back into his purple car. It's like Ben has forgotten to drive and fumbles with the keys, turning on the windshield wipers, the high-beams, before the engine actually starts.

A sound erupts from the swamp. Gurgling and broken-sounding, something stirring the water, coughing to life, possibly mechanical, possibly alive.

Zilch and Galavance wheel around in the direction of the approaching grumble of a revving engine . . .

Streaking across the swamp comes a hodgepodge of a vehicle, all patched together in varying bright colors and crisscrossed, incongruent racing stripes. The driver cannot be seen as a dozen fog lights all mounted to the front end and lined across the top of the windshield throw out 800-candlepower eye-melting shine. There's some music playing, a riff that triggers something in a part of Zilch's mind he still has left and it stings him to think about. The pain compass comes roaring back, momentarily blotting out the agony of being shot in the face with a harpoon. But it's nagging at him; he knows the song, but can't place the title, not until Galavance says:

"What is that?"

"That would be 'Flirtin' with Disaster' by none other than Molly Hatchet." He pauses. "Or did you mean that thing driving up out of the swamp?"

In time with the music swelling in volume, the car begins to climb, ascending up out of the swamp water, liquid pouring off its dented sheet metal. The cab is lifted up on stilts of some kind, a custom metal frame that stretches far beneath the water. It keeps climbing out, more and more emerging from the swamp. Soon a set of four enormous wheels are visible, wrapped in chain. The patchwork car is set atop stolen construction equipment wheels, making it into a tuner monster truck. The backhoe's tires. *That's* where they went, Zilch realizes, chagrinned.

"Wild guess. That's the thing Chev was talking about," Galavance says.

"Yep," Zilch says. "He was building a goddamn monster truck."

Galavance sighs. "Sunday, Sunday, Sunday."

With one grunt of the accelerator, the Frankenstein truck frees itself from the swamp mud and roars across the cul-de-sac. Beefy Ben tries to back them out of the driveway but his car's tires just throw smoke, spinning in place. Too late. The massive wheels are on them, easily climbing up over the hood and crushing the windshield down with a *spack*. The roof, as the truck eases the back wheel up onto the purple racer, crumples onto its passengers. There are screams, but they are mostly drowned out by the slapdash car-crusher's thunderous engine.

As "Flirtin' With Disaster" peaks, the vehicle pauses on top of Ben's car. The truck locks its front wheels and the rear right one, as tall as Zilch, begins spinning. The roof of Ben's car is flung away, slick as a tablecloth being ripped out from under a place setting. With his car roofless, Ben has a moment to escape. In a panicked scramble, he tries to climb up over the hood, but the truck thumps into reverse and backs up over him, pinning him to the hood. He screams. And the truck matches his bellowing with a few angry grunts of acceleration, in preparation of something awful.

"Jolby, stop!" Zilch shouts over the noise.

The front of the truck remains stationary, but the back wheel—set to a mighty roar of the engine—spins. Beefy Ben, with just a few quick revolutions, is rendered into pink porridge. Screaming, then not. A man, then paste.

Through with that task, the truck rolls down over the remainder of the car, leaving Beefy Ben's ride a flattened slab of wrinkled purple sheet-metal. Blood from the other men trapped inside flows freely under the doors and puddles on the asphalt.

The monster truck moves with surprising elegance, out across a few of the other lawns and makes a slow circle as it turns around.

The vehicle rumbles past, taking a second pass at Ben and his friends for good measure, slowly, as if Jolby is savoring it, and for a moment Zilch can see inside the passenger window. There's the outline of a large, angular head. Then, closer, massive brown eyes, the green pallor and face of Jolby, completely transformed.

"Is that what he looks like when he . . . ?" Galavance stammers.

The truck hesitates in the front yard of 1330 Whispering Pines for a moment, Jolby's frog face filling the side window, its eyes trained on Zilch and Galavance. Its darkly speckled eyes move around, scanning them, then slowly drift down toward their feet. Its eyes, if possible, go wider. A line of drool visibly cascades from its mouth, syrupy and long, reminding Zilch of a dangling shoelace. He looks down, and sees a spilled bag of Ben's takeout. Something yellow—melted cheese possibly—is smeared in with the mud and blood, partly crushed in amongst the smooshed remains of run-over French fries.

Quickly snapping up the bag, Zilch holds it overhead like one would showcase the freshly disembodied head of a fallen enemy. Jolby's eyes grow unmistakably hungrier. But when the bag's soggy underside splits and its contents splatter out back onto the ground, the frog-man seems to snap to, disappointed that the prized meal is sullied. It gives Zilch and Galavance one last withering glare, faces forward, then mashes the accelerator, the engine booming in immediate reply.

Zilch and Galavance both yell out at the same time. "Jolby, wait!"

The vehicular abomination roars across the cul-de-sac and back into the swamp. The bog is kicked out in front of the tires in a wall of stirred white water. The vehicle sinks in and rumbles along, exhaust billowing out from the redirected pipe jutting up out of the trunk of the car—a black cat-tail trailing up into the sky behind it.

Zilch breaks into a run, going to the edge of the water. *"Five second rule! Don't be a snob, come on back!"*

He fumbles with the harpoon gun, trying to get it reloaded.

Galavance rushes him. "What are you *doing*?"

"What we bought this thing for!" The thing feels poorly made in his hands; a lot of parts that should be tight are loose, and he could probably break the thing over his knee.

Zilch faces the retreating monster truck, the massive back end bobbing as it hits the water and momentarily loses speed.

He takes aim but, down an eye, knows he'll be about as accurate as if he threw a rock in the dark, but squeezes the trigger anyway. The bands snap and the harpoon sails through the air, lodging itself into the glass of the rear windscreen.

The vehicle presses on as if nothing happened, a bee-sting to an elephant. It gets out far enough into the swamp that soon it's just the chassis gliding across the top of the weedy surface of the water—out to the islands, where it moves into a grove of willows. the lights cut out, and the thing is completely invisible. A few tree tops in the distance shimmy, then go still.

The drilling sensation in Zilch's skull fades, then stops altogether. "Fuck."

When he turns around, Galavance is standing at the edge of where the cul-de-sac and swamp overlap. She's holding her hand, favoring it, her finger now swollen to double its size and bleeding.

Zilch trudges over, the mud trying to suck his shoes off. "Let's get some ice on that, huh?"

She glares at his face, at his new hole. "How about we get a bandage on *that*?"

Blood dribbling down the bridge of nose as he bends over, Zilch fetches Ben's waterlogged take-out bag bobbing in the loose mud. Holding up the crumbling paper bag to the setting sun, he lights up the restaurant's logo from behind the printing: FRENCHY'S.

WITH A BAG OF FROZEN PIZZA BAGELS ON HER HAND, GALAVANCE sits on the floor with her back against the wall, watching Zilch through the open bathroom door. There's a quiet wet pop and a clatter of metal as he yanks the six-inch harpoon out of his head and drops it into the sink. He leans into the mirror, dabbing at his bleeding eye with the collar of his shirt.

"Stupid redneck. Kind of glad he got squashed."

"So I guess we know what Jolby was doing with all those parts now," Galavance says, shifting the pizza bagels around since some of them are softening. "And where he's been all this time. He probably keeps to the shallow parts of the swamp and just *lives* in that thing."

Zilch leans into the mirror again, so close that his forehead nearly touches the glass. His black suit coat is soggy with swamp water, and his pants are clinging to his legs like they're painted on.

"I don't know if you saw the look on Jolby's face when he got a whiff of that bag of takeout," he says, "but there's no doubt in my mind anymore that stale Frenchy's is like catnip to him."

There was a moment in which Galavance, as crazy as it might have seemed, had interpreted Jolby's return in a positive light. After all, he'd come back and saved her, hadn't he? Maybe that was the little bit of the real Jolby still alive, fighting for control inside his frog body, trying to right his wrong and make amends for all the terrible things he's put her through. But with Zilch's words, she realizes how stupid that idea was: Jolby wasn't being a man of action after all—Beefy Ben and his friends were all killed because of territorial squabbling over food and not her. He hadn't been coming to her rescue.

Zilch emerges from the bathroom, toweling his hands, his right eye socket packed with a wad of red toilet paper that grotesquely stretches his eyelid. When he blinks, it looks like a grotesque little mouth trying, and failing, to chew an oversized marshmallow.

"We need fresh bait," Galavance says. "And unless we wanna drive to Raleigh, where the next-nearest Frenchy's location is . . ."

"We still have to deal with your regional manager, you know. She's not going to stop."

"I know, but think about it: Frenchy's would be the last place she'd expect to find us. She's probably on her way here. So if we go *there*, now . . ."

Staring at the far wall of the living room, Zilch's expression shifts from ready, perhaps even bravely resolute—to worried. Galavance spins on the bucket she's using for a seat to see what's got him concerned. The blue tarps covering the windows light up for a moment, then darken, and they can hear an engine rumbling outside, sounding poorly tuned and overworked.

"Too late," Zilch says.

As Zilch fights to load the harpoon gun again, Galavance moves to the window, peeling the tarp aside to take a peek.

A black sedan crawls past, taking its time.

"We have lights on," Zilch says, posting up next to Galavance at the window, peeking out with her. "She knows we're here."

"What's the plan?"

"You're asking me? She's your boss."

"Should we go out and talk?" She notices Zilch opening the beer cooler. "What are you doing?"

Zilch flops the two bagged parasites onto the seat of a lawn chair and undoes the knots in their bags. The two creatures splay and dangle from their thin plastic containers, drooling through the nylon strips of the lawn chairs and to the floor. One of them twitches a tentacle, making Galavance jump back.

"They're not dead?"

"Invertebrates can take a serious licking," Zilch says. "With no bones to break, they can go nighty-night and then patch themselves up pretty quick. Don't think I picked that up from working this job—I took a field trip to the aquarium in third grade." Zilch screws up his face as he pulls the knot of bloody toilet paper from his eye socket. "They had a whole thing about jellyfish and it's about all I remember from it. Weird how random shit like that suddenly comes in handy years later, huh?"

He squeezes the bloody wad over one half-dead parasite and as a few drops of blood land among the tangles of wet, waxy tentacles, the thing begins thrashing. Dripping more onto the second elicits the same reaction. Before either can slither away though, Zilch packs them both back into the bags and ties up the knots again, holding them by their handles as the bags bulge and threaten to rip.

"What's she up to out there?" he says.

Galavance peeks outside and watches as the car stops on the street. The engine dies, the headlights go dark. Patty doesn't get out. With the streetlight shining in through the back of the car, Galavance can see Patty's wrestling to get something on, like she's pulling a bag over her own head.

"There she goes, getting in her Ewok get-up again," Zilch whispers. "Keep an eye on her. She has a way of vanishing in that thing. I'm gonna go out through the garage and see if we can't negotiate."

"She has a gun, Saelig."

"Funny thing about getting shot already today," Zilch says, holding the garage door's knob, "is that the second time probably won't be much more than an annoyance." He holds up the bagged parasites squirming in his hand. "Meet bargaining chip number one and bargaining chip number two."

"No. She'll just use them to make more, won't she? No way."

"I won't actually let her have them. Do I look that stupid? She needs them and she'll probably do anything for them. She's hunted these things a while, according to what you said. I'm running out of time, and even if she is a huge piece of shit, she can still be useful. If she knows how the things spread, then she'll know the value of these disgusting critters. If she wants to retain her standing at Frenchy's, she'll have to produce results. I've catered big-wig corporate events, I've picked up a few things. Results are paramount. Synergy's important, too, whatever that is."

"All right," Galavance says. "I just hope you know what you're doing." She peeks outside again. The car's door opens and Patty steps out, rifle cradled in her hands, giving a quick scan to her surroundings. Swinging the door closed behind her with a knee-high swamp-traversing boot, the dome light behind her fades off—and she vanishes. Not even the streetlight helps. She's just *gone*, like a cheap movie effect, poof.

Galavance has a moment of panic, thinking Patty might've done a ninja-leap up through an upstairs window, silent, already in the house. She kills the work lights, throwing 1330 Whispering Pines Lane into complete darkness. Tripping over something, she bends over and finds a length of copper piping—already bent into a seven. Gripping it like a weapon, her back to the wall, she watches every tarp-covered window in the room around her for shadows, trying to force her breathing into some kind of a regular rate. Her finger hurts. Her back hurts. Her legs hurt. She's seen too many gross things today. It's been a bad weekend altogether.

I do not want to die here, in this unfinished, drowned new development neighborhood.

She starts to say something to Zilch but turning back where he'd just been standing, she sees the door to the garage pull shut behind him.

Galavance once heard that when someone is about to die, it isn't always their life that passes before their eyes. Sometimes, depending on the person, they think about everything they regret. It's not exactly a sunny thought, but it made sense to her when she first heard it. And not just regret for things they'd themselves done or failed to do, themselves, but regret for the things they'd allowed others to do to them.

But now, in the heat of the moment, Galavance realizes she doesn't want to sit around and spend her last potential moments alive regretting all the shit she let Jolby do to her. She wants to forgive Jolby. Badly. She doesn't want to take her anger with her. But she finds she can't let it go, not until she knows the truth, hears *from him* what he'd done. She can't live without getting that closure. Can't die without it, actually, she thinks morbidly. But what if she never gets it? What if Patty does a combat roll into the house, pops up, and fires a bullet into her head? Galavance wonders if that's how ghosts are made.

She hears Zilch clear his throat outside. "Excuse me, miss, but you're trespassing."

Patty—closer to the house than Galavance expected, nearly at the front door by the sound of it—gasps. "Oh. I'm sorry, I, uh . . . I work for wildlife control, we've had reports of—"

"I know what's out here," Zilch says. Through the tarps covering the windows, Galavance hears the soft twang of a harpoon pistol readying. "Unless you're willing to impart some helpful tips for luring were-amphibians, I'll have to ask you to leave."

"Were-amphibians? That's very clever."

"Thanks. So, cough up any helpful tips you have or take it on the arches, Patty."

"How do you know my name?"

"That isn't important."

There's a pause in the conversation.

"Where's Galavance?" Patty says.

"That isn't important either."

"You're the one she was talking about, aren't you? Who are you?"

"Jim Rockford."

Patty snorts. "All right, smartass, cut the shit. Who are you with? The Clown? The King? The Freckle-Faced Cooz? The Bell?"

"Let's say the third one."

"The Pigtailed Tyrant, huh? Dave Thomas is dead, and your company died with him. No wonder you're out here. You're itching for a hit, same as us. Have you figured out how to separate the fish taste?"

"Ohhh, I get it now; you mean *Wendy's*." Zilch, says, dropping his authoritative *basso profundo*. "Dave Thomas died? Man. When did that happen?"

There are a few squishes of boots in the mud, which is likely Patty turning with her rifle to face Zilch, Galavance assumes. "Who are you really working for?"

"The third one, like I said. Wendy's. Love that dead-eyed redhead. Square burgers and that fucking chili. Man, I could take a *bath* in that stuff."

"If you were actually employed by Wendy's, you'd have known about your company's founder's death. I've called your bluff, mister. I'd like the truth, please."

"Okay, fine. I don't work for Wendy's," Zilch says. "You got me. And since it seems it bears repeating, I'll say it nice and slow:

if *you* are not going to *help*, please reinsert your person within your *automobile* and take your *ass* on down the *road*. Understand?"

"What is that you're brandishing?"

"It's a harpoon gun."

"Get much luck with that?" Patty scoffs.

"It works well enough. See my lack of a left eye?"

"Proving you shot yourself with your own weapon hardly speaks of its qualities. Or yours. This is a Remington thirty-ought-six, sir. I've harvested nearly eight thousand pounds worth of meat, for my company, for its *patrons*, using this rifle. How many have *you* bagged?"

"I'm a slow starter."

"So, none."

"Look, lady. Can you help us bring him close? We just want to talk with him."

"At this point, Jolby Dawes isn't a him anymore. It's an it. Permanent transformation only takes three weeks. And judging by all this carnage around, I assume he's getting quite testy—his animal side taking over."

"Fine, you've made it clear you're not interested in helping. Then piss off. This one is mine."

"Who do you work for?"

"Goddamn, are you deaf? We're not going through that again. Leave. Go. Vamoose. Don't let the door hit ya where the good lord—"

"I could just shoot you," Patty says. "And Miss Petersen, too, wherever she's hiding. After I do that, nabbing this last known Lizard Man would be mine and mine alone. It's still young, it's glands are probably quivering, they're so full of the worm seed."

"God, do you *have* to phrase it that way? Wait—he's the last one?"

"There've been no other reports. I thought you would've known this. We need him, even more so now that we know how to get the aftertaste out of it now."

"Monster meat. Monster meat that carries parasites that in some cases turns people who eat it into one of them. But I'm assuming you're counting on that."

"Unless the former Jolby Dawes seeds, the rest of the raw meat will have to be undercooked for the next generation of parasites to blossom."

"Again, is phrasing everything the most disgusting way possible some kind of corporate branding, or do you come up with those labels?"

"I came up with them. And everything would've been fine, if we undercooked a meal now and again to let a few newborns pop up here and there, but because Food Safety likes to kick the little guy when they're down, they've been cracking down on us with an almost fascist enthusiasm. We've had to, unfortunately, during the meat's processing, cook all that good potential out. Which just leaves us with fish-smelling gamey junk meat. I need this last one alive, he still has his glands full of—"

"Do not say that word again. Listen, what if I could give you two—count 'em, two!—of Jolby's offspring? They're a little beat up, but still as squirmy as the day they were born from two strapping young men."

"You've obtained some of his seedlings?"

"If we *have* to call them that, yes."

Galavance listens as Zilch's oversized shoes clop on the driveway. She hears the rustle of plastic bags.

"May I touch them?" Patty says, sounding awestruck.

Galavance hears a little slap. "Look with your eyes," Zilch says.

"How?" Patty says. "From where? They're in beautiful shape, so young!"

"One was planted in Jolby's best friend, either before or after he killed him," Zilch began.

"Yes," Patty cut in, "they do that sometimes, to give the little darling a warm place to grow if the host puts up a fuss during impregnation. And from whom did this second darling gush forth into this beautiful world?"

"Me," Zilch says.

"You're lying. You managed to extract a seedling from yourself and survive?"

"I'm very talented," Zilch says. "Now I've showed you these two bouncing baby boys. Tell us how to bring Jolby in so we can talk to him, and you can have these to do with as you will."

"You're handing me a fortune, you're aware of that, right? From these two, I'll be able to keep Frenchy's in stock with sausage for decades, given enough time to breed them and place them with hosts. I hate to tell stories out of school, but we have a tank ready back at Headquarters waiting and ready so there won't be any more need to do this whole safari routine in these detestable backwoods towns."

"Not so fast, don't get grabby," Zilch says. "You scratch *my* back first."

"You may have survived giving birth to a seedling," Patty says, "but I doubt a rifle bullet fired into your heart at point blank range is something you could walk off."

"Try me."

"Give me the seedlings or I'll shoot you."

"Lady, I spent a good six and a half seconds coming up with this plan. Don't ruin it by getting greedy. Take these ugly fuckers, tell me how to bring Jolby to dry land, and we'll call it a day."

"Put the seedlings on the ground—gently—and back away slowly. I said put the seedlings on the ground!"

Galavance has heard enough. She tears open the plywood plank being used as a front door and emerges out onto the porch. Patty, in her ridiculous Swamp Thing getup, stands in the muddy front yard. The moonlight lights the three of them, and Galavance suddenly feels unprepared, realizing she's the only one who isn't armed.

Zilch seems disappointed that Galavance has shown herself, giving away the element of surprise, and takes a better aim at Patty in case she makes any sudden moves. Patty holds her rifle in her arms, ready to fire from the hip at Zilch.

"Miss Petersen, I'd like to extend you an offer," Patty says, her eyes still locked on Zilch. "Immediate push to corporate. You'll have an office of your own, relocation to New Orleans effective ASAP. We'll get you away from this swampy crossroads, and the pay is good. *Very* good. All you have to do is tell this gentleman here to leave the professionals to their work."

Galavance plugs an extension cord into the work light. The front yard is suddenly flooded in buzzing light, making both Patty and Zilch squint.

"She isn't interested," Zilch shouts at Patty. "She's done being a drone for a shitty restaurant chain. She—"

"Patty," Galavance says, "I don't think I'm Frenchy's family material. Please tell me how to help Jolby. If you don't want to help him, that's fine, but I'll have to ask you to leave. This is my boyfriend's property and while he's not here, that makes it mine."

"Don't be silly, girl." Patty peels off her ghillie suit mask. "This is your *job* you're talking about. You've been entrusted with some mighty big company secrets. And we take care of those who have made it to the inner circle of trust. Very good care."

"Consider this my resignation. Tell me how to help my boy-friend."

Patty shakes her head, looks at Zilch. "Misguided young people. Think they're going to rule the world with their fucking blogs and tweets and all that bullshit. What have you given your life for, Mister Whoever-You-Are? Huh? Anything?"

"I give it often, doing this shit," Zilch says. He raises the harpoon gun. "Now you can leave or *I'll* shoot *you*. And trust me, these little suckers hurt."

Keeping her aim square on Zilch, Patty clicks off the safety.

"Stop. I've only got one eye but it works," Zilch says. "Be smart."

"I have to have the seedlings. I need them."

"Fine. If you're gonna be so stubborn about it, here." Zilch winds back and as if launching a bowling ball, underhand tosses a bag over the muddy lawn to Patty. She fumbles as the work-lights on the porch blind her, her hands flailing, eyes squinting in the harsh electric light. The parasite in its volleyed bag slips right between her outreaching hands and the thing smacks right into her chest. The bag breaks open on impact like a water bal-loon hitting its target. The creature inside immediately grabs hold, suckers latching onto the hanging tendrils of Patty's cam-ouflage suit. And just as the first one latches onto her, Zilch lobs the second, hitting Patty low in the stomach.

"Oh, my goodness—just *look* at them," Patty says, staring down from chin to chest to look at the creatures fastened to her. Her hands come together, as if to hug them, stroking their slimy many-armed forms as they entangle with each other, reach-ing, their limbs telescoping, slow, like a worm moving over the ground, up around her neck, softly feeling for flesh. Patty gig-gles as they reach around her left ear, then her right. Drawing themselves up her chest, feelers extending to nuzzle her chin, their suckers pop and reaffix themselves in sequence, advancing.

"Saelig..." Galavance says, unsure if she wants to watch.

"Oh, they like me," Patty says, cooing. "They're trying to kiss me. Hello, babies. Hello there. My name is Patty."

"She asked for them," Zilch says, taking a squishy step back. "Now they're hers to do with what she wants."

Patty giggles as a tentacle touches her bottom lip, attracted by the warmth of her mouth, and tries to push inside. She pinches her lips together, laughing through her nose, but the things keeps pushing, working against her jaw, moving her head back. Patty's eyes shoot wide as she suddenly understands their intent. "No, dear," she says, muffled. "No, no, not me, heh-heh. I'm gonna to take you two home, so you can do this to someone else. Not me. Not me. Stop that now, stop. Stop. *Stop.*"

One of the griddle-singed tentacles, flaking its charred crust as it reaches, probes her ear—driving its length inside, jangling an earring. Patty is pushing back now but the thing is like elastic, it just extends itself to match the length of her pressing arms, its feelers and tentacles and papillae still angling for the warmth inside Patty's head. In its sudden eagerness, it slaps about Patty's face, knocking her glasses off.

Then, like Patty is sucking a large bundle of spaghetti—the entire thing disappears into its new host's gaping mouth. Her eyes roll back in her head. Her knees buckle. She splashes into the mud, face down. There are a few gurgles and pops, inside her, muffled. Galavance watches the entire process, wishing she hadn't.

"Is she dead?" she finally asks.

Zilch looks up and down the street, then back at Patty, her face planted in the mud, making bubbles. "No." He flips her body over with his foot. She's unconscious. Reaching out her nostrils and the corners of her mouth, two small strands squirm about, keeping guard over the entrances.

"Won't she turn into another were-amphibian?"

Thwap. Patty's head is flung to one side as an aluminum rod stakes her temple and her slow shuffling in the mud ends. Zilch lowers the harpoon gun. "Nope."

"What the hell did you do that for? She hadn't turned."

"She hadn't turned *yet*. Plus, I've tangled with a bunch of weird and wicked shit," Zilch says, "but she was easily in the top ten."

"She was a human being, Saelig."

"Fuck that. She sold her soul a while ago," Zilch says, and shrugs. "I don't feel bad. Wait, lemme check. Nope. Not feeling bad at all. I don't see why your knickers are all in a bind."

"This is fucked," Galavance says, staring down at a very dead Miss Patty. Shapes push around under her ghillie suit, the parasites likely feeling deceived, their new home already starting to go cold. "I can't believe you killed her."

"How many times have you imagined doing exactly that—or worse—to her? Be honest."

"A few," Galavance admits. "More than a few."

"Then consider me your fairy godmother. I make dreams come true. *Prang*, dead regional manager, just for you."

"More like an asshole genie. And don't put this on me—you *murdered* her."

"It was her or us." Zilch retrieves Patty's rifle from the ground and shakes the mud from it, pulls back on the lever, and turns the breach toward the work light. "This thing wasn't loaded with foam darts."

"Well, I guess it's too late to argue about it now. Still, though. Give me a warning next time, okay?"

Zilch agrees with a nod. "Fair."

"God, I feel sick. What . . . what're we gonna do with her?"

Saelig glances around again. The rows of half-constructed houses all stare, silent and unoccupied. Far down the unpaved lane where it connects with the main road, a car passes. It doesn't turn into the neighborhood. The crickets and frogs sing. The sky's clear, and this far from the smog of Raleigh, every star shines unhidden. Under different circumstances, it would be beautiful.

"She said were-amphibians are attracted to the meat of their own," he says at last. "Jolby was lured in by the scent of the take-out Beefy Ben and his boys had, so that checks out. And she mentioned something about having a trunk full of the sausage, didn't she?"

"Okay, so we have our bait. But that still doesn't answer my question: what about her?"

"Put her inside, get the bait set up at the edge of the water there, and when Jolby catches the scent, we . . . you know, get him."

"Get him," Galavance says and laughs. She nods over at Beefy Ben's flattened racer, covered by a tarp, only a foot high from how it used to stand. "He has a monster truck. That'll probably be our fate too if we try to just *get him*."

Galavance turns to look out into the swamp. The light on the porch only reaches to the edge of the yard, lighting up the still, dark water for a yard or so out. She can feel him watching. Perched out there in a tree, on the hood of the monster truck possibly. Maybe listening, if his hearing has also increased with his strength and insanity.

She faces Zilch. "I think I know what to do."

MONDAY.

THE SUN IS COMING UP, AND WITH IT, THE PROMISE OF A scorcher. The cicadas begin screaming and the crickets all pack it in. The hanging mist burns away and the dew darkening the deck fades, boiled off.

Zilch wraps a strip of duct tape around Patty's mouth, pushing hard to make sure it sticks. Galavance watches, her stomach in her throat; he's so casual about the whole thing. She thought she knew him, but he's proven himself to be more fucked up than she'd ever expected. He has Patty slumped mostly upright in one of the lawn chairs on the back deck, nearly spilling out of the thing, the harpoon still dug into her head. As he walks away, he pats Patty on her belly. The shapes inside, trying to push their way out, react with soft thrashes. "Don't go anywhere," Zilch says sarcastically.

"Do we really have to keep her around like this?" Galavance says. "Can't we put her in the garage with Chev or something?"

Zilch tears open one of the boxes of the sausage Patty brought with her, his one remaining good eye going squinty as the smell wafts out. "She'll serve as a container. The people I work for might be interested in a look, for research." He coughs into a fist, looks at it, and goes back to rummaging through the box of sausage, tearing through the thick plastic bags as if on the hunt for some prize he might find under all of the thawing pink cubes of meat. "I might get some extra credit out of it."

With each passing hour, Galavance has noticed, his pallor changes. When she first met him, he had a slight olive tint. Now he's gray as oatmeal. His hair looks thin at the temples, grayer in spots than it was before. When he speaks, she cannot help but notice his teeth are long, the gums flaring red and sunken down into his jaw. His remaining eye looks buried in a tunnel of his collapsing socket, ringed by purple bruising. His hands are bonier than before, his movements rattling and unsure. Taking the rifle down off his shoulder, he opens it again, closes it, and sets the safety.

"We all set?" he asks, and coughs.

She nearly got sick getting the sausage out of the boxes and slopped with a ladle onto the TV tray they have set on the far side of the deck, near where the swamp is starting to creep over the edge. A few more inches higher and it'd likely start trickling into the house—one more bout of rain is all it'd take. Galavance shovels the meat cubes, trying to think of it like dog food—anything but people meat. Its juices are thick and syrup-like, the smell like a harbor on a hot day. "Is that enough?" she says.

Zilch nods. "Turn on the fan."

Jamming the fan's plug into the extension cord, the oscillating fan they have set behind the TV tray with its pink bounty sitting ready begins to spin on its highest speed. Galavance and Zilch, standing to either side of Patty's corpse baking in the morning sun, watch for any movement in the distant willows, for ripples in the water, for the grunt of a monster truck's engine sparking to life.

Galavance leans over the railing with her elbows on the wood and stares out. *Out there in all that muck and terrible nastiness is my boyfriend.* It's a shitty thing to think, especially given that she can still hear Tammy Wynette in her head. Once she knows the truth—direct, from Jolby—maybe then a new song can be allowed to start. Maybe Nancy Sinatra's "These Boots Were Made for Walking."

She thinks of the cartoons where they turn smells into visible fumes and pictures red wisps drifting out over the bog, scouring for Jolby like a heat-seeking missile. The fan blows around her hair. She sweeps it behind her ears—and hears something.

She turns off the fan. In its silence, as if playing along, the swamp's fauna goes quiet. Even the wind seems to still, holding its breath to listen. The second of quiet is broken by a far-off rumble, an engine waking—terrible, loud, and angry.

With a sick feeling in both her stomach and heart, Galavance makes sure the harpoon gun is wound. She doesn't want to use it. Looking out over the swamp, filtering up through the tops of some trees across the way, white smoke rises in a stirring fog. Headlights spark bright between the trunks, like eyes opening. The engine bellows when the gas is hammered, and churned swamp water sprays out from Jolby's hiding place—a spot Galavance had passed her eyes over many times before without noticing anything. Broken limbs snap and tumble as the monster truck, with terrifying ease, makes the swampland bow down to its might. It emerges from the copse of willows, moss and bark sliding away from its asymmetrical front end, its grille like a broken, grinning mouth. When the tailpipe is lifted from the water, it gurgles free some of the water that'd snuck in and a coughs a plume of black smoke into the sky.

Zilch presses his remaining eye to the rifle scope and flicks the rifle's safety off.

"Thar he blows."

Heart hammering, Galavance watches the truck rumble closer, submerged in the water up to its cab, a white wall of water pushing out ahead. The thing seems to grow as the massive tires climb the shallows. Only when it's nearly a stone's throw out from the deck does she realize Jolby has no intention of slowing down.

"We might consider removing ourselves from the present location," Zilch says and pulls her back closer to the house and away from the railing. Patty's belly swells, the creatures inside—perhaps with their own type of pain compass—sensing their father drawing near.

The still-moving truck's windshield flops up like a mail slot hatch, and Jolby—green and dressed in rags—climbs over the wheel and onto the hood of the vehicle, squatting there poised on the edge of the grille, his head cocked back, nostrils flaring and narrowing.

The truck, though now driverless, continues to roll forward closer and closer. By the look on Jolby's face and the cascading lines of saliva falling from the corners of his mouth, he's honed onto the location of the scent.

Zilch lefts his finger back onto the rifle's trigger. Even as Galavance's sensible side calls her an idiot, even though she can think of a hundred different reasons to stand back and let the cards fall where they may, she just can't. She steps forward, putting herself in front of Zilch's scope.

Swinging the barrel away, Zilch's eyes are wide, trained on Jolby, but he glances at her long enough to blurt: "*What are you doing*?!"

They would've tussled over the rifle, Galavance would have said something about not wanting Jolby hurt right now, but all of that becomes a moot point because Jolby seizes the moment of confusion and springs from the hood of the truck, launching himself ahead of it—too impatient to wait any longer for the treasure sitting on that TV tray. Zilch shoves Galavance aside and steps into Jolby's arc—right between him and the pile of cubed sausage.

When Jolby connects the two go tumbling backwards in a pile of grunts and oofs, the were-amphibian pressing its feet into his chest and taking Zilch's head in its hands. Galavance picks up the fallen rifle and cracks Jolby on the side of the head with the stock. Jolby doesn't so much as flinch.

Zilch screams as a cracking sound rises from his skull, and one of the teeth from his crushed jaw tumbles free. Galavance hits Jolby again, this time winding up. Jolby takes one web-fingered hand off Zilch to swat her away. Twisting to glare at the annoyance, his large eyes double in size—there's something over her shoulder. Before she can turn to look, a shadow splashes across the deck.

There is the sound of wood breaking, of a chrome bumper making contact with the railing. It splits and the monster truck is still advancing, sending the TV tray and the meat on it flying. Patty's corpse slumps out of the lawn chair and is taken by the swamp. The deck, under them, begins to buckle as the truck starts to lever the wooden planks. All of them are now sliding down as Jolby's creation of stolen steel and sheet metal tries to pull itself up out of the water.

Galavance pulls Zilch to his feet and in through the back door of the house. Jolby drops into a squat and shoots himself with a jump up over the house. Galavance watches through the open back door as the truck overtakes the deck. She hopes the back of the house is strong enough to stop it, or even just slow it.

The home shudders as the vehicle makes contact, and she hears something upstairs fall over. Next to her, a crack darts across the wall, a black lightning bolt in the dry wall shooting across the kitchen and into the living room. A thin dribble of dust falls from the ceiling. Zilch's teeth are red and his gouged eye has started to bleed again. "We need to get out of this house," he says, mush-mouthed.

They backpedal into the living room, watching Jolby's creation continue to push its way closer to the house, the shattered deck throwing planks of wood going every which way, geysers of brown water pushing in through the back door in pounding gouts. Upstairs, or maybe on the roof, they can hear Jolby shrieking and growling. To Galavance it sounds disheartened, as if something of great value has been irretrievably lost. For a lightning-quick moment she's sad, because she thinks it's *her* that Jolby is upset about losing, but then remembers the bait, the sausage bits, and how they just got run over by the truck and were probably ruined, falling into the dock wreckage and swamp water.

The churning tires show no signs of stopping. Outside the kitchen window, over where a double sink might've been one day, they're still advancing, the nubs in a constant downward spin like a waterwheel after a big rain. The house around them moans and shakes, things knocking loose, beams in the ceiling buckling and snapping, portions of the wall crushing in on themselves like accordions, pipes bursting and water bleeding out from the house's injuries in hissing sprays. Together, Zilch and Galavance take another step back, watching in horror.

"That thing can't get all the way through . . . can it?" she murmurs.

As if in direct reply, the vehicular abomination finds a weak spot in the wall and pushes against it. *The entire house leans.*

"We should probably get outside," Zilch says.

They turn and make for the front door just as it shoots up, the entire living room lurching. They slide back, away from the door and toward the truck's maw as it patiently continues to push its way into the house. With the living room floor now at nearly a forty-five degree angle, the entire place raises up onto its end. The front door lifts, showing sky as the makeshift door swings open on its hinge.

Galavance charges toward it, running uphill with arms and legs pumping, but it's too difficult. Zilch cups her hands and boosts her up to the front window as it becomes a skylight. Below them, as the rear of the house shatters apart and they can only see the turning wheels of the truck, he gives her a shove with what little strength he has left and her fingers snatch onto the window sill. Outside, the entire house shaking under her, she reaches back down. Zilch leaps, grabs her hand, and she screams from the effort of hauling him out. They run down the front of the house as it continues to pivot, capsizing, and jump. The soggy yard breaks their fall.

Zilch helps her to her feet, then they turn and watch as the truck, locked with its gas pedal at a full tilt, finally hits something immovable, then rears and upends. The wheels spins freely and the engine, somewhere down inside the house it's being swallowed by, roars. The entire structure, meeting its breaking point—not built correctly to stand upright, let alone at this irregular tilt—breaks free of its foundation completely and the truck, essentially wearing the house, tips, and together they stand upright like a sinking ship, nose high in the air. For a heartbeat there is the impossible sight of a house on its end, balanced as gracefully as a dancer pausing *en pointe*, before gravity has had enough of this unnatural display and brings both crashing into the swamp. Zilch and Galavance are hit with the splash, drenching them.

They stand staring at the crumpling mountain of broken wood, splintered drywall, and snapped plastic siding standing and smoking in the bog. Once everything settles, deep underwater, they can hear the monster truck putter out, drowned. Surprisingly, a section of the house has remained intact, one side of the place hasn't broken and forms a sort of crooked ramp, a new roof.

"You okay?" someone asks near her and for a moment, Galavance's heart races—not with fear, but with hope. Maybe it could be like the movies and Jolby would come strolling out, unharmed, the shock of the carnage he caused freeing him from his monstrous other self. But it was Zilch, bending down next to her and helping her to her feet.

"Yeah," she says.

"Sure?"

She nods. *No, actually, not really.* But he does the guy thing and doesn't bother to read the signals or body language, just takes her words and lets the gentle clasp he had on her arm go. Not that she would want him to ask any further, because Jolby has just died, and really she doesn't know, even for herself, how she feels about it. "I'm fine."

The entire place looks like a dashed arts and crafts project; a punted house of popsicle sticks. Smoke curls from one window, a split portion of walling bleeding pink insulation out into the water. Zilch, limping, takes a step toward it.

"Where are you going?"

"In there," Zilch says as if it should've been obvious. "I have to make sure." He lost the rifle, Galavance realizes, at some point, and she lost the harpoon gun, too.

"There's no way he survived that. You did your job."

He turns to face her, and puts a hand on her shoulders. "I have to make sure. I need proof. Otherwise, I'll just be sent back." Maybe he hears how that came out and adds: "I didn't want it to go like this. But it did."

"I know."

"Let me go see," he says. "I'm not getting anything on the compass, but maybe he's still . . . you never know."

She didn't even get a chance to say goodbye, she realizes. "Okay."

ZILCH DOESN'T KNOW WHAT TO SAY TO HER OR IF HE SHOULD say anything at all. It's always hard to tell with women. Do you listen when they say they just want to be left alone to think, or is that a hint to pester them until they tell you what's really wrong? She's unable to look at the house, her arms curled around herself. He stares at her back, covered in tiny scratches from their escape, mud caked up to her knees, but under all that, her posture is clear: she's upset all right. *Of course she is, dumbass.* In one weekend, her life—which already wasn't great—became *completely* fucked.

The morning sun is glaring out over the houses across the street. His heart is beating slow. He considers again saying something to Galavance, wonders what *could* be said to make any of this better, decides the correct answer is "nothing," and so begins looking for an easy way into the rubble.

The front porch is at least twenty feet above his head. In the side-yard, he splashes through the ankle deep water to a point where the truck can be partially seen amongst the remnants of the kitchen and living room. The cooler bobs by, spilling Budweiser life rafts and a flotsam of Ramen noodle packets. He steps out deeper, stepping on something solid that sinks under his foot. Bubbles froth the water, and Patty, twisted and crushed, surfaces among the debris. The tape over her mouth has come free and her stomach isn't bulging—or moving—as it was before. *Ugh. Fucking fantastic.*

Climbing up onto what used to be the roof of the house, a chain reaction of sounds echoes all across the wreck, including several particularly unnerving moans and cracks. Zilch freezes, wide-eyed, hands out to his sides, waiting for the house to resettle again before moving any further.

"It's goddamn Jenga." Another few steps and he crests the roof then stops again, not liking what he sees. Or hears. Not the debris settling, but something down there's moving around, struggling, trapped.

"What's wrong?" Galavance shouts from below, startling him.

He doesn't answer. He listens. He can hear the engine clicking as it cools, somewhere deep in the water, so he begins weaving his way toward the low breathing sounds, the wet slapping about—which has now gone quiet, as if it has heard Zilch is on approach. He takes it carefully, testing each place before putting his whole weight down. Even having died many, many times before—it's never pleasant. That moment when the heart stops and your vision starts to fade, like the way the screen of an antique TV fades, the sound dropping away—the ultimate defeat is never easy to swallow, no matter how times you experience it. *This is nearly through, don't fuck it up now.*

Making it to one of the massive backhoe tires, Zilch decides he could use it like a ladder to climb down. Reaching his foot out, he places one heel between the nubs of the enormous tire, and then with a small hop, the other. His blood runs cold when he hears the steady metallic click and genuinely feels the wheel begin to turn under him.

"Shit," he hisses. His arms pinwheel, trying to keep his balance. Trying to outrun its tire's spin is impossible; it's operating like a massive gear and the cogs are all gripping him, pulling him straight down to the underside of the truck—where everything is hot.

Falling into the cave that the truck has buried itself into, Zilch lands in a pile of settled planks of wood and broken cabinetry and raining shards of glass. It's hot in here, very hot. He can smell smoke. Only some light is leaking though in narrow, unhelpful shafts.

"Jolby?" His voice doesn't go far; it's like screaming into a closet full of fur coats. Considering he may've decided to retreat to the closest refuge, his vehicle, Zilch decides to begin his search there.

Jolby must've looked up schematics for actual monster trucks online or something, because up close, this thing is just like the ones Zilch has seen at car shows, the entire floorboard of the cockpit a single sheet of Plexiglas. He can see very little inside, just tangled bits of seaweed and a steady trickle of dark water. Zilch bends down to his knees and begins trying to work the window open, kneeling with the axle of the front wheels crushing his back and the exhaust line under his knees.

The thing is bolted down good. One kick, then another, does nothing. Above him, all around him, is the deep, guttural moan of things shifting again. A single bolt, one pinched nail—anything could cause this whole thing to collapse.

He dares one more kick and the Plexiglas gives on one side. He tears it open and climbs inside. It's dark in the belly of Jolby's creation. Zilch plunges a hand down into the flooded, upside-down vehicle and feels around for Jolby's body—a hand, foot, anything. Finding nothing, Zilch lays down flat on the hot underside of the inverted truck and stares into the water, swishing debris out of the way.

The water next him boils as there is a sudden rush of something lifting out of the swamp. Zilch remains lying with the gas tank pressed against his chest, hoping that Jolby's vision is just as bad as his with all the smoke-choked darkness. But when he feels a webbed hand clamp down on his ankle, Zilch closes his eyes and gives a resigned sigh.

Jolby rumbles, "You again."

"Yep. I'm a two-flusher."

Zilch rolls over to look up at Jolby. He's badly cut up, across the chest and stomach. He spots something hanging out of the corner of Jolby's wide mouth—a small yellow string, or cord. It would be easy to mistake it for more electrical wiring or car parts, if it wasn't slowly moving, squirming around. Jolby packs it back into his mouth with a finger before saying, "Still trying to fuck my girlfriend?"

"What *is it* with you and that?" Zilch says. "No, I'm not, and I never was. I'm trying to help her. Do you know what kind of shit she's been through because of you? I doubt it, seems like you can only fucking think about yourself, you ass-hat." Even as the words come out, Zilch realizes that the barbs he's spitting Jolby's way could've easily been aimed at a mirror, just a few years back. That sudden ironic thought actually makes it easier. "Fucker, I'm through with this. Do you want me to help you get this thing out of your guts or not? Because I'll gladly beat you to death with something we find in here. All the same to me, honestly. I'll even let you pick the thing I do it with."

Jolby peers into Zilch's face, giving him an almost dazed, absent stare.

It's hard to be convincingly suave and sarcastic when dangling upside down by the ankle, held by something that can support your weight with one hand with ease, but Zilch tries. "Listen, don't ask me why, but Galavance wants you to get better. She wants to hear it from you what you did. She doesn't even seem to care you're like . . . this, only that you weren't faithful to her. She *might* be willing to forgive you."

"Like what way?" Jolby says. Each time he speaks, the finger-wide tentacle peeks out of the corner of his mouth again, like overcooked pasta that still hasn't been swallowed.

"Like this, Jolby," Zilch says. The blood is staring to run to his head. "You're not in good shape. The thing is trying to leave—you're too beat up. You aren't a hospitable environment for it anymore—"

"I found the other ones," Jolby says. "Inside that lady. They were crying for me. They're back with me now. I'll let them grow until they're ready to be planted. Maybe if I talk to Galavance, tell her we can be together again—new people with new lives—she might want to join me."

"You know, I haven't known Galavance as long as you, so take this with a grain of salt, man, but I kind of doubt she's going to be down for that."

With the hand not holding Zilch upside-down by the ankle, Jolby stuffs the searching yellow finger back into his mouth again. He swallows, with difficulty, closing his eyes momentarily to do so, but when he opens his mouth the worm flops right back out again. "I don't think I'm going to extend the same offer to you."

"That's fine. My answer, if you're wondering, would have been 'Fuck, no.'"

"Dude, sorry to do this to you, but I'm gonna eat you now, okay?"

240

"Wait—!"

Jolby pulls Zilch in close, toward his mouth. Zilch can hear the pop of his jaw dislocating, the were-frog's chin extending low, nearly to his belly. He can feel the heat of his open mouth radiating out and Zilch stares into the pink tunnel leading down into Jolby's innards.

So this is how this one ends, huh? Son of a bitch.

But at the root of his tongue, just over the cusp down into his gullet, Zilch watches a writhing mass of tentacles surge forward, operating like additional tongues, snapping onto his face with their myriad suckers. Zilch brings up a hand and lets them coil around his wrist and forearm.

He then punches the wrapped arm into Jolby's throat, burying it to the shoulder, driving his hand as deep as it can go, snatching and grabbing. Jolby shudders in surprise—Zilch is sure he probably wanted to chew him first before swallowing all of the pokey boney parts—and tries to shove Zilch away. Instead, Zilch pulls his other arm around Jolby's neck into a headlock, and digs deeper. Every time he gets a tickle of the worm between his fingers, the little fucker moves and he has to start all over again. He grabs it and twists his wrist to get it reeled back onto his arm. Then he is pulling and he can hear a voice, drooling profusely and gagging, begging him to stop. Each plea sounds less froggy and monstrous—and more like an overweight stoner that would much rather be sitting around eating some fast food right now.

"Yeah, this isn't very much fun for me either," Zilch says through gritted teeth, managing to get another few feet of the worm wrapped around his arm. He keeps pulling, one vicious tug at a time. With each one, Jolby is messing himself, really cutting loose. A surge of orange puke, littered with bugs and squirrels and other waterlogged fauna, comes spraying out on Zilch, gushing against his face and chest, body-hot and acidic.

Yard after yard of the parasites emerge, like tape on an end-less spool. They've coiled together, braiding their tentacles, and it's hard to tell where one ends and other begins. Which is fine, Zilch will just take them together or separate—but he's not giving up until this is through. It gets harder to pull as the tentacles, closer to the bodies of the parasites, become thicker. It almost would've easier to go in from the other end, he considers grimly.

Jolby's stomach gurgles, he heaves, and another spray of vomit erupts. Zilch is pelted with a soggy dead chipmunk, then half a rabbit, then the other half. He glances down at the steaming menagerie accumulating at his feet. In there, also, is a kinky length of a chewed snake, some wires, a gear shifter, and a tree-shaped air freshener.

"Thattaboy. Let it all out." Zilch turns his head away as the purging continues—they're making good progress here. And sometimes, progress hurts. The "little darlings" come free, Zilch is happy to see, but only two. The two he gifted Patty with. There's one more, Jolby's main man, his steadfast compadre, parasite zero. Zilch waits for it to emerge as Jolby hacks and sputters, freeing more woodland creatures—a blackened coil of a half-digested water moccasin, then an actual moccasin, one you'd wear on your foot—but no final darling.

Jolby's complexion clears, losing the pickle-like bumpiness and the green cast to skin bleeding away like bruises healing in fast-forward. He's becoming as pasty and doofy-looking as before. But another sputter, another yack session, and there's still no third little darling making an appearance among the ankle-deep pile of spew he's produced.

Zilch groans, pats Jolby on the back. "Looks like we might have to get a little more invasive, bud. Wouldn't happen to have some Crisco on you, would ya?"

Jolby's bloodshot eyes angle up at Zilch. "Huh?"

"Crisco. Because, as things are looking, we're about to become very close friends."

Still looking up at him, orange drool hanging from his lip, Jolby's eyes shift—bloodshot and blue one blink, then spotty and dark, frog-like again the next. Apparently for being well entrenched in the guy's stink-hose, the parasite was still able to eavesdrop.

GALAVANCE CAN HEAR A LOT OF COMMOTION, TWO VOICES yelling. It doesn't sound like it's going well, but since it's more than just Zilch yelling in frustration, since it's actually two voices, she knows that Jolby must have actually still been alive. Her legs are moving her forward, her hands finding holds on the wall of the house, prying her fingers between the broken pieces of vinyl siding to climb. She is cut, but keeps at it, and before long she's on the top of the heap. She spots the wheels of the truck and with careful steps, moves in that direction, careful to avoid stepping into any open windows or places that look like they may not be able to support her weight.

She reaches the opening where the wheels poke out and looks inside. Zilch is pulling at something, but she cannot tell from where. She leans to one side, trying to get a better vantage. Then she sees Jolby, still fully frogified again, with what looks like a length of pale vein-covered tube of flesh protruding from his mouth. His howls are horrible, shrill and painful both to the ears and to the heart. She begins to climb down.

Zilch notices her and calls up, "Careful, that's gonna—!" But it's too late—the slow shift of the wheel has already started, and for an embarrassing moment she's trying to hold onto it and climb it like a hamster, but it's no use. She falls into the cavern of wreckage, and groaning at the bottom of the heap, sees that Zilch is wearing what appears to be a full-arm cast made entirely of some worm-thing stretching out from Jolby's mouth. "What the hell are you doing down here?"

Jolby seizes the moment while Zilch is distracted to reach out with his own hands and grab the worm suspended between them and pull. Zilch is yanked off his feet, crashing through the broken wood and glass, and dragged on his belly toward Jolby as he reels him in one yank at a time. Galavance charges forward just as Jolby seizes Zilch by the throat and uncoils the worm from around his arm, packing the balled mass back into his gaping mouth.

With Zilch kicking and struggling, Jolby takes him over to a split two by four that's jutting up from the floor, raises him over it, and disregarding his pleas entirely, drops him onto the skewer. The wooden spike erupts out of Zilch's chest, squarely in the middle, surely piercing his heart and pulping anything else it may've just charged through. Within a moment, Zilch's eyes—one socket empty, the other full and shocked—shift from wide with surprise to empty. A raspy breath trails out of him, punctuated by a tiny cough, then nothing.

"*Oh my God,*" Galavance cries, "*you . . . why . . . ?*"

Jolby's face, as his faces her, is two-thirds the were-amphibian, and one third . . . himself. One eye has partly lost its staining and the shining happy sky blue of the Jolby she knows shines out, the skin surrounding it not a brownish green as a rotten leaf, but pink and . . . human-like.

"Gal," he says, the living noodle slurring his speech. "What are you doing here? I'm trying to work. If you want me and Chev to sell this place, we need to get back to it."

Jolby's expression face softens and he steps forward, hands out, his color now fully shifted to amphibian shades again. "I promise this place will sell," he says. "I promise everything will be fine just as soon as I sell this and . . . look at this," he gestures at the truck proudly. "I'm going to sell this too and take the money from it and put it into the house, make this place amazing, and when someone buys it, we'll be okay, and everything will be good again, like it was before. I can provide for you, see?"

Galavance scrambles backwards. "That's not going to happen," she says softly. "Everything's not going to be okay. You're sick." Even in this dire situation, Galavance is aware of the enormous understatement of those words.

Jolby frowns and drops his chin. He's gesticulating at her, making wiggling motions with his fingers. It's horrifying to witness, but immediately recognizable to her: he's trying to give her the Cuddle Bear move. "Come on, Gal. Don't be like that, babe."

"Don't come near me." She wants this command to sound fierce, but can't find the courage. She can barely breathe she's so afraid, backed up as far as she can go—trapped. She has no choice but to watch as he draws in closer, closer.

She turns her face away and prays that, if nothing else, it'll be fast. She hears a crunch and peeks back with one eye to see Jolby lowering himself onto his knees.

"Let me do something for you," he says. "Let me make it up to you." He pulls, sudden and rough, and her shorts come down some more. It's like he thinks she's playing a demented game of hard-to-get, and he demonstrates his intentions by opening his mouth and flopping his grotesquely long tongue up and down. The pale worm-shape, beside it, tangling and untangling, lashes about. She almost vomits.

Hands on her hips, he tries pushing his mouth closer. It's all she can take and puts a foot on his chest and kicks with all of her strength.

He weighs considerably more than her, so instead of pushing him away she actually launches herself backwards, through the makeshift wall she was backed against. Her shoulder collides with a standing pillar of debris. Something heavy somewhere above them . . . *shifts.*

"I'm going to die if I don't get out of here, Jolby," Galavance pleads. "Just let me go, I swear . . . I swear I won't bother you at work ever again."

"It's all right, babe, I'm actually glad you're here," he replies cheerfully with a shrug, and then winks. "Chev's out doing something and, I mean, I always *wanted* to do it in this place. Look at all these rooms, all this space. So much more space than our place where we can get crazy."

Galavance loses all track of what she wants to say to Jolby for a moment, because over his shoulder behind him, she can see Zilch, still impaled on the broken stud, move. The lid of his one remaining eye is fluttering, and he's attempting to sit up but is quite literally nailed in place, like a pinned insect.

"Galavance?" Jolby says, leaning to put his eyes in the path of hers. "You said we needed to talk. And even though I don't think we really have anything to talk *about*—I think everything's just fine—I'll listen, I'll be happy to listen."

She looks at him squarely. "Did you cheat on me?" Something blunt as a hammer might just shock him back. No talk about jobs or anything of the bullshit that had piled up between them—the truth, the heart, the thing that made a relationship work. She questions, for the first time, directly to him, the trust binding them together.

His face flips through a series of expressions. Surprise. Mild anger. Frustration. Disbelief. Guilt. And then a non-expression, blanked. Acceptance, clarity? But maybe not, given what he rolls out next.

"I don't even know how to respond to that," Jolby says. "That hurts, babe. Like, really hurts. But if you were like me, you'd see that pain can't find you when you're swimming deep. It's like dreaming. Down under the water, nothing hurts. It keeps the air from reaching the cut. Don't you want that, babe?"

"No, Jolby, I don't. I want to know what you did. I don't care if you're sorry, I just need to know that *you* know what kind of pain you caused me."

"Gal, I . . . I messed up."

Behind him, Zilch locks eyes with Galavance over Jolby's spotty shoulder. He remains quiet as he awkwardly attempts to lift himself off the wooden spike driven through his back, with only one working arm.

Jolby stops in his shuffling tracks for a beat. His hands come up and touch the sides of his head, roughly where his jaw connects to his skull. A half-inch of worm pulls itself between his lips, and Galavance watches his throat swell as he swallows. When he looks up at her again, any trace of blue in his one eye is gone. The green has absorbed any scant shade of human flesh, and he is completely a were-amphibian once more. Looking down at himself, he smiles proudly, then cocks his eyes up at Galavance and the smile broadens, bad thoughts communicated, wordless.

WHEN CONSCIOUSNESS FLOODS BACK TO HIM, ZILCH FINDS himself unable to get up; the odd angle at which he's lying and the piece of wood he's been speared onto, naturally, make this difficult. Wiggling around does nothing but give him internal splinters. A few open-handed smacks crack it somewhat, but freedom still feels impossible—all the while, twisting to look over one shoulder, he watches, helpless, as the were-amphibian closes in on Galavance. She kicks him back and he reels, nearly stumbles, but recovers, determined and patient.

The thing advances another step, hands out as if meaning no harm, while the look on its face says otherwise.

Zilch wrenches his upper body to one side, then the other. The spike of wood cracks again, louder, fragmenting. Digging in one heel, he presses off, taking the snapped-off piece with him. Thumping himself on the chest as if trying to dislodge a belch pushes it out his back, landing slicked end to end with red Zilch fluid. The buggies go to work, mending what they can, but with so few of them left, the yawning cavity in his chest only reduces itself to a sleepy pucker.

With a broken spindle from the crushed staircase in hand, teeth gritted, Zilch raises it overhead and brings it down like a cartoon mallet over the were-amphibian's head, the blow fueled more by annoyance than anything.

Fighting to catch himself with a wide side-step, Jolby, head wavering, trips and stumbles over. His impact when he hits the floor makes the wall above them all crack and moan; in terror, Zilch and Galavance watch as it suddenly drops by a foot, raining dust and broken nails.

Pointed Zilch's way is the were-amphibian's bare ass. Zilch thinks about what he considered earlier, about how it would've been easier to go in the other end. *When life gives you lemons . . .* he thinks cynically, balls a fist, and with a two-count heave-ho, makes himself Jolby's ventriloquist.

What happens after that is highly unpleasant. There is lots of shouting, fishing blindly this way and that. When he can feel he's got a worm cornered somewhere in Jolby's large intestine, Zilch grabs it and pulls, hard. Once free, he tosses it aside. It scuttles for the edge of the water, where the deck lies crushed.

"Mind getting that?" Zilch says, nodding at the critter making its blind race for freedom.

Galavance drops her bare foot onto it. It whips about, shrieking, as Galavance grinds her heel. Something pops and a gush of green shoots out its side, and it stills, able to wriggle a few tentacles but not much more.

"Now for number two," Zilch says, and goes back in. This one is bigger, birthed from his own gashed belly, and it's really up inside Jolby. Snatching one tentacle, threatening to tear it, Zilch pulls, and yard after yard comes out until finally, *snap*. The parasite breaks free and Zilch falls over backwards. Jolby's grunting and swearing about as much as you'd expect, maybe a little less, all things considered.

The last remaining parasite, sensing it has to make a break for it, uncoils from Zilch's arm and begins scurrying across the hot metal of the monster truck's underside toward the cab's opening—the freedom of the open swamp ahead. Dodging Galavance's stomps, it leaps. Zilch reaches out and tries to catch its tail as it slithers away, pushing off of what he can, ducking under the axel again and—no, it slips over the edge into the cab, and with a splash, is in the water.

But just before vanishing into the churned brown water and seaweed and debris, it's speared with an aluminum bolt—not killing it, but preventing its escape. Stepping inside the truck's cab, Galavance turns the harpoon gun around and as the parasite whips about, squealing and trying to free itself, she brings the gun's grip down on it. Just then the second parasite, mustering up its energy, drops from the slanting debris above, possibly to the rescue of its sibling. As it coils itself to spring toward Galavance's face, to force itself down her throat, she snags it out of the air and spikes it to the ground alongside the first one she's already halfway killed. She pounds both over and over with the harpoon gun's grip, snarling and growling with each strike.

They're in smashed pieces when she's finally through and stops to catch her breath. They fall into the water in chunks, mealy strands that bob along but finally sink. She's falling over, arms shaking from the effort she put into this Amazonian display.

"Whoa," Jolby says. "That was awesome, babe."

"Jolby, shut *the fuck* up."

"We need to get him out of here," Zilch says and notices that despite everything, and especially given that it would appear they'd managed to save Jolby without killing him, she looks rather solemn, her arms crossed over her chest. Jolby is visibly improving by the second, returning to his normal pinkish hue. But by the look on Galavance's face, Zilch wonders if she even cares whether he's dead or alive at this point.

Barely above a whisper she asks: "Is he going to be okay?"

"I think so," Zilch says.

"Was that all of them . . . ?"

"Yes. He's cured—by one definition or another."

She only nods. Comforted by that news or not, he can't tell.

GALAVANCE HELPS JOLBY INTO THE PASSENGER SIDE OF HER car. It had barely escaped being pulled into the wreck when 1330 Whispering Pines Lane sunk. She waits until he meets her gaze, and when he does, she can see the guilt practically radiating off him.

"You look pissed," he says, legs dangling out of the car.

"There's probably a reason for that."

"*Are* you pissed?"

"Yes, Jolby, I am."

"I wanted to tell you what was going on with me, but you saw what I looked like, I—"

"Not that, Jolby. Though that wasn't great either."

"Then . . . I don't understand. If we're not gonna talk about me being sick . . ." How much he remembers doing—like dismembering and impregnating the corpse of his best friend—Galavance cannot tell. He certainly remembers something, though, because his gaze goes distant and he holds his forehead in his hand, lips curling with disgust. Something in that noggin is taking shape.

"That wasn't you," she says. "And right now, I don't care about that, because that's over."

"Okay," he says, visibly relieved, off the hook. "Good. I'm glad you're being so cool about this, Gal. I mean, I really had no idea I was doing any of it, it all just sort of happened. I mean, I was just hanging out with Chev one day and I started feeling weird and then I got the shits and then every once in a while, just out of the clear blue, I'd—"

"I don't *mean* that, Jolby. Would you listen to me?"

"Gal, come on. Don't use my name. You know I hate it when—"

"Jolby," she snaps, "I may be partly responsible because I was bringing leftovers home from work for you. But that's just one part of it."

"Wait, what? I didn't get it from . . ."

"From what?" she says.

"I kind of thought it was from, you know . . . like herpes."

She nearly dusts her teeth grinding them so hard. "So you were aware. You were fully aware, the whole time?"

Jolby's eyes dart around. "Do we really have to talk about this right now, right here? I don't feel that great. I think I'd like to go home, lay down for a while."

For a moment, she wishes she could shoot lasers from her eyes. "Yes. Here."

"Okay, so . . . what? What do you want to talk about?"

"You cheated on me. And you knew you were cheating on me."

"Uh . . ." his face goes through that kaleidoscope of emotions again. Confused. Hurt. Angry. And finally, guilty. His chin goes down but her hand flashes out quick to take it before it can reach his chest. She makes him look at her.

"Yes or no," she says.

"I knew. Look, Gal, I—" Jolby tries.

But Galavance is standing, wiping as much mud off herself as she can, then turns away. She goes around the side of the wrecked house, and has to wade out into the swamp just to get to the back. Patty floats by in the water, then a small ripple of bubbles surfaces from under the ghillie-suited regional manager and she sinks, taken by the swamp. Galavance swallows her disgust and the twinge of shame she feels for her death, and with high steps, makes her way to the side of the house where Zilch stands on the slanted roof, looking out over the water. He notices her wading up next to the place, below.

"You're gonna get leeches," he says.

"He knew he was doing it," she says, but doesn't want to talk about it more than that. "Anything else we need to do around here? I'd like to leave now."

"You and me both," he says, coming to the edge and dropping down. "A piece of advice: with Beefy Ben and his friends sitting squashed in the driveway, plus what's left of Chev in the

garage . . . and your regional manager, wherever she's floated off
to . . . you might want to, you know, distance yourself from this
place. Give it some room, to breathe, so to speak."

"No problem there," Galavance says.

His torn coat hangs open, and she can see through him.
Where his heart should be is a hole, and sunshine's coming in from behind him. A part of the skin on his chin has
been torn away, pale bone showing. He runs his hand back
through his mud-caked hair, and shakes his head, staring out
over the bog.

"Susanne and I used to drive past this place—before it was a
cul-de-sac—all the time. Right over there. I'd drive her to work
sometimes when she worked the late shift. We'd be going along
the road over there and she'd roll down the window so she could
hear the frogs. She'd close her eyes and put her seat back and just
smile."

"Will you get to see her again?"

"I don't know. And that's all right, if not."

"You don't think you . . . deserve to, by now?"

"You're asking me that, after what you just dealt with this
weekend? I'd figure you'd be done with men—and our excuses
and apologies."

"People can change."

"So you're taking the high road, huh? Shame." He smiles.
"But will Jolby change, you think?"

"Maybe. I hope so."

Zilch looks back out across the swamp, trailing the road
across the water, Kit Mitchell Road, and Galavance wonders if
he's possibly painting himself and his wife in their car over there,
cruising along late at night.

"Say, uh—I should thank you. You could've just killed him
instead of . . ."

"Jamming my hand up his ass? Sure. But part of me thinks, looking at you now, you might've preferred if I'd just done him in."

"No. The bad stuff—the truly bad stuff, like killing Chev—was because of that thing. Him cheating on me, while really screwed up, doesn't mean he should die." She pauses. "So, like, are you done? You finished the job, didn't you?"

"I am. Just dragging my feet now. I missed this neck of the woods more than I thought I would."

"Do you get need to go anywhere special to, you know, check out?"

"They prefer it if I finish back where I started. Makes less paperwork for them or something. If I could bum one last ride, I would appreciate it."

"No need to ask. I was gonna offer."

It's not a half-beat after Zilch drops down before the house falls in on itself. Smoke shoots out of every gap it can find. One tongue of fire moves across the shingles, another spouts up to light a broken window like a jack-o-lantern. The smoke shifts from white to black. In a couple of hours, if no one comes to call in the blaze, there will be nothing left. If that happens, Galavance wonders, maybe Zilch's employees won't have to come out then to cover things up, make things tidy. Maybe they'll give him a pat on the back for making that one aspect of their job just a little bit easier. *He's earned at least that much*, she thinks.

Galavance drives, while Jolby lays sprawled in the back and Zilch reclines in the passenger seat, his arm hanging out the window. She can't be sure, but it looks like he's listening to the frogs and crickets. They pass the swamp, and it falls behind them, growing quiet outside the car except for the rush of wind. Zilch raises the window, like he's heard enough.

They don't listen to any music, and no one talks. They're all exhausted, and with the air conditioner blowing full blast, the entire car is filled with a fug of their collective stink. But no one points fingers; they just drive.

Jolby sits up to put his head between the front seats. "Sorry I tried to kill you, dude."

Zilch coughs trying to laugh. "I appreciate that."

"Did I fall on something? My ass really hurts."

Galavance and Zilch exchange a knowing look.

A few miles further, Jolby's hand creeps over the back of Galavance's seat and onto her shoulder. His fingers play with her hair, tweak her earlobe. She tolerates it for a whole three seconds before flicking him away. Her hand returns to the gear shifter, stroking the chrome skull with the ruby eyes, happy there on its own.

"What happened to Chev?" Jolby asks.

Between glances at the road, Galavance reaches down into the cup-holder between them and takes out a quarter, handing it to Zilch. "I call heads." It comes up tails, and Zilch, for a few miles' worth of driving explains, to Jolby what he did with his best friend. They soon have to pull over so he doesn't get vomit all over the car.

The cemetery is empty of visitors. Jolby remains in the car, by Galavance's request, and she and Zilch pass through the squeaky gate and up the slight grade where the headstones line the gravel path.

They come to the edge of the disturbed earth, broken pieces of Zilch's casket still lying around in the dirt. Galavance doubts anyone's even been up here in the past few days. One dead parasite lies near the plot, the second still bearing its griddle burns, and the third winding Zilch's disembodied arm—which, holding by the wrist, he cradles close to his chest like it's a priceless, auto-graphed baseball bat.

"So what's the plan for Miss Petersen?" he asks her, kick-ing at a broken piece of casket near his feet. "Not planning on changing that to Missus Dawes, are you?"

Galavance sweeps some hair back, finds a dead leaf in it, and flicks it away. "Nope. We're done. I'll break the news to him in a minute."

"Can't say I'm sad to hear that. Stick to it, though."

"Stick to what?"

"If you break up with him," he says. "Stick to it. There won't be any changing for him. I'm speaking from experience here."

"He might make someone a good husband someday—a very *patient* someone. Just not me. My patience is well past its expi-ration date."

Nodding, Zilch takes a step back so that the heels of his shoes are set on the edge of the grave. Reaching into his inside pocket, he withdraws the employee delivery module, clicks it and snaps forward a long needle, then jams it into his chest. He looks up at Galavance and cocks an eyebrow. "How do I look?"

"Like a chef who just had the worst shift of his life."

Zilch is laughing at this, really belly-laughing—even as a loud buzzing begins to emanate from somewhere deep in his body, louder than the cicadas around them. He rolls his head back, still laughing. The device sticking out of his chest lights up, green. A wave ripples over him, from the soles of his feet up to his head, leaving behind the dull gray color of death. When it reaches Zilch's laughing face, the only trace of his fun-loving guffaw Galavance hears is an echo.

A white line connecting his tumbling ashes to the sky arches high above, its progress marked by a winking green light—the needle device as it's sucked back up wherever he was sent from.

The standing Zilch-shaped statue of ash crumbles in a whoosh, the more solid parts falling down into the grave, filling in the low spots, bones clacking as they tumble, and the borrowed carbon all going back to approximately from where it had been raised.

Galavance blinks, and the grave suddenly looks untouched, the grass over the slight mound in the earth not missing a single green blade, like the whole thing had never happened. She straightens the bouquet someone had left before the grave marker—flowers not meant for Saelig Zilch, but ones she feels he deserves all the same.

"Let him see her, okay?" she says to the sky. "It'd do the goofy bastard some good. That's just my two cents."

Passing through the cemetery's gate and squeaking it shut behind her, Galavance sees Jolby is in the front seat of her car now, half-asleep. He stirs when she pulls the door closed and starts the engine. He looks around.

"Where'd that dude go?"

"Dropped him off."

"At a cemetery?"

"Yes, Jolby."

He slides down in the seat more, thumbing back the harness strap from under his double chin. He closes his eyes. "What do you think, babe? Head home, talk about this, maybe over some breakfast? It's been a while since you made your world-famous pancakes for me."

"Get out," Galavance says.

"Huh?"

"Get out of my car."

"Well," Jolby scoffs, "technically it's *my* car, but . . ."

"No, all of this *shit* is yours. This and this and this and this," she begins ripping off every chintzy addition he Krazy Glued to the interior of her car, the mirror in the shape of a supine lady and the chromed vent-covers and the hanging disco ball mirror ornament—and shoves the whole chintzy heap at him. "But the car is mine. I've made 90 percent of the goddamn payments on it."

"You're seriously going to break up with me? I was drunk. Every single time, Gal, I was just drunk. I wasn't me. It was like when I had that thing in me—and thank you for helping me with that—but instead of some worm-thing it was beer and I—"

"Shut up." Galavance looks into his face. He looks puzzled, as if all of this is some massive surprise, a trick, a prank maybe. She leans across the emergency brake and takes his soft, whiskered cheeks in her palms.

"What're you doing?"

"Let me see something," she says and closes her eyes and kisses Jolby. She breaks the vacuum between their lips with a pop and says, "What do you know—you're still a frog."

"Huh?"

"Jolby, please take your shit and get out of my car," she says. "I'm going to be happy, even if it fucking kills me."

ZILCH WAKES STANDING. HE's IN A CHEF'S JACKET, CHECKERED pants, and clogs. He has a knife in his hand, and on the cutting board before him is a half-diced onion. The air is heavy with steam, and all around him are others in similar garb, no one paying him a second glance. He doesn't recognize anybody else in the kitchen. Waiters shove through, nab plates waiting for pickup, and move back out. For a lack of any better ideas, Zilch decides to blend in for the time being—try to remember when he was hired here, or even the name of this restaurant. Chopping up the rest of the onion is pleasantly mindless, the motion of his hand second nature, as rapid as it is effortless. He doesn't even need to watch what he's doing, so he scans around through the shelves ahead of him, peeking through at these other cooks he doesn't know the name of, not a single one.

A waiter pushes through, turns sideways to slip behind Zilch, and deposits a dirty plate in the sink full of suds. Zilch thinks he's gone, but then the man is suddenly right alongside him, watching him chop like it's his first day and he's never seen anyone do this before. Someone has a radio up loud down at the other end of the kitchen, and over the classic rock the waiter leans in close to Zilch's ear and whispers, "It's me."

Zilch looks at the young waiter, who cracks a big smile. "And who would that be?"

"That hurts my emotion-part, Saelig."

"Oh. Eliphas Dungaree." Zilch sets the knife down, many memories resurfacing, nearly overwhelming him. The kitchen around them continues to bustle—people calling out for order up, cooks requesting certain spices, some singing along to the radio. Zilch had been so caught up in the moment that he'd been worried he was going to get yelled at a second ago for not helping. But this isn't real. Of course it isn't real.

Zilch faces Eliphas and crosses his arms. "You look happy."

"You helped me win the bet," Eliphas says. "I thought I'd repay the effort, but I didn't think xabfarbs would be of any interest to you—that currency isn't used on Earth yet."

"Do I get to be done?" Zilch says. "Because anything other than that, frankly, I don't think I'd be real interested."

"You wouldn't be interested in speaking to one of our diners? She says the meal you prepared is worthy of some accolades. She'd like to give them in person, if you can find the time to go speak with her."

"Don't fuck with me, man," Zilch says. "Not with that."

"No fuckings-with intended," Eliphas says. "Table five, whenever you're ready."

"If I go out there and the room's on fire or there's a big sign that says 'sucker' on it, I'm gonna come back here and teach you how to swallow swords using this," he says, waggling the ten-inch knife under Eliphas's nose.

"Go and see," Eliphas says, his smile refusing to break. "I doubt you'll be disappointed. Setting this up took some finagling, but I wanted to thank you."

Zilch hesitates before stepping out into the dining room. When someone yells, "Order up!" he flinches, stepping away from his station in the line and pushing through the swinging door. The air is colder out here. The windows stand tall around the large, low-lit dining room. The walls are painted in a filigree of gold over red, and each table has a votive candle burning, under-lighting the faces of smiling diners.

Zilch notices the little number set to the edge of each table. He passes tables two and three, turning a corner to see table four standing empty, and then there's table five. A woman is seated alone, her back to him. Her dark hair hangs about her strapless dress. She has an untouched glass of red wine in front of her and an empty plate set to one side with a fork crossing it. Zilch can hear his pulse in his ears. His eyes feel hot. He remembers not only her name, but everything about her. But trying to say her name, much less anything else, hitches in his throat.

He takes a step forward.

SOUNDTRACK

"Sick, Sick, Sick" – Queens of the Stone Age
"Outside Chance" – Heavy Trash
"Head over Heels" – The Go-Go's
"Black Mold" – The Jon Spencer Blues Explosion
"The Future Strikes Back" – Restavrant
"The Wind Cries Mary" – The Jimi Hendrix Experience
"O' Be Joyful" – Shovels & Rope
"Supernaturally" – Nick Cave & The Bad Seeds
"Pills I Took" – Hank III
"Shake Your Hips" – The Legendary Shack Shakers
"I'm Alive" – John Oszajca
"Vacation" – The Go-Go's
"There She Goes, My Beautiful World" – Nick Cave & The Bad Seeds
"Black Betty" – Spiderbait
"She Said" – The Jon Spencer Blues Explosion
"Flirtin' with Disaster" – Molly Hatchet
"Bumble Bee" – Heavy Trash
"Bad Moon" – Restavrant

Thank you, Cory Allyn, and the Skyhorse Publishing team.

Andrew Post spent the countless study halls of his formative years filling notebooks with science fiction and horror stories. Now he is the author of, among others, the sci-fi thriller *Knuckleduster* and the YA fantasy series The Fabrick Weavers. Andrew lives in the Twin Cities area of Minnesota with his wife, who is also an author, and their two dogs.